THE LAST GUNFIGHTER
KILLING GROUND

THE LAST GUNFIGHTER
KILLING GROUND

William W. Johnstone
with J. A. Johnstone

PINNACLE BOOKS
Kensington Publishing Corp.
www.kensingtonbooks.com

PINNACLE BOOKS are published by

Kensington Publishing Corp.
850 Third Avenue
New York, NY 10022

PUBLISHER'S NOTE
Following the death of William W. Johnstone, the Johnstone family is working with a carefully selected writer to organize and complete Mr. Johnstone's outlines and many unfinished manuscripts to create additional novels in all of his series like The Last Gunfighter, Mountain Man, and Eagles, among others. This novel was inspired by Mr. Johnstone's superb storytelling.

ISBN-13: 978-0-7860-1837-6
ISBN-10: 0-7860-1837-2

First printing: October 2008

10 9 8 7 6 5 4 3 2 1

Printed in the United States of America

Chapter 1

It was good to be home again, Frank Morgan thought as he reined in at the top of a hill overlooking the mining settlement of Buckskin, Nevada. A mighty pretty place, nestled in those pine-covered foothills as it was, with majestic, snowcapped mountains looming around it.

And it struck Frank, as it always did at moments like this, how odd it was for him to be thinking of Buckskin as home. For so many years, he had been on the move, wandering from place to place with a natural restlessness that had helped earn him his nickname—The Drifter.

Since he had settled down in Buckskin and accepted the job as town marshal, though, he had experienced a contentment unlike any he had known for quite a while. When circumstances took him away from the settlement, as they had recently when a dangerous job had sent him down to Arizona Territory, he was always anxious to get back.

"There it is," a man's voice said from behind

Frank. "The famous Buckskin, Nevada. It doesn't appear to have changed much since our last visit."

Frank turned his head to look back at the buggy where his son, Conrad Browning, and Conrad's wife, Rebel, rode.

"The big silver boom is over," Frank said. "The settlement should keep growing, but it'll be slower and steadier now, instead of going from being a ghost town to busting at the seams practically overnight."

"Especially since it has a famous town-taming marshal now," Conrad said, and Frank wasn't sure if there was a faint note of sarcasm in the words or not.

For years father and son had been estranged, even after the death of Vivian Browning, Frank's first wife and Conrad's mother. Vivian had left half of her vast business holdings to Frank, making him one of the richest men in the West even though nobody would ever guess that from his well-worn range clothes and the even more well-worn Colt .45 that was holstered on his right hip.

No, Frank Morgan was a gunfighter—some said the last real, true gunfighter in the West—not a tycoon. One of the few men faster on the draw than him was the legendary Smoke Jensen, who had, in these waning days of the nineteenth century, done what was almost unheard of. Jensen had put his gunfighting days behind him and was living a life of peace on his Colorado ranch.

That was the sort of thing Frank Morgan aspired to. That was why he had decided to put aside his drifting ways and settle down in Buckskin.

But the violence that had surrounded so much of his life kept trying to pull him back. Maybe it hadn't been a good idea to pin on a lawman's badge. Maybe as long as he wore it, there would always be some no-good son of a buck who needed killing. Maybe he would never know true peace, Frank sometimes thought during dark nights of the soul, until he was dead. Then he would have the peace of the grave . . .

Sometimes things could change, though, he tried to remind himself at times like that. Just look at him and Conrad. His son had flat-out hated him when they first got to know each other.

It didn't help that Conrad had been raised by another man, his mother's second husband, and hadn't even known Frank until he was grown. But circumstances, namely their shared business interests, had led them to fight side by side on several occasions, and Conrad had developed a grudging respect for his father. Frank liked to think that at times Conrad was beginning to feel a little real affection for him. Time would tell about that.

"Perhaps I should visit more often," Conrad went on. "Since the Crown Royal mine started production again, though, I've had good men looking out for my interests, like Garrett Claiborne."

"And like your father," Rebel pointed out.

She was a beautiful blonde, a Western girl born and raised, and Frank thought that marrying her was just about the best thing that could have happened to Conrad. She wore a stylish, expensive traveling outfit at the moment, with a modish hat perched on her upswept blond curls, but give her a chance and she'd be in buckskins and jeans and a Stetson again, riding like the wind.

"Yes, that's right," Conrad said, his voice a little gruff. He and Frank got along better than they used to, but he wasn't the sort of man to get all sentimental. That was fine with Frank, since he wasn't that kind either.

He heeled the horse into motion and started down the hill with Conrad and Rebel following in the buggy. Frank hadn't taken either of his regular horses, the big stallions Stormy and Goldy, with him to Arizona, but the rented mount he rode now, a big blood bay, was a good horse. He would be glad to see Stormy and Goldy again, along with the massive, shaggy cur Dog, who had been one of his trail partners during many of the long, wandering years.

Frank Morgan was a medium-sized, compactly built man with the broad shoulders and lean waist of a natural-born horseman. He wore comfortable boots, jeans, a faded blue work shirt, and a cream-colored, high-crowned Stetson with a slightly curled brim. Thick dark hair lightly touched with gray was under that hat. His features, tanned and weathered by years spent outdoors, were a little too rugged to be called handsome, but he was a man with a compelling, powerful presence anyway. Not a fancy man in any fashion. The revolver on his hip had plain walnut grips, and the Winchester rifle he carried in a saddle sheath had obviously seen plenty of use. When a grin spread across his face and his eyes twinkled with good humor, it was obvious that Frank was a good man to have as a friend.

When the grin went away and his eyes turned icy and hard as flint, it was equally obvious that Frank Morgan was a bad man to have for an enemy.

Frank was smiling now as he rode toward Buckskin, glad to be back, but wary, too. The only reason Conrad and Rebel were here was that the situation in Buckskin was rather unsettled at the moment. Trouble might be brewing that could affect the interests of the Browning Mining Syndicate—Frank and Conrad, in other words.

"There are rumors that someone is going to dispute the ownership of one of the mines in the area," Conrad had explained to Frank a week earlier, down in Arizona Territory. "I don't know which of the mines it is, though. I don't see how it could possibly be the Crown Royal. Our title to the claim is completely free and clear, as far as I know. But if there's a chance we'll have to defend it in court, I want to know about it so we can begin making preparations for the case."

Frank wasn't that well versed in legal matters himself. He had lawyers in Denver and San Francisco who looked after his business interests, and that was the way he liked it. He was perfectly happy to have Conrad and Rebel come back to Buckskin with him, though, and if there *was* any trouble that threatened the peace of the town, that was definitely his business as the marshal. He hoped the deputy he had left in charge, the crusty, capable old-timer called Catamount Jack, hadn't run into any problems he couldn't handle.

Frank pulled ahead of the buggy. His horse could make better time than the vehicle, which had to take the descent slow and careful-like. There was a road that the stagecoach from Carson City used, but it was narrow, twisting, and badly rutted in places.

The fresh scent of the pines, the arching blue sky, and the laughter of an icy, fast-flowing stream filled Frank's senses. The horse underneath him stretched its legs eagerly, and Frank let him run.

The slope leveled out into a meadow covered with grass that came fetlock-high on the bay. Tiny flowers dotted the grass colorfully here and there.

Altogether, it was much too pretty a picture to have death intrude on it.

Or at least, it should have been.

But it was at that moment Frank heard a sinister whisper next to his ear and recognized it as the wind-rip of a bullet passing close by his head. Instinct made him haul back on the reins and yank the horse into a tight turn.

He didn't know where the shot had come from, but his first concern was the buggy following him— and its occupants. He saw that the buggy had just emerged from the trees and started across the meadow with Conrad at the reins. Frank sent the bay lunging in that direction.

"Get back!" he shouted to Conrad as he stood up in the stirrups and waved urgently. He knew that made him a bigger target, but he had to make sure that Conrad saw him and realized something was wrong.

Conrad must have, because the buggy suddenly slowed. The bay lurched at that same instant as a bullet smashed into its chest, and Frank immediately kicked his feet out of the stirrups.

It was a good thing he did, because the bay went down, its front legs folding up underneath it. Frank was thrown forward over the horse's head. If he hadn't freed his feet when he did, he would have been dragged down with the bay, and it probably would have rolled over on him or caught him with one of its wildly flailing hooves.

As it was, Frank flew through the air and landed on the ground hard enough that all the breath was driven from his body. He was able to roll over several times and break some of the force of the fall, though, and when he came to a stop on his belly he was shaken but not stunned. His brain was still working.

It told him he was in a bad spot, and that was confirmed a second later when another slug plowed into the ground beside him. He heard the sharp whipcrack of a rifle this time and knew the shot came from his left somewhere. The bay had stopped thrashing around, so Frank scrambled toward the fallen horse. Its lifeless body was the only bit of cover available out here in the meadow.

Another slug sizzled past Frank's head, but he was moving too rapidly for the bushwhacker to draw an accurate bead on him. He threw himself behind the horse corpse and hunkered as close to the ground as he could. Twisting his head, he saw that the buggy had vanished back into the thick pines on the hillside, and was grateful for that. Conrad and Rebel ought to be safely out of the line of fire now.

With that worry off his mind, Frank turned his attention to the son of a bitch who was trying to kill him. When he heard another shot and then the thud of the bullet into the horse's body, he risked a quick look. Powder smoke hung over a cluster of rocks at the base of the slope about two hundred yards east of the place where the trail reached the meadow.

Frank waited for another shot, then lunged up and reached for the Winchester that was still in its sheath strapped to the saddle. Luckily, the bay hadn't fallen on that side, or Frank wouldn't have been able to get the rifle out. As it was, the bushwhacker almost levered another round into his weapon too fast, because he got another shot off before Frank could duck back down. The bullet tugged at the sleeve of Frank's shirt on the arm he had extended to snag the Winchester and jerk it from its scabbard.

He stretched out flat again. A fighting smile plucked at his lips. The odds were a mite more even now . . . and he was mad. That bay had been a fine horse, and it deserved a better end than being cut down by some slimy bushwhacker.

Frank thrust the Winchester's barrel over the horse and opened up, cranking off three rounds as fast as he could work the rifle's lever. He directed his shots toward the rocks where the would-be killer was hidden. He didn't think he would hit the bush-whacker, in all likelihood, but if he could get some slugs bouncing around in there, it would make things mighty hot for the varmint.

Several more shots sounded, but these came from the trees where the buggy had disappeared. Frank knew there was a rifle in the buggy, so Conrad must be taking a hand in this fight. As always, it made Frank feel good to know that his son was siding him. He continued peppering the rocks with lead.

This must have been more of a fight than the bushwhacker expected, because after a few min-utes, during a lull in the firing, Frank heard the swift rataplan of hoofbeats coming from the direc-tion of the rocks. When he risked a look, he saw dust haze rising into the air. The bushwhacker was giving up and taking off for the tall and uncut.

Or at least, that was what he wanted Frank to think. Frank had too much experience to leap up and make a target of himself just because it ap-peared the rifleman had fled. He hoped that Conrad had sense enough not to come out of the trees just yet. Even if Conrad didn't, he figured Rebel would know better anyway.

Minutes dragged by. Frank waited with the patience of a man who knew his life might depend on it. The buggy didn't come out of the trees either, so Conrad and Rebel were playing it safe, as he had hoped.

After about ten minutes, Frank heard horses coming from the direction of Buckskin. He rose up enough to take a look and saw four men riding out from the settlement. Frank's keen eyes recognized the rangy, buckskin-clad figure in the lead as Cata-mount Jack.

If the bushwhacker wasn't already gone, the arrival of the men from Buckskin would chase him off. Frank decided it was safe to stand up now. He got to his feet and waved the rifle over his head, catching the attention of Jack and the other men. Then he walked over to his hat, which had flown off when he was thrown from the mortally wounded horse, and picked it up. By the time Jack and the others galloped up and reined their mounts to a halt, Frank had brushed off the Stetson and donned it again.

Jack's leathery, bewhiskered face split in a grin under the battered slouch hat he wore.

"When I heard all the shootin' from up here, I said to myself Frank Morgan must be back in these parts," he declared. "I surely did!"

Chapter 2

Jack dismounted and stuck out a knobby-knuckled hand. Frank gripped it firmly, glad to see the man who had become his deputy and good friend.

"That wasn't a very friendly welcome," Frank said. "Downright hostile, in fact."

Jack nodded as his grin disappeared and was replaced by a dark frown.

"Yeah, that's the way things have been around here lately, downright hostile . . . and gettin' hostilerer all the time!"

Frank looked at the three men who had accompanied Jack and recognized them as Amos Hillman, the owner of the livery stable, Henry Burton, the former professor from back East somewhere, and Junior Ledyard, who worked for Amos as a hostler. He shook hands with all of them, glad to see them, but noted that they shared some of Jack's grim demeanor.

"It's good to be back anyway," he said.

"You may not feel that way when you hear what's been goin' on," Jack warned. "We got all kinds o' trouble. You may want to turn around and ride the other way."

Frank said, "I doubt it. Help me get my saddle off this horse, and you can tell me all about it."

Hillman motioned for Junior to give Frank a hand, and as the hostler was doing that, Jack said with sudden alarm in his voice, "Somebody comin'."

Frank glanced up and saw the buggy rolling out of the trees.

"Don't worry," he assured the deputy. "That's my son and daughter-in-law."

Jack's bushy eyebrows lifted in surprise.

"Conrad's back? He didn't seem too fond o' the place last time he was here. He must'a heard about Brighton."

"Who's Brighton?" Frank asked. All he knew, and all Conrad knew, was that there was some question about the legitimacy of the ownership of one of the silver mines near Buckskin.

At one time, during the settlement's first boom days, there had been dozens of mines around here. But then the veins of silver had seemed to play out, the mines had closed down, and Buckskin had almost dried up and blown away. Only a handful of stubborn folks had remained in the settlement, among them Thomas "Tip" Woodford, the owner of a busted mine called the Lucky Lizard.

Then silver had been rediscovered, and with the advances in mining techniques that had been made since the first boom, three of the claims had become highly profitable again, including Woodford's Lucky Lizard and the Browning Mining Syndicate's Crown Royal. The third mine was the Alhambra, owned by Jessica Munro, widow of Hamish Munro. Jessica was an absentee owner, since some folks around here still held grudges because of all the gun trouble and bloodshed caused by her late husband. She had hired a competent superintendent to run the mine, and things had settled down again.

But they never seemed to stay that way for long, Frank reflected as he watched the buggy approach. Conrad was still handling the reins, and Rebel had the Winchester across her lap. He wondered if she was the one who had taken those shots at the bushwhacker, instead of Conrad. It was certainly possible, given Rebel's feisty nature.

"Fella name of Dex Brighton," Catamount Jack said in answer to Frank's question. "He showed up a while back and started tellin' folks that he's the real owner of the Lucky Lizard."

So it was Tip Woodford's claim somebody was trying to move in on. That was a relief in one way, Frank thought, but still mighty bad news. Tip was the mayor of Buckskin and a good friend. The settlement might not even still be here if it weren't for Tip Woodford.

"Hold on and wait for Conrad and Rebel to get here so you'll only have to tell the story once," Frank told Catamount Jack.

The old-timer snorted.

"I'd just as soon not have to tell it at all, but I reckon you'd better hear about it. If Brighton gets away with his thievin', he's liable to go after the other mines next."

That was one of Frank's worries, too. An outlaw who went unchallenged usually kept trying to grab more and more.

Of course, he didn't *know* that this fella Brighton

was an outlaw, he reminded himself. As a lawman, he was supposed to keep an open mind.

But it was hard to believe that anything about Tip Woodford's operation wasn't honest and above-board.

Conrad brought the buggy to a halt.

"Frank, are you all right?" he asked, and Frank thought he sounded genuinely concerned.

"Probably picked up a bruise or two when I hit the ground, but I'll be fine," he said. "How about the two of you?"

"That varmint didn't even take any potshots at us," Rebel replied. "Looked like it was you he was after, Frank."

"Appeared that way to me, too." Frank looked at his son. "Did you let anybody here know that we were coming?"

Conrad shook his head. "Not really."

"What does that mean?"

Frank must have put the question a little sharper than he intended, because he saw Conrad's back stiffen.

"I sent a letter to Garrett Claiborne a couple of weeks ago, while you were still involved in that Ambush Valley business, advising him that we would be paying a visit to Buckskin once you returned. It's possible that he's received it by now."

Frank thought it was likely. There was no telegraph line into Buckskin yet, but mail deliveries on the stage line that ran down here from Carson City were pretty dependable.

Catamount Jack shook his head. "I saw Claiborne just a couple o' days ago, and he ain't said nothin' to me about you bein' on the way back here yet,

Frank. I reckon he would have if he knew. Could be he never got the letter."

"But somebody else could have gotten his hands on it," Frank mused, "and decided that he wanted to give me a hot lead welcome when I came back."

"Makes sense," Jack said with a nod. "And I wouldn't put a little dry-gulchin' past that son of a bitch Brighton." He tugged on the brim of his hat as he nodded at Rebel. "Beggin' your pardon, ma'am. I sometimes forget to watch my language."

"It's easy to forget when you're talking about a son of a bitch," she said with a smile. "Don't worry, Jack. I heard a lot worse than that from my brothers every day when I was growing up."

Conrad looked a little scandalized, though. Frank figured that in some respects, Conrad would never completely get used to the rough-and-tumble ways of the West.

"All right, Jack," he said to his deputy. "Tell us about Brighton."

"Wait a minute," Conrad said. "Do you mean to conduct a serious discussion out in the sun, right next to this dead horse?"

"It'd be a mite more pleasant in the Silver Baron, all right, Marshal," Jack said. He licked his lips, no doubt thinking of the cool beer available in the saloon as well.

Frank chuckled. "All right. Let me just climb up in the back of the buggy . . ."

He stepped into the vehicle, crouching in the area behind the seat. Conrad got the pair of horses moving again, and they set off for town, accompanied by Catamount Jack and Professor Burton. Amos Hillman and Junior Ledyard remained behind to finish stripping the gear off the fallen bay. They would dispose of the horse's body later.

A lot of people in the settlement had heard the shooting from the meadow, which was only about half a mile away. Because of that, there were quite a few curious folks still on the street when the buggy and the two riders arrived.

As they went past the hotel, Frank noticed a man standing on the building's front porch, a shoulder leaned casually against one of the posts holding up the awning. The man studied the newcomers with a cool but intent interest. He was well dressed in a brown tweed suit, matching vest, and dark brown Stetson. His face was tanned, in sharp contrast to the white hair under the hat. That hair color was premature, though, because Frank estimated that the man was no more than thirty-five years old.

The townspeople flocked around the buggy to find out what had happened, and within seconds the word was going through town that Frank Morgan was back in Buckskin. Conrad stopped the buggy at the hitch rack in front of the Silver Baron Saloon, which was also owned by Tip Woodford, and when Frank swung down from the vehicle the townspeople crowded around him, eager to shake his hand and welcome him back.

Frank still enjoyed that, because it was so different from the way he had been treated in so many places he had visited. In most settlements, people had shunned him and been afraid of him because he was a gunfighter. The local badge-toter usually showed up pretty quickly, often carrying a shotgun, to warn him about causing trouble and suggest that it would be better for all concerned if he would just vamoose out of town. Women stared at him like he was some sort of monster, and children stared wide-eyed at him as if they could see the blood of all the men he had killed on his hands.

Not here, though. Here he was a respected member of the community. Quite a change. So Frank made sure he shook hands with and spoke to everyone who wanted to greet him before he made his way into the saloon and took a seat at a big table in the rear along with Conrad, Rebel, and Catamount Jack. Conrad looked like he didn't care for the idea of his wife being inside a saloon, but give the boy credit for *some* brains, Frank thought. Conrad had figured out by now that it wasn't going to do any good to argue with her.

Johnny Collyer, the head bartender and the fella who ran the Silver Baron for Tip Woodford, brought over a pitcher of beer and some mugs himself, rather than sending the drinks with one of the waiter gals. He shook hands with Frank and said, "It's mighty good to have you back, Marshal. Buckskin just hasn't been the same without you."

"Thanks, Johnny. Is Tip around?"

Collyer shook his head. "Out at the mine, I reckon. Miss Diana, too."

Diana Woodford, Tip's daughter, kept the books and ran the mine office. Like Rebel, whom she actually resembled slightly in her blond beauty, she was a bit of a tomboy, and she'd had quite a crush on Frank Morgan when he first came to Buckskin. Frank was old enough to be her father, though, and he had successfully deflected her interest to Garrett Claiborne, who was younger and a more appropriate beau for her.

Johnny Collyer poured beers for everybody, even Rebel, and then went back behind the bar. Frank sipped from his mug, enjoying the way the cool beer cut the trail dust. He wasn't much of a drinker, preferring a good cup of coffee or even a phosphate to hard liquor, but sometimes a beer went down just fine.

He said, "All right, Jack. Tell us about Dex Brighton."

Jack took a healthy swallow of beer, his corded throat working as he swallowed, then lowered the mug and wiped the back of his other hand across his whiskery mouth.

"Fella rode into town about a month ago, not long after you left for Arizona Territory, Frank," the old-timer began. "Nobody paid much attention to him at first. You know how it is, folks come and go all the time."

Frank nodded. Ever since the silver boom had gotten rolling again, new folks showed up in Buckskin nearly every day.

"Brighton wasn't a miner or a cowhand or anything like that," Jack went on. "You could tell that by lookin' at him. I took him for a gambler maybe, and sorta kept an eye on him for a day or two, just to make sure he wasn't a tinhorn who was gonna try to set up a crooked game or anything like that. I reckon he was just gettin' the lay o' the land, though, before he sprung his surprise. He went into Tip Woodford's office one day and told ol' Tip that he was the real owner of the Lucky Lizard."

"That's not possible," Conrad said. "Mr. Woodford has owned the Lucky Lizard claim for years, ever since the first silver boom in Buckskin."

"Yeah, well, that ain't the way Brighton tells the

story. Y'see, Tip Woodford bought that claim from a fella years ago, before there ever was a Lucky Lizard Mine, before anybody had found any silver in these parts at all. Brighton says that his pa was partners with the hombre Tip bought the claim from, and that they had a deal so that they could only sell out to each other, not to anybody else. So accordin' to Brighton, it weren't legal when Tip bought the claim, and since both o' the original partners is dead, that means the Lucky Lizard belongs to him."

Frank frowned in thought. The story was a bit convoluted, but no more so than plenty of other circumstances surrounding various mines and mining claims in the West. Disputes over the ownership of such rights were commonplace.

"What did Tip do?" he asked.

"Well, I reckon he wanted to throw Brighton out on his ear, but Diana was there so he didn't. He just told Brighton he figured he was mistaken about that and even offered to show him all the paperwork provin' that Tip owned the mine. Brighton said that that didn't mean anything, but he appreciated ever'thing Tip did to get the mine operatin', so he said he was willin' to let Tip keep a one-quarter share for himself. He said he figured that was a mighty generous offer."

"I'm guessing Tip didn't see it that way."

Jack snorted. "Not hardly. He got a little hot under the collar finally, and told Brighton to go peddle his papers elsewhere. Brighton said he'd be sorry for that and said when he took over, Tip wasn't gonna get nothin'." The old-timer's bony shoulders rose and fell in a shrug. "That's how things stand, as far as I know. Brighton's still hangin' around town tellin' folks that he's the real owner o' the Lucky Lizard, and there's not much Tip can do about that. Word is that Brighton's got some fancy lawyer comin' in to take Tip to court and try to take the mine away from him that way. But Brighton's been seen talkin' to some hard-lookin' hombres, too, and Tip's a mite nervous. He thinks Brighton might try to take over the Lucky Lizard with hired guns, if it comes to that."

"It won't," Frank promised with a grim look on his face. "Not if I have anything to say about it."

"Well, maybe you can start now," Jack said. He nodded toward the batwings at the saloon's entrance, which had just been pushed aside to let a man stroll in. Somehow, Frank wasn't surprised to see the hard-faced, white-haired gent from the hotel porch walking toward them as Jack added, "Here comes Brighton now."

Chapter 3

Dex Brighton came straight toward the table where Frank sat with Conrad, Rebel, and Catamount Jack. Frank rose to his feet as the man approached, wanting to meet Brighton on an equal basis. Brighton stopped a few feet away and gave Frank a curt nod.

"You're not wearing a badge, but I assume you're the town marshal. Frank Morgan, right?"

"That's right," Frank said.

Brighton extended a hand.

"I'm Dexter Brighton. It's good to meet you, Morgan. I've heard a lot about you."

His affable manner didn't extend to his eyes, which remained cold and hard. Frank hesitated before shaking his hand, but only for a second. If Brighton was trying to cause trouble for Tip Woodford, then Frank had to regard him as an enemy, because Tip was his friend.

At the same time, it was possible that Brighton had legal grounds for his claim on the Lucky Lizard, in which case Frank was sworn to uphold the law. He gripped Brighton's hand, which was hard, dry, and strong. The man was well dressed and had the look of money about him, but he had done plenty of hard work in his life, too.

"I've heard a few things about you, too, Brighton," Frank said.

Brighton chuckled, but again, the humor didn't reach his eyes. "I'm sure you have." He nodded to Catamount Jack. "Hello, Deputy."

Jack just grunted.

"Don't believe everything you hear, Marshal," Brighton went on.

"I generally don't. I like to see things with my own eyes before I make up my mind about anything—or anybody."

Brighton nodded. "That's wise. I think you'll find that I'm just a man who wants what's rightfully his."

"We'll see," Frank said.

Conrad cleared his throat.

Frank half-turned and waved his left hand toward the table. "My son, Conrad Browning, and his wife."

Conrad stood up and shook hands with Brighton as well. "Mr. Brighton," he said.

"Conrad Browning of the Browning Mining Syndicate," Brighton said with a smile. "Owner of the Crown Royal Mine. You see, I looked into the situation here in Buckskin before I ever came out here. I hope we'll be friendly competitors once I take over the Lucky Lizard. Enough silver to go around for everyone, eh?"

"Your business affairs are your own, Mr. Brighton," Conrad replied, his voice cool. "They have nothing to do with the Crown Royal or the Browning Mining Syndicate."

"And we'll have to see about that claim of yours on the Lucky Lizard," Frank put in. "I haven't seen anything to indicate that it doesn't belong to Tip Woodford free and clear, just the way it always has."

"Not always," Brighton said, and for the first time a tone of clipped anger crept into his voice as his polished façade slipped. "And as far as evidence goes, I have the partnership agreement between Jeremiah Fulton and my father, Chester Brighton. It clearly states that if either of them wanted to sell his share in the mining claim they owned jointly, it could only be sold to the other partner. Fulton's sale of the claim to Woodford was in violation of that agreement. Therefore, the sale was null and void. The agreement also states that in the event of the death of one partner, his share would pass to the other partner. Fulton died first, so legally the entire claim went to my father. And when *he* died, it passed on to me. It's just that cut-and-dried, gentlemen."

"You talk like a lawyer," Frank said. His tone of voice made it clear he didn't think that was a good thing.

Brighton smiled and shook his head. "No, I'm a businessman, not an attorney. But I *have* had some excellent legal advice on this matter."

"Where's that partnership agreement you mentioned? You're going to have to produce it if you want to convince me or anybody else that you're telling the truth about your claim on the Lucky Lizard."

"In due time, Marshal. When the time is right."

"And when is that going to be?"

"I believe a circuit court judge is due to arrive here in another week or so on his usual rounds," Brighton said. "My attorney should be here by then, too."

So that was his plan, Frank thought. He wasn't sure why Brighton had come to Buckskin ahead of the judge, instead of showing up at the same time and springing his surprise then, so that Tip Woodford wouldn't have had any time to prepare a defense. But if this was the way Brighton wanted to play it, that was all right with Frank.

He nodded and said, "I reckon we'll let the court settle it then. In the meantime, there's no need for you to be stirring up trouble around town."

Brighton spread his hands. "What have I done to stir up trouble?"

"I hear you've been talking to some hardcases. Hired guns maybe, in case this legal challenge of yours doesn't work out and you try to take over Tip's claim by force."

Brighton's face darkened with anger. "That's scandalous talk, Marshal. I haven't broken any laws, and I don't appreciate being treated as if I have. I think it's obvious, too, that you're not going to be impartial in this matter since you and Woodford are friends. He's the one who hired you for your job here, isn't he?"

"That doesn't have anything to do with me warning you not to cause trouble," Frank snapped.

"Doesn't it? Before you pinned on a badge here, you were nothing but a cheap, drifting gunman, isn't that right, Morgan? It seems to me that if anyone's got a hired killer on his side, it's Woodford, not me."

Frank tightened the reins on the anger that welled up inside him. Catamount Jack wasn't as restrained. He leaped to his feet.

"Why, you slick, no-good polecat! You can't talk that way about Frank Morgan!"

He started toward Brighton, his hands balling into knobby-knuckled fists.

Frank moved quickly to get between Brighton and his deputy before Jack could throw a punch. It wouldn't make a judge any more kindly disposed toward Woodford's case to have one of the local lawmen physically attacking Brighton. That could make it look like Tip was trying to use his position as Buckskin's mayor to intimidate his opponent— even though Tip really had nothing to do with it.

Putting a hand on the old-timer's chest to hold him back, Frank said, "Take it easy, Jack. That won't do any good." He looked over his shoulder at Brighton. "I think you'd better move along, mister."

An arrogant smile appeared on Brighton's face as he said, "As far as I know, Marshal, this is a public place, and you don't have any right to order me out unless I'm causing a disturbance."

"You're causin' a disturbance, all right," Jack said, lifting a fist and shaking it. "You're makin' me mad as hell, you damn tinhorn."

Brighton ignored him and continued looking at Frank with that challenging, coolly mocking smile. He stood motionless, his thumbs hooked in his vest.

"He's right, Jack," Frank told the deputy. "He hasn't broken any laws, so I guess he's got a right to be here. Why don't you go on back over to the office, and I'll see you later."

Jack looked like he was going to put up an argument, but after a moment he nodded.

"All right, but watch yourself, Marshal," he said.

"This fella's like a snake, all coiled up and just waitin'. You never know when he's gonna strike."

"Don't worry," Frank said. "I've stomped plenty of snakes in my time."

Brighton stiffened at that, but he didn't say or do anything. Still glaring darkly, Catamount Jack stalked out of the saloon, sort of like his namesake.

"Well, Marshal, this has been a very informative conversation," Brighton said when Jack was gone. "I knew that your deputy didn't like me, and now I see that I have to regard you as an adversary, too, because of your connection to Woodford."

"I'm sworn to uphold the law, Brighton," Frank said, echoing his earlier thought. "If the circuit judge supports your claim, you'll have no trouble from me, regardless of what I might think of you personally."

"I hope that's true, Marshal. I think you'll see in time that we don't have to be enemies." Brighton turned to the table, tugged on the brim of his hat, and said to Rebel, "Ma'am, it was an honor and a pleasure to make your acquaintance. I apologize for any discomfort or embarrassment I might have caused you."

Rebel gave him a cool smile. "Don't worry about it, Mr. Brighton. I'm not uncomfortable or embarrassed." She paused, then added, "You see, *I've* stomped a few snakes in my time, too."

Surprise flared briefly in Brighton's eyes before he controlled it. Rebel wasn't the beautiful ornament that clearly he had taken her for. He managed to chuckle and said, "I'll bet you have, ma'am." Then he nodded to Frank and Conrad. "Gentlemen."

They waited until he was gone, then sat down again. The saloon had quieted down some during the confrontation at the rear table, as the Silver Baron's patrons turned to watch. The noise level in the place gradually returned to normal as they realized that there wasn't going to be a brawl or a shootout after all.

"I don't like that hombre," Rebel said. "He's got some of the coldest eyes I've ever seen."

"But he certainly acts like a man with the law on his side," Conrad said. "He seems confident of winning his case once the judge arrives."

Frank nodded. "Yeah, but if that's true, why show up ahead of time like he did? Why not come into town with his lawyer just before the judge gets here?"

"That's a good question," Conrad admitted. "Really, though, it's none of our business."

"None of *your* business maybe. *I've* got to keep the peace here."

Conrad shrugged. "There's no law against what he's done so far."

"You almost sound like you're on his side," Rebel said.

"Not at all. I don't like the man either. But perhaps I'm more accustomed to dealing with his sort than either of you are. I've done business with plenty of men that I didn't necessarily like or even trust."

"You won't be doing any business with him," Rebel snapped. "At least I hope not."

Conrad shook his head. "I don't see any reason why I would be. If his claim has no legal standing and is thrown out of court, then he's a nonentity as far as we're concerned. If it's upheld, then as he said, he's a competitor. Either way, he's got nothing to do with the Browning Mining Syndicate or the Crown Royal." He smiled. "Which is a great relief, because it means that we can go ahead and get out of here and go home to Boston."

"So soon?"

"We've been out here for two months. Isn't that long enough?"

"I wouldn't mind staying out here for good," Rebel said softly.

Conrad frowned.

Frank sensed that the question of where they should live was an ongoing discussion between Conrad and Rebel. It was also none of his business, so he stood up to leave.

"Reckon I'll go on over to the office and see if there's any paperwork I need to catch up on. I knew I could trust Jack to keep the peace around here while I was gone, but he's not much on reading and writing."

"We'll see you later," Conrad said. "We'll be staying at the hotel tonight. Perhaps you'd like to join us in the dining room for dinner?"

Frank would have preferred eating at the Chinaman's hash house or the café run by Lauren Stillman, Ginnie Carlson, and Becky Humphries, the three soiled doves who had retired from the world's oldest profession and settled down in the second-oldest—filling the bellies of hungry men.

But he wasn't going to turn down the invitation from Conrad, so he smiled, nodded, and said, "Sure. I'll see you there."

He stopped at the bar on his way out to pay Johnny Collyer for the beer, even though the bartender tried to say the drinks were on the house. Frank had to pause and shake hands with several of the men at the bar, too, since they wanted to welcome him back to

Buckskin. Claude Langley, the dapper, goateed Virginian who ran the undertaking parlor, said in his Southern drawl, "Things just haven't been the same around here with you gone, Marshal."

"Not as many bodies to bury, huh?"

Claude frowned. "Well, that's not exactly the way I meant it, but now that you mention it . . . and I mean no offense, Marshal . . ."

Frank clapped a hand on his shoulder.

"I know you don't, Claude. I'll see you around."

And probably all too soon, Frank thought, if his past history was any indication.

He went to the entrance and pushed the batwings aside to step out onto the boardwalk. The afternoon was well advanced by now, and night would be falling soon. Some of the workers from the mines would show up for an evening's raucous entertainment. Quiet hung over Buckskin at the moment, though, almost as if the settlement was holding its breath.

As the batwings flapped closed behind Frank, the quiet in the street was shattered by a hoarse shout. He looked around and saw a man running toward him.

"Marshal, you'd better come quick!" the townie called in an urgent voice. "Tip Woodford's about to kill that Brighton fella!"

Chapter 4

Frank caught hold of the man's arm to stop him as he stumbled.

"Take it easy," he said. "Catch your breath and tell me what's going on."

The man nodded and dragged in a lungful of air. Frank recognized him as Vern Robeson, who worked at Amos Hillman's livery stable.

After a moment Robeson was able to say, "I was runnin' down to the marshal's office to fetch Catamount Jack. I'd heard you were back in town, Mr. Morgan, but I didn't know where you were. Just lucky I ran into you, I guess."

"What about Tip Woodford and Brighton?" Frank prodded.

Robeson's eyes widened.

"Oh, yeah! They're down at the Lucky Lizard office. I heard Tip say he was gonna shoot Brighton if he didn't get outta there!"

Frank nodded and let go of Robeson's arm. He took off at a fast walk toward the building that housed the mining company's office, saying over his shoulder, "Go get Jack anyway and tell him to hurry on down there."

"Sure thing, Marshal!" Robeson said as he broke into a run again.

It wasn't far to the Lucky Lizard office, and when Frank got there he saw that the confrontation had spilled out of the building and into the street. Tip Woodford stood on the sidewalk, an old-fashioned cap-and-ball revolver in his hand. Red-faced with anger, he brandished the heavy gun, threatening Dex Brighton with it as Brighton stood a few yards away in the street.

Thomas "Tip" Woodford looked more like a miner than a mine owner. He had graying red hair, and his blocky body was clad in overalls, a slouch hat, and work boots, the same sort of outfit he had worn when he was still a penniless prospector. He had made a fortune, lost it, then made another one, and stayed pretty much the same throughout. His wealth hadn't changed him and probably never would.

His daughter Diana, wholesomely pretty in a gingham dress, clung to his left arm with a scared expression on her face. Tip shrugged her off and jabbed the old revolver's barrel toward Brighton.

"I'm sick and tired o' you, mister!" he bellowed like a wounded buffalo. "You come around here bother-in' us again with that line o' bull you been spoutin', and I'll blow a hole in you, I swear I will!"

Brighton didn't appear to be frightened, even though he had to know that an old horse pistol like that was a touchy weapon and might go off at any moment. Frank certainly knew that. He slowed as he approached, not wanting to spook Woodford, and called, "Tip! It's Frank Morgan! Put that gun down before you hurt somebody."

Woodford's eyes darted toward Frank for a second, but he didn't lower the gun and his attention went right back to Brighton.

"Heard you were back in town, Frank," the mayor said. "Good to see you."

"It's good to be back. At least, it was until you started threatening to ventilate folks."

Woodford grunted. "This thievin' varmint don't qualify as folks. He's like a hydrophobia skunk that you got to shoot before it gets in your chicken house."

As cool and calm as ever, Brighton said, "You heard the man, Marshal. He's threatened my life. I want you to arrest him."

"There's no need for that," Frank said. "Tip's not going to hurt anybody. He's just mad, and *he's going to put the gun down!* Do it now, Tip."

Diana took hold of her father's left arm again.

"Please, Pa," she said. "It's not going to help anything if you shoot that fella. Then you'll just go to prison for murder."

"Or the gallows," Brighton gibed

Frank said, "You're not helping matters, Brighton."

He moved forward, holding his hand out toward Woodford, palm down, making gentle motions toward the ground. The mayor didn't lower the gun, though, until Frank eased between him and Brighton.

"Dadgum it, Frank," Woodford said. "You've been gone. You don't know what this varmint's been up to."

"I've heard quite a bit about it already. Why don't you give me that hogleg, and we'll go in the office and talk about it."

Woodford hesitated, then finally shrugged and placed the cap-and-ball in Frank's hand.

"Aren't you going to arrest him, Marshal?" Brighton demanded from behind Frank. "I'll swear out a formal complaint."

Frank swung around to face the man.

"Back East you might get away with that, Brighton, but not here. No harm's been done, so move along. Anyway," he added, "you shouldn't have come down here and provoked the situation. I want you to steer clear of the Lucky Lizard office from now on."

Brighton sneered. "You're a poor excuse for a lawman, taking sides this way, Morgan. Maybe I should get in touch with the authorities in Carson City and request that a U.S. marshal be sent down here to restore some real law and order."

"You go right ahead and do that if you want to, mister," Frank bit off. "You just go right ahead."

He wasn't worried about Brighton's threat. Getting a U.S. marshal in here might even be a good idea. Most of the federal lawmen who worked west of the Mississippi were tough, competent, and had some common sense.

Tip Woodford stepped around Frank and said, "You'll never get your hands on the Lucky Lizard with your legal trickery, Brighton. That mine belongs to me, fair and square. Jeremiah Fulton had every right to sell it to me. He never even said anything about havin' a partner!"

"Of course he didn't. He knew he was swindling you." Brighton laughed curtly. "But this will all come out in court. You're a fool, Woodford. You could have had a quarter-share in the mine, strictly out of the goodness of my heart, but now I'm going to take all of it away from you. Every last penny. You and your daughter will be left with nothing, you pathetic old oaf."

Tip's face flushed a dark brick-red, and he moved with more speed than Frank anticipated. He didn't have the old revolver anymore, but he still had a big, beefy fist and the strength that came from swinging a pick thousands of times. He lunged at Brighton and smashed a blow into the Easterner's jaw.

Brighton appeared to be taken by surprise by Woodford's attack, just as Frank was. The punch rocked him back a step, but he didn't go down. As he caught his balance he struck back, hammering a left into the mayor's midsection and then chopping a sledging right across his face.

"Pa!" Diana cried.

Woodford was driven back by Brighton's powerful blows. He outweighed Brighton, but the other man was younger and stronger. As Woodford sagged to one knee, Brighton closed in on him, drawing back a leg to kick him in the face.

Frank grabbed Brighton's shoulder and shoved him away instead. "That's enough, blast it!"

Brighton's face was dark with fury. He ignored Frank and went for Tip Woodford again. This time Frank caught him around the middle. The muscles in Frank's shoulders bunched as he flung Brighton back. The man fell this time, his hat flying off as he rolled in the street.

Brighton came up spitting curses. With a visible effort, he brought his rage under control and pointed a finger at Woodford.

"You saw it, Marshal!" he shouted at Frank. "If pointing a gun at me wasn't enough, now he's physically attacked me! If you're a real lawman and not just Woodford's lapdog, you have to arrest him!"

Frank felt like taking a punch at Brighton himself. The hombre just rubbed him the wrong way.

Unfortunately, Brighton was right. Tip had crossed the line, and the crowd that had gathered around to watch the angry confrontation had seen the whole thing. Tip hadn't left him with any choice.

Stepping over to the mayor, who was still on one knee, Frank reached down and took hold of his arm. "Come on, Tip," he said.

Woodford stared up at him. "You're arrestin' me, Frank? *Me?*"

"You shouldn't have taken a poke at Brighton. That's assault and disturbing the peace."

"He's the one who's disturbed the peace o' this town!"

Tip was right about that, Frank thought, but that sort of disturbance wasn't against the law, worse luck.

"Frank, you can't do this," Diana said as Frank helped her father to his feet.

"The law says I do," Frank replied heavily.

Woodford brushed himself off and straightened his shoulders, achieving a rough dignity despite his work clothes.

"It's all right, Frank," he said. "We hired you to be the marshal and enforce the law, and I reckon that's what you got to do, whether any of us like it or not."

"And I sure don't," Frank said under his breath.

"Are you taking him to jail?" Brighton demanded.

Frank turned toward the man.

"That's right."

Brighton sneered. "And I assume you'll let him go as soon as you get there. This is all for show, isn't it?"

"Nope. Mayor Woodford will be treated like any other prisoner. He'll stay in jail until he posts bail, and then his case will be heard by the circuit judge when the judge holds court here."

"Who's going to set the amount of the bail?"

Tip laughed harshly.

"As the mayor, I gen'rally do that. Reckon this time it'll be up to the marshal."

Frank nodded. "You usually set bail at twenty dollars for offenses like this, Mayor. So to make sure there aren't any complaints about favoritism . . ." He shot Brighton a dark look, then continued. "I'm going to set bail at fifty dollars for you."

"That's a joke!" Brighton protested, flinging a hand angrily toward Woodford. "He can pay that without any trouble."

"I've more than doubled the usual bail," Frank said. "If that's not enough to satisfy you, Brighton, then you can take it up with the judge when he gets here."

"Don't think for a second that I won't."

Still holding Woodford's arm, Frank steered him toward the squat stone building that housed the marshal's office and town jail.

"Come on, Tip."

Woodford looked at his daughter and told her, "Get the bail money from the office and bring it over later, honey. No need to get in any hurry about doin' it, though. I don't mind sittin' in jail for a while. It's been a long time since I been behind bars."

Frank led the mayor away. He cast a glance over his shoulder to make sure that Dex Brighton didn't try to bother Diana Woodford.

The Easterner didn't even look in Diana's direction,

though. He just picked up his hat, slapped it against his thigh to remove some of the dust from it, clapped it on his head, and strode off toward the hotel.

"That was a damn fool stunt, Tip," Frank said under his breath to his prisoner. "You didn't leave me any option except to arrest you."

"Doggone it, I know that, Frank, and I'm sorry I put you in that spot. That Brighton hombre just makes me so mad I can't see straight. I reckon I went plumb loco."

Frank grunted. "Can't say as I blame you. Fella waltzes in here and tries to take away what you've worked years for. That's enough to make anybody loco." Frank paused. "Problem is, he may have the law on his side."

"I don't believe it for a minute! Brighton's crooked. You can tell it just by lookin' at him."

For Tip's sake—and for the sake of the town—Frank hoped that the mayor was right. He had a feeling that Buckskin would be worse off with Brighton as the owner of the Lucky Lizard. Tip had always funneled some of his profits from the mine right back into the town, although not very many people knew about that.

They met Catamount Jack on the way to the jail. "What'n blazes is goin' on here?" the deputy asked. "Frank, it looks like you're arrestin' the mayor!"

"That's what I'm doing. Tip got into a ruckus with Brighton. He threw the first punch."

"It was a good one, too," Woodford said with a smile. "Felt it all the way up to my shoulder."

"I sent Vern Robeson to fetch you," Frank went on. "How come you're just showing up now, Jack?"

"I was, uh, indisposed. Sorry, Marshal."

Frank knew that Jack must have been in the out-house behind the jail when Robeson came looking for him.

"That's all right," he said. "It happens to the best of us."

They reached the building and went inside. Frank waved toward the old sofa that sat against the front wall and told Woodford, "You might as well have a seat while we're waiting for Diana, Tip. I don't think there's any need to put you in a cell."

Woodford shook his head. "No, I want you to lock me up just like you would anybody else. Brighton's already got it in for you, too. I don't want to give him any more ammunition for when Judge Grampis gets here."

"Suit yourself," Frank said as he reached for a ring of keys hanging on a nail on the wall behind the desk. "The bunks in the cells are probably just about as comfortable as that sofa anyway. At least they don't have any broken springs sticking up through them."

He unlocked the door to the cell block and put Woodford in one of the cells, all of which were empty at the moment. Woodford himself pulled the door shut with a clang.

"Any coffee in the pot, Jack?" Frank asked.

"Always coffee in the pot," the deputy answered. "Question is, is it fit to drink?"

"Well, is it?"

"Only one way to find out. I'll get cups for both of you."

Jack brought the coffee while Frank sat down on a stool in front of the cell where Tip Woodford had lowered his bulk onto the blanket-covered bunk.

"I'll go take a turn around town," Jack said. "The

fellas comin' in from the mines need to see a badge to remind 'em that Buckskin's a law-abidin' place."

He went out, leaving Frank and Woodford sitting on opposite sides of the bars. Frank sipped the strong black brew from the tin cup in his hand and then said, "What about it, Tip? Is there any chance that Brighton is telling the truth? Is it possible he actually does own the Lucky Lizard?"

Woodford sighed. "I don't know, Frank. I honestly don't. I thought the deal I made with Jeremiah Fulton all those years ago was on the up-an'-up, but I reckon it's possible Fulton lied to me. If he really was partners with Brighton's pa, and if they had a signed agreement like Brighton says . . . well, then, much as it pains me to say it, he might be right."

"I'll have to see that document with my own eyes before I'll believe it," Frank said. "And even then, it's going to have to convince the judge and your lawyer, too."

"What lawyer?" Woodford asked with a frown. "I don't have a lawyer. Never needed one."

"You do now. And you're going to have one as soon as I can get word to San Francisco. You'll have the best lawyer that the Browning Mining Syndicate can provide for you."

Woodford looked doubtful. "I sure do appreciate the offer, Frank, but I ain't sure how that boy o' yours is gonna feel about it."

"You let me worry about Conrad," Frank said.

Chapter 5

"Absolutely not. That's a private dispute between Brighton and Mr. Woodford. The Browning Mining Syndicate can't afford to become involved. If Brighton prevails in court, we would have made an enemy of him from now on."

"It's a mite late to be worrying about that," Frank said as he looked across the table at his son. "Brighton already knows we don't like him."

They were in the hotel dining room with plates of roast beef and vegetables in front of them. A short time earlier, Diana Woodford had posted bail for her father, and Frank had released Tip with a warning to go right back to the big house on the edge of town where he and Diana lived and avoid Dex Brighton.

Conrad studied his father's face for a moment and then said, "You've already promised Mr. Woodford that we'll provide legal representation for him, haven't you?"

Frank shrugged. "Pretty much."

Conrad put his fork down so hard that it rattled against his dinner plate.

"Blast it, Frank! You seem to forget that Woodford is our competition, too. We don't owe him any favors."

"Garrett Claiborne is convinced that the veins of silver being mined by the Lucky Lizard and the Crown Royal don't come anywhere near each other," Frank said. "So it shouldn't matter to us one way or the other whether Tip's mine is successful."

Conrad nodded. "That's exactly the point. It shouldn't matter to us. You offered to help him simply because he's your friend."

"And what's wrong with that?" Frank asked without denying Conrad's charge.

"It's not good business."

"There are some things more important than business."

Rebel had been pretty quiet up to this point, but now she laughed.

"Don't say that to Conrad," she told Frank. "He considers it heresy."

Conrad flushed. "I do not. I just take a more practical approach to these matters than either of you do."

"You were quick enough to ask me for help when you had trouble with that railroad spur you were building and when Cicero McCoy stole all that money," Frank pointed out. "Anyway, I'm not asking you or the Syndicate to pay for Tip's lawyer. I figured to send for one of my personal lawyers. Turnbuckle and Stafford are already on retainer; I reckon they might as well earn some of that money I've been paying them."

Conrad's eyes widened.

"Turnbuckle and Stafford are two of the top attorneys in San Francisco! In the entire country, for that matter. You'd drag them out here to this frontier town for a simple mining dispute?"

"You've got to remember that there's a lot of money at stake here," Frank said. "Maybe it wouldn't be that much to hombres like Leland Stanford or J.P. Morgan or ol' John D. Rockefeller, but it's not like a penny-ante poker game either. Anyway, I'm only going to drag one of them out here from San Francisco. The other one can stay there and hold down the fort."

"Hold down the fort," Conrad muttered. "You refer to tending to the affairs of one of the top law firms in the country as holding down the fort."

"Call it whatever you want. I've already sent a rider to Carson City with a message to wire to San Francisco. With any luck, one of those fellas will be on a train heading in this direction before the day is over tomorrow."

Conrad shook his head. "I should have known there was no reasoning with you. You're as stubborn as ever."

"I'd say the apple doesn't fall far from the tree," Rebel commented.

Conrad frowned at her. "You could at least be on my side. You're my wife, after all."

"I'm always on your side, Conrad." She smiled. "Except when you're wrong."

"I give up. And I hope you two enjoy your dinner." Conrad looked around the table at them. "This is liable to be the last peaceful evening in Buckskin for quite some time!"

Frank couldn't argue with that.

Things never seemed to stay peaceful around him for very long, no matter where he was.

The next morning, Frank rode out to the Crown Royal Mine to talk to Garrett Claiborne. Stormy, the rangy gray stallion that had carried Frank over so much of the West, was clearly glad to be reunited with his master, and he stretched his legs and capered like he was a young horse again as they followed the trail out to the mine.

Dog, the big, shaggy, wolflike cur, had reacted in much the same fashion, rearing up to put his forepaws on Frank's shoulders and eagerly licking his face. To some people it might have looked like the dog was trying to tear out the man's throat, but Frank knew better.

Dog loped alongside, occasionally dashing off to check out some intriguing scent or give chase to a rabbit or prairie dog he didn't really want to catch. He didn't go very far, though, before returning to Frank's side.

Frank saw smoke rising before he reached the mine. He knew it came from the chimney of the cookhouse. Feeding a barracks full of hungry miners kept the two Mexican cooks busy most of the time.

He heard the rumble of the stamp mill, too, and the sound of the donkey engines that pulled the ore cars out of the mine along the narrow-gauge steel rails. When you got right down to it, a mine of any sort was a noisy, smelly place, and sometimes Frank wasn't sure that having them spread all over the West was a good thing.

Whenever mines and railroads and all the other

sorts of industry arrived, the frontier was never quite the same afterward, and for those who remembered it the way it used to be, as Frank Morgan did, there was a certain nostalgic melancholy associated with the march of progress. With each passing year, the places where a man could pause on a hilltop and watch an eagle wheeling through a pristine blue sky and know that he might well be the only human being within a hundred miles were becoming fewer and fewer.

Trying to stop civilization, though, or even slow it down much, was like trying to bail out the Mississippi with a tin cup. It just couldn't be done.

Frank reined to a halt and swung down from the saddle in front of the log building that housed the mine superintendent's office. He looped Stormy's reins around a hitching post, told Dog to stay, and went up the steps to the little porch and the door. He didn't knock but went on inside.

Garrett Claiborne, who hailed from Georgia, was on the smallish side, but he was muscular and could handle himself in a fight. He had tousled dark hair and a close-cropped beard. He was standing in front of a big, angled drawing board that had a diagram of some sort pinned to it. Frank didn't know much about such things, but he thought he recognized the drawing as a cutaway diagram of the Crown Royal's network of tunnels and shafts.

"Frank!" Claiborne exclaimed. "I mean, Mr. Morgan."

"Frank's just fine." He shook hands with the mining engineer. "How are you, Garrett?"

"Good, good," Claiborne said, nodding his head.

Frank gestured toward the diagram. "Thinking about expanding?"

"Yes, I believe the vein we're following in this tunnel right here"—Claiborne traced it on the paper with his finger—"is assaying out at a rate that makes extending the tunnel worthwhile. I was a little concerned about the stability of the rock strata, but I believe I've worked out some modifications to our bracing systems that will alleviate the extra strain."

Frank nodded. "That's good, I reckon . . . even though I barely understood what you said."

"Don't worry, I know how you and Mr. Browning insist on proper safety procedures being followed. There's always going to be a considerable amount of risk when you're working underground, of course, but I do my best to minimize it." Claiborne paused. "You know that most mine owners don't give much of a damn about such things."

"All I know is how you run the Crown Royal, Garrett, and I'm satisfied with that."

Claiborne stepped away from the drawing board and over to the desk.

"Some of the men told me you and Mr. Browning arrived in Buckskin yesterday afternoon. If you had let me know when you were getting here, I would have ridden into town and delivered a report on the mine's operation to both of you."

"Time enough for that later," Frank said with a wave of his hand. "Anyway, it wouldn't surprise me if Conrad drove out here later today in his buggy to look the place over." He frowned slightly. "You didn't get my letter telling you that we were on our way back from Arizona?"

Claiborne shook his head. "Not at all. This is the first time I've heard of any such letter."

That didn't come as a surprise to Frank. He hadn't forgotten about that attempt on his life the day before. Unless it had been a random holdup or something like that, which seemed unlikely, that bushwhacker must have been laying up in those rocks, waiting for him.

That meant someone hadn't wanted him to reach Buckskin alive, and the most reasonable explanation for how they had found out he was on his way was that the would-be killer—or someone he worked for—had filched that letter before Claiborne ever saw it.

The question remained, though, who that might be. And even more important, who wanted him dead?

Frank spent a while longer talking with Claiborne, then got back on Stormy and rode away from the Crown Royal. He wanted to take a better look around the site of the ambush.

The day before he had been more concerned with getting Conrad and Rebel on to Buckskin safely, and then the whole troublesome business with Brighton had come up. Now he wanted to see if he could find anything that might give him a clue to the bushwhacker's identity.

Instead of returning to the settlement and then following the road to Carson City, Frank cut across country instead. He had ridden around this region often enough so that with his frontiersman's instinct he wasn't likely to get lost. His route took him near the Lucky Lizard, but he didn't detour in order to pay a visit to the rival mine.

Frank's eyes were always in motion as he rode, searching the rugged countryside around him for any sign of danger. The man who had taken those shots at him had failed once, but the odds were that whoever he was, he would try again. Frank's natural wariness, honed by years of riding perilous trails, was in full force now.

Nothing happened, though, and he saw no sign of a trap as he approached the boulders where the rifleman had hidden. When he reached the rocks, he reined in and spent several minutes in the saddle before he dismounted, studying the area and getting the big picture set in his mind. From here he could see all the way across the expanse of meadow where he had been riding when the shooting started. The bushwhacker had come pretty close with his bullets—but not close enough.

Frank swung down from the saddle and hunkered on his heels, taking a closer look at the ground, which was hard enough so that it didn't take prints very well. He saw a few marks left by a horse's hooves, but there was nothing unusual about the prints and no way of knowing whether they had been made by the bushwhacker's mount or the mount of some other rider. When Frank was satisfied that he wasn't going to turn up anything important, he said, "Dog, search."

It was time for someone with senses even more acute than The Drifter's to take a hand—or a paw, in this case.

The big cur started nosing through the rocks, his muzzle close to the ground. After a moment, his hackles rose and he started growling, as if he smelled something that he didn't like. Frank had long since learned to trust Dog's instincts, even when they seemed almost supernatural. He mounted up again and called, "Dog, trail!"

Dog took off like a shot, bounding over the ground, darting around rocks, and leaping over deadfalls. Frank followed as best he could, although sometimes he had to call out for Dog to stop and wait while he and Stormy caught up. The trail wound back and forth, but led gradually up and over a ridge, then along a dry wash.

After half a mile or so, the wash came to a creek that was flowing, the stream that had formed the wash when it was in flood. Dog ran back and forth along the gravelly bank, barking in frustration. Obviously, the rider he had been following had entered the creek, making it impossible for the big cur to trail him.

"Let's go across and see if you can pick up the scent, big fella," Frank said to Dog. He sent Stormy splashing across the shallow stream.

The three of them cast up and down the stream for a mile in each direction without locating the bushwhacker's trail again. Frank was disappointed but not surprised. There was no telling how far the rifleman had followed the creek before emerging from it. Locating his trail again might take all day, and even then it would be just a matter of luck. They might not ever find it.

"Remember that hombre's scent, Dog," Frank told his canine friend. "You're liable to run across him again one of these days, and if you do, I'll be counting on you to let me know about it."

Dog seemed to grin at him. Frank knew the big cur wouldn't let him down.

In the meantime, he supposed they might as well start back to Buckskin. He wanted to keep an eye on the situation there and make sure no more trouble broke out between Tip Woodford and Brighton. There might be other problems that needed the marshal's attention, too.

And as he rode toward the settlement, he wondered if that telegram had reached the law offices of Turnbuckle and Stafford in San Francisco yet . . . and if it had, just what sort of reaction it had caused.

Chapter 6

Claudius Turnbuckle wasn't really a fire-breathing dragon, but Luther Galloway felt as if he were about to enter the lair of such a mythological creature as he approached the door of Turnbuckle's private office with a yellow, sealed envelope in his hand.

A lad wearing the uniform of Western Union had delivered the envelope to the law offices a short time earlier and said that the envelope contained an urgent telegram. Luther had worked for Turnbuckle and Stafford for almost two years now and knew that almost all telegrams were urgent—or at least, the people who sent them *thought* they were.

Mr. Turnbuckle might not agree, and if he didn't, Luther would take the brunt of his roaring displeasure. The telegram wasn't addressed to either of the partners in particular, and he would have much preferred dealing with Mr. Stafford, who, while pompous and stuffy, wasn't nearly as frightening as Mr. Turnbuckle.

Unfortunately, Mr. Stafford was away on business for the firm, down in Los Angeles, so Luther had no choice except to draw a deep breath and rap on the heavy oak door.

"What is it, damn it?" Turnbuckle's deep, powerful rumble penetrated the thick panel easily.

Luther turned the brass knob and eased the door open a couple of inches.

"Telegram, sir. The boy who delivered it said it was urgent."

"Well, bring it in."

Luther pushed the door back far enough for him to enter the dark-paneled office with its shelves of equally dark-spined legal volumes. The lone window was covered with thick drapes. Every time Luther came in here, he thought that he would go mad if he had to spend all his time in such a gloomy, oppressive place. Maybe that was why Mr. Turnbuckle was so short-tempered. He seldom saw the sun.

Turnbuckle sat behind a massive desk piled high with papers. A veritable flood of documents passed through the office every day, threatening to wash away the half-dozen clerks who worked in the outer office, Luther being the senior among them. Those young, would-be attorneys seldom stayed for very long, which was why it had taken Luther less than two years to move up in the ranks to his current position. He would have left by now, too . . .

If he had been able to pass the bar exam. Unfortunately, that had not yet been the case.

Turnbuckle peered over the half-spectacles that perched on the tip of his nose and extended a big, rough hand. Legend had it that the burly, balding, bushy-eyebrowed attorney had once worked on the docks here in San Francisco, loading and unloading the ships that came here from all over the world, and

Luther could easily believe it. Turnbuckle looked like he could physically break in half most of his opponents in court, which added to his intimidating presence and his impressive record of success.

"Well?" he snapped now. "Don't just stand there gawping, Galloway. Give it here."

Luther hurried forward and leaned over the big desk to hand the envelope to Turnbuckle. The lawyer ripped it open with long, blunt fingers and took out a yellow telegraph form. As his eyes scanned the words printed on the flimsy, those bushy eyebrows rose in surprise. Luther was equally surprised, or perhaps even more so, when a smile appeared on Turnbuckle's rugged face.

He ventured a question. "Good news, sir?"

Turnbuckle grunted and then said, "Frank Morgan needs our help."

The name was familiar to Luther, of course. He had seen it on countless documents.

"The . . . the gunfighter, sir?"

"The client whose business interests account for a significant amount of income for this firm, you mean," Turnbuckle scolded.

"Yes, sir, of course," Luther said quickly.

Still, he was shocked. He knew quite well that Frank Morgan was an equal shareholder with his son Conrad Browning in the many and varied Browning financial holdings, which included banks, railroads, mining ventures, shipping, and numerous other enterprises.

But Luther was equally aware of Morgan's notorious reputation as a gunman. There was no way of knowing how many men Morgan had killed during his long, blood-soaked career. Probably only a handful of people knew of his status as a tycoon, but everyone who had ever read one of the dime novels about him, or seen an article about him in *Frank Leslie's Illustrated Weekly* or *Harper's* or *The Police Gazette,* knew Frank Morgan as The Drifter, one of the deadliest gunfighters to ever roam the West.

Luther had read those stories. He had even perused some of the cheap, yellow-backed novels. It gave him a secret thrill whenever he handled legal documents relating to Morgan's affairs. However, he wouldn't have admitted that to anyone, because his interest in such violence was also something of a secret shame.

"What does Mr. Morgan want us to do for him, sir?" Luther asked now. "Some business dealings that need our attention perhaps?"

"You could say that," Turnbuckle said as he dropped the telegram on the desk, where it immediately threatened to get lost in the sea of other papers. He chuckled . . . actually *chuckled*, something that had never happened in Luther's experience. "He wants either me or Stafford to come to Nevada and help a friend of his defend a mining claim. Since Stafford's busy, it'll have to be me. Or rather, us, I should say."

Luther's eyes widened. There was so much to be amazed at in Turnbuckle's statement that he didn't hardly know where to start.

"N-Nevada, sir?"

"That's right. Buckskin, Nevada. I know you've heard of it, Galloway. The Crown Royal Mine is located quite near there."

"Yes, sir, of course. But . . . us?"

"You're going with me. I'll need a clerk to handle some of the details for me, and you're the most experienced one we have."

"But . . . but wouldn't it be better to leave me here to make certain that the office continues functioning smoothly, sir?"

Turnbuckle swept a hand crossways in a curt, slashing gesture.

"The office can run itself for a while, and you damned well know it, Galloway. This is a chance to get out and see some of the country. Besides, I've always wanted to meet Frank Morgan. He's supposed to be quite an individual."

Quite a killer, Luther thought. And what was this about seeing some of the country? Turnbuckle kept himself shut up inside this office as if he didn't care if he ever saw anything else.

"Get down to the depot and purchase tickets for us on the next train to Carson City," Turnbuckle went on. "Morgan needs us there as soon as possible. The circuit court judge is due to arrive in about a week, so we'll need time to prepare our case. Once you have the tickets, send a messenger to my house with our departure time, then go home and pack your bag."

"But sir, I can't just drop everything—"

Turnbuckle's head snapped up, and his familiar thunderous scowl appeared.

"And why not? You're a single man, I believe, with no family responsibilities."

"That's true, sir."

"And your responsibilities at work are what I say they are, isn't that true?"

"Yes, sir, certainly."

"Then get cracking, son!" Turnbuckle boomed. "There's no time to waste. I want to be on our way to Nevada before this day is over."

There was nothing Luther could do except nod feebly and say, "Yes, sir. Of course, sir."

Like it or not, he was going to Nevada.

But at least Mr. Turnbuckle had said the case involved defending some sort of mining claim for one of Mr. Morgan's friends. That was prosaic enough. Review the facts of the case, research the applicable legal precedents, prepare a brief, perhaps assist Mr. Turnbuckle with the arguments he would present to the judge . . . that was all it would amount to, and Luther was confident he could perform all of those tasks in a competent, efficient manner.

Just because Frank Morgan was involved didn't mean there would be any . . . gunplay . . . or killing . . . or anything like that.

When Dex Brighton first came to Buckskin, he had made arrangements to rent a horse from the surly proprietor of the local livery stable. Not that the man had been all that surly at first, but ever since he had found out about Brighton's claim on the Lucky Lizard, he'd been decidedly hostile, probably because he was friends with Tip Woodford. But a deal was a deal and he hadn't tried to back out of the one he'd made with Brighton.

Because of that, Brighton had a mount available whenever he needed one, a big gray gelding with white stockings and a white blaze on its face. He had ridden out to the Lucky Lizard several times to look over the mine that would soon be his. Today, though, he went the opposite way out of the settlement, heading into a rugged area where several played-out mines were still shut down. The renewed silver boom hadn't extended to them. The claims were still worthless and abandoned. No one went around them anymore.

They were perfect for Brighton's purposes, in other words.

He saw the outthrust sandstone brow of a ridge ahead of him and headed for it. As he drew closer, the black mouth of a mine tunnel entrance became visible at the base of the ridge, under the overhang. Brighton rode right up to the tunnel and dismounted.

The man who stepped out of the tunnel had a gun in his hand. He wore a black vest over a shirt that had once been white, and a black Stetson was tipped back on his head so that dark, wiry curls spilled out in front of the hat. The man's face was weathered and seamed by exposure, even though he wasn't more than forty. A misshapen lump of a nose that had been broken several times jutted out over a thick mustache and a wide, arrogant mouth.

"I thought I recognized you, Boss," the man greeted Brighton as he holstered his gun. "Wasn't gonna take any chances, though."

Brighton nodded. "That's good. No one knows you're here, Stample, and I want to keep it that way." He reached into the saddlebags slung over the back of the rented horse and brought out a couple of bottles of whiskey. "I figured you could use some provisions."

Stample threw back his head and laughed. "You do know how to take care of a fella, Boss." He reached for the whiskey. "These'll come in handy when the boys get here tomorrow . . . assumin' that there's any left."

"I was going to ask you about that. You're still expecting the rest of the men tomorrow?"

Stample nodded and jerked his head toward the mine entrance. "Yeah. Come on in and have a drink with me while you're here."

Brighton followed the man into the tunnel. Several crates were stacked about twenty feet inside. Brighton knew they contained food, ammunition, and other supplies.

He knew that because he had paid to outfit Stample and the other men who would be showing up here soon. You had to spend money to make money, as the old saying went, and although Brighton didn't like the spending part all that much, he was willing to do it if it would help him get his hands on a fabulously valuable silver mine.

It could still turn out that he wouldn't need any help from Stample and the other men he had hired, if he was successful in pressuring Woodford into agreeing to a settlement, but it was better to be prepared. And he was going to get *some* use out of them, because he had a job that he was going to explain to Stample right now.

They sat on empty crates near the remains of a campfire. Stample found some tin cups and splashed whiskey into them, then handed one to Brighton. As they sat there, Brighton heard Stample's horse moving around, deeper in the tunnel.

He gestured toward the sound with the cup in his hand.

"You've got your horse back there?"

"Yeah. The tunnel widens out considerable, right around that bend. Plenty of room for my horse and for the others, too, once they get here."

"What about the smoke from the fire?"

Stample pointed along the tunnel.

"Got some little ventilation shafts back yonder, too. You can feel the draft from the tunnel mouth."

Brighton nodded.

"It draws the smoke on through the tunnel," Stample continued, "and it filters out up on top of the ridge. Nobody'll notice it. Nobody will ever know we're here, Boss."

"That's the way I want it for now, so don't get careless," Brighton warned. He took a healthy swallow of the whiskey he had bought at one of the other saloons in Buckskin, not the Silver Baron. He didn't want to give his opponent in this fight any of his trade. "I've got a job for you."

Stample grunted. "About time."

"Woodford's determined to make a court case out of this. He's going to take it before the circuit judge next week."

A frown added creases to Stample's already lined forehead. "I thought you didn't want to go to court. You said you'd run a bluff on Woodford and make him turn over his mine to you. That phony partnership agreement you got ain't gonna stand up in court."

"We don't know that," Brighton snapped. "I paid good money to the man who faked it. But I'd rather not have to rely on that alone, and you're my insurance so that I won't have to, Stample."

"Keep talkin'," the hired gunman said.

"Woodford can't take the case to court if there's no judge, now can he?"

Stample's eyes widened. "You want me to kill a circuit court judge?"

"He'll be coming in on the stagecoach next Tuesday morning," Brighton said. "That's the only way to reach Buckskin since there's no rail line yet. That stagecoach is going to be held up by masked outlaws, and there'll be gunplay during the robbery. Tragically, the judge will be cut down by a stray bullet."

Stample looked intently at Brighton for a long moment and then nodded. "Yeah, I can see that happenin'," he said.

"That will give me more time to wear down Woodford and get him to settle this without going to court. Just be sure that no one can identify you or any of the other men, and don't let them trail you back here."

"Morgan never found me, did he?"

"And you didn't kill Morgan the way I asked you to," Brighton pointed out. "You missed."

Stample glared and then tossed back the rest of his whiskey before reaching for the bottle again.

"I had a good bead on the son of a bitch twice," he muttered. "He's just lucky, that's all."

Brighton finished off his drink.

"I can promise you one thing," he said. "If Frank Morgan keeps sticking his nose into my business . . . his luck is going to run out."

Chapter 7

When Frank got back to Buckskin, he found that the settlement was relatively quiet. Even though it was still considered a boomtown, with new people coming in all the time, word had gotten around that the marshal was a dangerous man to cross. In fact, he had quite a reputation as a gunfighter. Because of that, even the roughest hombres tended to walk a little softer and think twice—or three times—before they started trouble.

The exceptions to that were the hombres who came to Buckskin *because* Frank Morgan was the marshal. The ones who wanted to make a name for themselves by gunning down the man known as The Drifter.

Like the two who showed up the next morning.

Frank was still in the office, having a cup of coffee. He had been out earlier and had breakfast at the café, then returned here while Jack made the morning rounds. Frank sat at the desk with his feet propped up, flipping through the stack of wanted posters that had come in while he was gone to Arizona.

As usual, it was a pretty sorry assortment of owlhoots. But his own face had graced a wanted poster from time to time—always unjustified, but there nonetheless—he reminded himself. Some of these fellas might not be as bad as they were made out to be. But most of them probably were.

The door opened and Jack came into the office, hurrying enough so that Frank knew something was wrong. He took his feet off the desk and sat up straight.

"What's wrong?" he asked his deputy.

Jack pulled at the tuft of whiskers on his chin.

"Couple o' hombres are over at the Silver Baron jawin' about how they come to Buckskin to try you out, Frank. They think they're fast guns, but they're just young and stupid, as per usual."

"Did you talk to them?"

Jack shook his head. "Nope. Just heard about it from Vern Robeson."

"Vern gets around, doesn't he?" Frank chuckled, apparently unconcerned, but a grim look lurked in his eyes.

He had long since grown weary of killing young, ambitious men who wanted to make a name for themselves. And there was always the chance that one of these days, one of those would-be gunslingers would turn out to be faster and more accurate than him. It was inevitable that someday Frank would run into someone who could beat him to the draw . . . unless he hung up his guns and somehow made it stick.

That was mighty unlikely.

"All right." Earlier, he had dropped his hat on the desk rather than hanging it from the nail on the wall. He reached for it now as he went on. "I'll go see about it. Maybe I can talk some sense into their heads."

Catamount Jack snorted. "You'd be more likely to fill up a rat hole by poundin' sand down it. It wouldn't be as empty as those young fellas' heads are o' brains."

Frank put his hat on as Jack went to the wall rack and took down one of the shotguns hanging there.

"What do you think you're doing?" Frank asked.

"Goin' with you, o' course."

Frank shook his head. "There's no need for that."

"What if those varmints try to gang up on you? You might need me to handle one of 'em whilst you deal with the other." Then Jack grimaced and went on. "But if they do that you'll just have to kill 'em a mite quicker, won't you?"

"You're the law in this town if anything happens to me," Frank pointed out. "And even at this time of day, there are probably enough people in the Silver Baron that you don't need to be firing a scattergun in there."

"And in a gunfight, I can't haul out this old percussion pistol o' mine fast enough to do you much good as a partner," Jack said with a bitter twist in his raspy voice. "You're tryin' not to tell me that I'd be more of a liability than a help."

"I've never thought of you as a liability, Jack," Frank said honestly. "If I did, I never would have gone off and left you in charge here like I did. It's just that I'm better suited to handle some things than you are, and vice versa."

"Yeah, I'm better at bein' a useless ol' geezer."

Jack started toward the door, an angry look on his face.

Some genuine anger of his own welled up inside Frank. He caught hold of his deputy's arm and snapped, "Blast it, Jack, you're blowing this way out of proportion. You're about as far from useless as anybody in Buckskin. I could take this badge off right now and leave you in charge permanently, and I wouldn't lose a bit of sleep worrying about leaving the town in your hands."

"I couldn't handle gunnies like those two in the saloon, and you know it."

"You wouldn't have to if I wasn't here. The only reason men like that even come to Buckskin is to try their hands against me."

Jack couldn't argue with that. They both knew it was true. From time to time a crooked gambler set up a game, or some miners got in a fight, or somebody got knocked out and robbed in an alley after leaving some soiled dove's crib, but that was just about the normal extent of trouble in Buckskin these days. Jack was tough enough, and respected enough, to handle things like that.

But the would-be shootists and pistoleros were a different story. Those were Frank's responsibility.

And he had two of them waiting for him now.

"Come along with me if you want," he told Jack, "but leave the Greener here and stay out of the fight, if there is one."

"Oh, there'll be one," Jack said with grim certainty. But he went back to the rack and hung up the shotgun again, then fell in step beside Frank as the two of them started down the street toward the Silver Baron.

Even after all these years, it never failed to amaze

Frank how quickly word could spread of impending violence. As he and Jack approached the saloon, he saw several people gathered on the boardwalk in front of the place. More were headed in that direction.

Vern Robeson was one of the men peering in the Silver Baron's front window. He turned to greet Frank with an eager grin.

"Looks like there's gonna be two more notches on your gun pretty soon, Marshal!"

"I don't carve notches on my gun, Vern," Frank snapped. "I don't know any real gunfighters who do."

Vern's grin disappeared. He shuffled his feet and looked down at the boardwalk.

"Sorry, Marshal. I didn't mean nothin' by it."

"I'll bet Amos is wondering where you are."

"I'll go on along down there to the stable . . . in a few minutes."

Frank knew what the hostler meant. He was going to stay right here to see what was going to happen. If anybody died this morning, Vern Robeson wasn't going to miss it. And that was his right, Frank supposed. Vern wasn't breaking any law by standing on the boardwalk.

Frank pushed the batwings aside and stepped into the saloon. Catamount Jack was right behind him. Every nerve in Frank's body was alert, every muscle taut and ready for action. It was always possible in a situation like this that the men who were waiting for him might slap leather and start their guns blazing as soon as he walked into the room.

They didn't, though. In fact, the two young men standing at the bar didn't even realize he was there until they saw Willie Carter, the only bartender working at this time of the morning, looking intently at the door. Even then, they leisurely finished the drinks in front of them before they turned to face The Drifter.

Instantly, Frank saw the resemblance between them. They were brothers, probably no more than two or three years apart in age. Sleekly built, flashily dressed, handsome in a cheap way. Saloon gals probably fawned all over them. And when they grinned, the expressions reeked of arrogant confidence.

"Well, if it ain't the marshal," the older one said.

"See, Rand?" the younger one said. "I told you he wouldn't be scared to face us . . . even though he oughta be."

"You were right, Brock. I figured Frank Morgan was so old that he would've lost all his guts by now."

"If he ever had any to start with. Maybe he backshot all those fellas he's supposed to've killed. I mean, jus' look at him. I wouldn't put it past him, would you?"

Rand shook his head. "Nope. I reckon he never was any more'n a puffed-up bag o' shit."

Frank laughed, causing both brothers to look surprised. He couldn't help it. They had probably rehearsed those lines before they ever rode into town.

His reaction had thrown them off stride. They were confused and angry now.

"What the hell's the matter with you?" the one called Rand snapped. "You gone soft in the head, Morgan?"

"Nope," Frank said. "I've just heard that sort of garbage so many times, for so many years, that it just sounds foolish to me now. What do you reckon every would-be gunslick does when he decides to face me down? He tries to needle me into drawing, just like you two are doing. He tries to get under my skin, to make me mad, to make me careless." Frank shook his head. "It's never worked that way before, and it's not going to work now." He chuckled again. "But you boys go right ahead with whatever routine you've worked out. You might get me to laughing so hard that it *might* just give you a little bit of an advantage. I don't think so, but you never know."

"Why . . . why you crazy old fart!" Rand sputtered. "Don't you know who we are?"

"He's Rand Johnson, and I'm Brock Johnson," the younger brother said. "We're the Johnson brothers!"

Without looking around, Frank asked, "Those names mean anything to you, Jack?"

"Not a damned thing," the deputy replied. "I never heard of 'em. But then, I can't keep up with every loco kid who thinks he's fast with a gun."

"I killed Sammy Carlisle!" Rand said. "And Brock gunned Wichita McHenry and Pete Cragg! We're gonna be more famous than Frank and Jesse James or the Daltons!"

"I think I sorta heard o' that McHenry fella," Jack said, "but I ain't sure."

"I saw Pete Cragg in Yankton a few years back," Frank said. "He was a two-bit owlhoot and slow as mud on the draw. Carlisle's a new one on me. He must not have been around for very long."

Both of the Johnson brothers were red in the face with fury now.

"Quit your jabberin', damn it!" Brock said. "You'll know who we are when you got our lead in your carcass, blast you! Now fill your hand, Morgan!"

Frank shook his head. His joking demeanor was gone as he said, "I don't want to kill you, son. But that's what's going to happen to you and your brother both if you don't get on your horses and ride out of here right now. What you're doing is foolishness, sheer foolishness, and I don't want any part of it. Go find somebody else to kill you, if you're that determined to die."

For a moment, he thought they were going to listen to him. He thought this might be one of the rare occasions when his words actually got through those lying dreams of fame and glory that had led many a young man to the grave.

But then Rand and Brock Johnson both snarled and grabbed for their guns, clawing the weapons out of their holsters.

Frank had no way of knowing which one was faster. Brock claimed two kills while Rand had mentioned only one, so Frank took him down first, smashing a slug into Brock's chest that caused the young man to stumble back against the bar.

Then, faster than the eye could follow, the muzzle of Frank's Colt tracked to the right and spewed flaming death once again. Rand was moving and trying to bring his gun up as Frank fired, so the bullet hit him on the right side of the chest instead of dead center in his heart. It tore through his lung, though, and instantly filled that organ with blood. Rand gasped in shock and pain as he began drowning in it. He managed to stay on his feet and tried again to raise his gun.

Frank fired a third shot, and this time the bullet found Rand's heart, putting an end to his suffering as he crumpled to the floor. The sawdust that normally soaked up spilled beer caught the crimson stream that flowed from the young man's mouth instead.

Brock was still on his feet, leaning against the bar. He should have gone down by now, but somehow he had found the strength to stay upright. His gun slipped from nerveless fingers and thudded to the floor as he gasped, "You . . . you . . . nobody's that . . . fast!"

"That was your mistake, son," Frank told him. "Somebody, somewhere, is always that fast."

Brock's eyes rolled up in their sockets, and he pitched forward on his face, dead when he hit the floor.

"Son of a gun," Catamount Jack breathed. "Neither of 'em even got a shot off! Not that I was expectin' 'em to," he added hastily.

Frank took fresh cartridges from the loops on his gunbelt and replaced the spent rounds in the Colt's cylinder.

"I imagine somebody's gone to fetch Claude Langley already," he said, "but if they haven't . . ."

"I'll take care of it," Jack said.

Frank holstered his gun and looked at Carter behind the bar.

"Sorry, Willie. I'd just as soon not kill people in here if I didn't have to."

"It's all right, Marshal. You gave those two every chance in the world to light a shuck outta here. It's their own dumb fault that they didn't."

That was true . . . but it didn't make Frank feel any better about adding two more graves to Buckskin's Boot Hill.

People crowded around to congratulate him as he left the saloon, of course. They always did. Frank accepted their words with polite nods, but then the sight of a rider trotting along the street caught his attention. The man on horseback was the fella he had sent to Carson City with the wire for his lawyers in San Francisco.

"Howdy, Phil," Frank hailed him. "You get a reply back from that telegram?"

"Sure did, Marshal," the man said as he reined in. He reached into the pocket of his cowhide vest and took out a folded paper. "Here you go."

"I'm much obliged." Frank took the paper and handed Phil a gold eagle in turn. The man had worked as a miner until he developed a cough that kept him from spending long hours underground. He still had a family to feed, though, so Frank had him doing odd jobs and running errands such as this whenever the need arose.

Frank opened the message, read it, and nodded in satisfaction.

"What's it say?" Catamount Jack asked.

"Leaving immediately for Buckskin, stop. Will arrive Friday latest, stop. Am confident of victory, stop. Look forward to meeting you Morgan, stop. Signed, Turnbuckle."

"That's one o' those lawyer hombres, right?"

Frank nodded. "One of the best lawyers west of the Mississippi, or at least he's supposed to be. I reckon we'll find out whether he is or not." He looked around. "Claude Langley?"

"Here he comes with that meat wagon o' his right now."

More work for the undertaker, Frank thought. All because two young fools had thought more of gun glory than they did of their own lives.

He bet his coffee was cold by now, too.

Chapter 8

Luther Galloway's head was spinning from the speed with which he and Mr. Claudius Turnbuckle, Esq., had departed from San Francisco.

He had purchased the tickets at the train station, sent a messenger to the offices of Turnbuckle and Stafford with the information that the train on which they were booked departed at 11:30, and then rushed to his rented room to pack. He didn't even return to the office, just went straight to the train station again to wait for Mr. Turnbuckle.

The lawyer arrived at 11:15 in a hack loaded with baggage. The driver, several porters, and Luther himself were pressed into service to get everything loaded onto the train on time while Turnbuckle supervised the operation, frowning darkly and leaning on his silver-headed walking stick. They made it—barely—and then Luther had to deal with the fact that he hadn't been able to obtain a private compartment for them at the last minute.

"You expect me to ride sitting up all the way to Carson City like a common person?" Turnbuckle demanded angrily as he and Luther stood in the vestibule of the car where their seats were located. Those sentiments, expressed in the lawyer's usual loud, ringing tones, drew several resentful looks from the other passengers.

"Please, sir," Luther said. "You said you wanted to leave on the earliest possible train, and this is it. Unfortunately, they had no private compartments available. I would have checked with you to see whether you wanted to wait for a later train, but the ticket clerk said that if I tarried, these seats would be gone. Then you would have had no choice but to wait."

Turnbuckle wore a tweed overcoat and hat despite the relatively warm weather. He glowered at Luther under the pulled-down brim of the hat and growled, "All right, all right. I suppose we'll just have to make the best of the situation. Where are our seats?"

Luther consulted the tickets as he led the way down the aisle.

"Right along here, sir."

The seats were on the left-hand side of the car, about midway along the aisle. They were nicely upholstered and appeared comfortable to Luther, but of course they were much less luxurious than Turnbuckle was accustomed to. At least, Luther supposed that was the case. In the time he had worked for Turnbuckle and Stafford, Mr. Turnbuckle hadn't done any traveling. In fact, Luther had never even seen him outside the office until today.

"I'm sitting beside the window," Turnbuckle declared, and naturally, Luther didn't argue with him. He sat down beside the attorney, being careful not to let his shoulder touch Turnbuckle's. Neither of them would have been comfortable with that level of familiarity.

The Central Pacific train rolled out of the station on schedule, lurching into motion with a slight jolt. It would travel first to Sacramento, then across the Sierra Nevada Mountains into the state of Nevada. Luther had determined that Carson City was the closest rail terminal to their destination. He wasn't sure how they would get from Carson City to the settlement called Buckskin, but he assumed there was some sort of coach service.

He hoped they wouldn't have to rent mounts and travel by horseback. He had ridden a few times in one of San Francisco's parks, but he was no horseman. In fact, he had lived the entire twenty-five years of his life in the city and wasn't that comfortable with the idea of visiting a frontier settlement to start with.

That worry nagged at him until he felt he had to say, "Sir, we're not likely to encounter any, ah, hostiles, are we?"

"You mean Indians?" Turnbuckle grunted a couple of times, and it took Luther a moment to realize that the lawyer was laughing. "The only hostiles still on the loose anywhere are a few renegades in Arizona and New Mexico, and maybe in West Texas. All the others have been pacified."

Luther tried not to sigh.

"That's a relief, sir. I wasn't sure what the situation was."

"Now outlaws, on the other hand . . . There are still roving gangs of bandits, and they've been known to hold up trains. You can worry about *them* if you want to, Galloway."

Luther's jaw clenched and his fingers knotted together. He knew that Turnbuckle was making fun of him, and he didn't like it. At the same time, the idea that they might be in danger from bandits *was* worrisome. But it was too late now to do anything except hope for the best.

Turnbuckle distracted him by saying, "I took a few minutes before leaving the office to skim through the Nevada statutes regarding mining claims." There were volumes in the office's law library detailing the statutes of almost every state in the nation. "Of course, I don't know the specifics of the case Morgan wants me to take, but I thought it would be a good idea to get an overview of the law."

"That was a very good idea, sir."

"When we get to Buckskin and have all the details, I may have to send you back to Carson City to research the law for me."

"Of course, sir. I'm prepared to accomplish whatever tasks you give me."

Luther was *really* starting to hope there was a stagecoach or something similar that ran between Carson City and Buckskin. The idea of riding back and forth by himself, at the mercy of the elements, savage beasts, and even more savage humans, made his mouth go dry with terror.

"You've been a good clerk, Galloway," Turnbuckle said with what sounded like grudging respect. "Even if you *weren't* able to arrange private accommodations for us on this train. When are you supposed to take your test to see if you can pass the bar?"

Luther's mouth opened and closed, but no words came out. Turnbuckle didn't even know that he had already taken the bar examination twice and failed to pass both times?

But why should Turnbuckle be aware of that? Luther certainly hadn't spoken of it around the office. He was too ashamed of his failures.

"Once you're licensed to practice law," Turnbuckle went on without waiting for an answer to his question, "there might be a place for you at the firm as an associate. No guarantees, you understand. Stafford would have to agree, and he can be a cantankerous old pelican."

As far as Luther had been able to see during his time at the firm, Mr. John J. Stafford was much more pleasant and easier to work for than Mr. Turnbuckle. And yet here was Turnbuckle talking about how cantankerous he was. Perhaps in private, between the two partners, there might be some truth to that. Luther didn't know.

He thought he ought to say something. "Thank you, sir," he replied, managing not to stammer. "I appreciate that vote of confidence."

"Well, let's see how you do helping me with this case," Turnbuckle said. "Frank Morgan is one of our more important clients, and I don't want to let him down."

"No, sir. Of course not. Just let me know anything I can do to help."

Turnbuckle grunted again, but it wasn't a laugh this time. "Right now you can open this window. There's not a breath of fresh air in this car."

"Of course." Luther got to his feet and reached over Turnbuckle, again being careful not to crowd him, and unlatched the window. He pushed the pane up several inches to let in some air.

Unfortunately, that air wasn't very fresh. It stunk of smoke from the engine, and there were even a few cinders from the locomotive's stack floating in it. Turnbuckle began to cough and snapped, "Shut it! Shut the damned thing!"

The outburst drew more looks from the other passengers. Luther tried not to sigh in dismay as he hurriedly reached over Turnbuckle and lowered the window. The trip to Carson City was supposed to take approximately twenty-four hours, which meant they would reach their destination around the middle of the day tomorrow.

It was beginning to look like it was going to be a long trip.

Luther was right. Turnbuckle became more and more irascible as the journey continued, and after a night spent trying to sleep sitting up, he was an absolute bear. If it occurred to him that his clerk was in the same uncomfortable situation, Luther saw no sign of it. The lawyer was concerned with his own problems and no one else's.

The train was still in the mountains when morning dawned. Luther peered past the grumbling Turnbuckle and watched the spectacular scenery rolling past. Snowcapped mountains clawed at the very heavens, climbing high into the clear blue vault of the sky. Thickly wooded slopes formed dark green curtains. Valleys plummeted to dancing streams where fast-flowing water broke whitely on jagged rocks that thrust up from the creek beds. Luther thought he could tell just by looking at the streams that the water was so cold it would take a man's breath away. Maybe it would wash all of his problems away, too . . .

The train began climbing, following the steel rails that curled around the side of a mountain. Luther figured that when it reached the top of the slope it would cross a trestle so high that looking down into the valley below would send shivers of fear through him. The same thing had happened several times already during the trip. He really hadn't been aware that heights bothered him so much until now.

The steepness of the ascent meant that the train had to slow down to a crawl as the engine labored to haul the massive weight to the top. To the left rose an almost sheer wall of rock; to the right, the earth dropped away, falling several hundred feet to one of the twisting valleys that meandered through the mountains.

From where Luther sat, when he looked out the windows on the other side of the coach, it seemed only nothingness was out there, and it made him dizzy and disoriented when he looked in that direction for too long. It appeared that there was nothing to support the train. It ought to fall right down the side of the mountain.

So even though the view didn't amount to much, he looked out the left-hand window beside Mr. Turnbuckle instead. The lawyer was dozing with his head tipped forward, his chin on his chest. An occasional snorting snore came from him. Luther sighed as he looked at the rocks now creeping by outside the window.

Suddenly, movement caught his eye. A ledge ran along the slope, and a man stood on that ledge, poised as if to leap. He wore a short coat, a hat with a wide brim that was pulled down low over his eyes, and a bright red bandanna that was pulled up and tied around his head so that it covered the bottom half of his face. He gripped a revolver.

Luther had seen similar figures on the covers of dime novels. The man was an outlaw!

Even as that realization soaked in Luther's stunned brain, the man on the ledge disappeared. A heavy thump on the roof over his head told Luther what had happened. The masked bandit had jumped from the ledge onto the roof of the railroad car.

The train was about to be held up!

That conclusion was inescapable. Even Luther knew that one man couldn't stop and rob a train by himself, so there must have been other outlaws hidden on the slope, ready to make the daring leap onto the cars as the train crawled past. Even now some of them were probably closing in on the engine so that they could drop down into the cab and force the engineer to stop the train. The others would be making their way into the cars to loot the passengers' valuables at gunpoint!

Forgetting for the moment that he was just a lowly clerk and Turnbuckle was one of the leading attorneys in the entire country, Luther grabbed his employee's shoulder and gave it a hard shake.

"Sir! Wake up, sir! We're being robbed!"

At that moment, as if to punctuate Luther's warning, a woman screamed somewhere in the rear of the coach, and a gun blasted. The report was deafening, and it was followed immediately by more screams from the female passengers and angry shouts and curses from the men.

"Everybody stay right where you are!" a harsh voice bellowed, easily overriding the uproar in the coach. "Nobody move! Rattle your hocks and I'll put hot lead in your damn gizzard!"

Luther stiffened. An overpowering curiosity forced him to look around. He saw the man from the ledge stalking up the aisle, brandishing two heavy six-guns now. As the outlaw drew closer, Luther could see that his eyes were wild, filled with the lust to kill. At least the right one was; the left eye canted off at an odd angle, and Luther wasn't sure the outlaw could see anything out of it.

"Cough up the loot!" the bandit shouted. "Now!"

Luther was prepared to hand over his wallet and his watch, the only things of any value that he was carrying. He hoped that Mr. Turnbuckle—and everyone else in the car, for that matter—would proceed in such a reasonable manner. If the masked desperado began shooting, there was no telling who might be hurt.

Unfortunately, the legends about Claudius Turnbuckle were mostly accurate. He had indeed spent several years working on the docks and was a veteran of the wild days along the Barbary Coast. And as Turnbuckle surged up out of his seat with a roar of anger and turned toward the bandit, Luther saw to his dismay that his employer wasn't going to cooperate.

Not by a long shot.

"Put those guns down or I'll have you behind bars for the rest of your life!" Turnbuckle bellowed at the outlaw. He shoved past Luther, who clutched feebly and futilely at his coat. Turnbuckle lifted his walking stick and shook it. "By Godfrey, sir, do you know who I am?"

"Yeah," the bandit said, his wild eye rolling. "You're a stupid son of a bitch who's about to die!"

With that, the guns in his hand came up, and both weapons roared thunderously as smoke and flame erupted from their muzzles.

Chapter 9

Luther was too stunned by the roar of the guns assaulting his ears to do anything except sit there and watch as the bullets slammed into Turnbuckle's body. The lawyer clutched at the back of a seat and tried to stay upright, but he was too badly wounded. He slumped to the floor of the aisle and lay there gasping in pain.

Luther wasn't the only one shocked by this wanton display of brutal violence. The other passengers were silent now as they stared in terror at the train robber. Mothers clutched their children to them and husbands tightly embraced the shoulders of their wives as they waited to see what would happen next.

"Don't be like that dumb bastard," the outlaw said as he used his left-hand gun to gesture at the fallen figure of Claudius Turnbuckle. "Stand and deliver, and maybe you'll live through this!"

He holstered the left-hand gun and used that hand to pull a canvas sack from behind his belt. Thrusting the sack at Luther, he said, "You! Four-eyes! Take this and open it up. Get everybody's valuables. Make it snappy now, or I'll ventilate you, too!"

It had been a while since Luther had been called Four-eyes. Childhood, in fact. But the insult was just as painful and unjust now as it had been then. It wasn't his fault that his eyes were a little weak and he had to wear spectacles.

Of course, under the circumstances it would be foolish to worry about a little name-calling, Luther realized, when Mr. Turnbuckle was lying there dying on the dirty floor of a railroad car and a crazed bandit was threatening *his* life, too. He forced himself to his feet and took the canvas sack with trembling hands.

"Don't drop it," the bandit jeered, and even though the bandanna masked the lower half of his face, Luther could well imagine the ugly grin that must be on his lips.

Luther opened the bag, and with the outlaw prodding him in the back with a gun barrel, he went up and down the aisle, collecting wallets, pocketbooks, watches, rings, and other jewelry from the other passengers. Everyone cooperated. They would have been insane not to, Luther thought.

When he was finished . . . when the car had been looted to the bandit's satisfaction . . . the man said, "Now you, Four-eyes."

"I . . . I beg your pardon?" Luther's strained voice sounded odd to his ears, as if it didn't even belong to him anymore.

"It's your turn. Empty your pockets into the bag." The bandit nodded toward Turnbuckle. "And don't forget that son of a bitch either. Clean him out, too."

Luther followed the man's orders, taking out his

own valuables and adding them to the collection in the sack. Then he knelt next to Mr. Turnbuckle's body.

The lawyer wasn't thrashing around and moaning anymore. He lay there gray-faced and motionless, either unconscious—or dead. Luther thought Turnbuckle was still breathing, but he couldn't be sure. As the outlaw loomed over him, he went through Turnbuckle's pockets, removed his wallet, took the watch and chain from his vest, slid a couple of rings from Turnbuckle's fingers. Everything went into the sack.

"That'll do," the desperado growled. He thrust his free hand at Luther, who gave him the sack. The outlaw looked down at him, that blind, off-kilter eye rolling wildly, and lined his pistol on Luther's face.

Luther stared into the barrel from only inches away as the bandit pulled back the weapon's hammer and said, "You're so scared I reckon I'd be doin' you a favor if you put you outta your misery, Four-eyes."

At that moment, Luther was sure, absolutely certain, that he was about to die. His life had only seconds remaining in it. He knew he ought to do something, anything, but fear and dread had frozen him in place as he knelt next to Claudius Turnbuckle's body.

Then the outlaw laughed and eased the gun's hammer back down.

"But you ain't worth a bullet," he said. With that he turned and stalked toward the rear of the car, glaring at the frightened passengers on either side of the aisle and causing them to shrink away from him as he passed.

Luther lost his precarious balance and sat down

hard in the aisle next to Turnbuckle. His heart pounded so hard it seemed to be on the verge of bursting out of his chest. He couldn't hear anything except a roaring in his head, and he didn't seem able to draw enough air into his lungs. He gasped like a fish out of water.

The outlaw vanished into the vestibule at the end of the car. Luther gradually became aware that the train wasn't moving anymore, but he didn't know when it had come to a stop. Shortly after the robbery had begun, he assumed. The gang of thieves must have horses hidden somewhere nearby, he thought. They would gather there as soon as their looting was complete and ride away into the godforsaken wilderness of the Sierra Nevadas. They probably had a hidden stronghold somewhere the law would never find them.

"Gal . . . Galloway . . ."

The tumult in Luther's head had subsided to the point that he was able to hear the strained whisper that came from Turnbuckle. The lawyer wasn't dead after all.

But with two bullet wounds in his chest, surely he wouldn't last much longer. Luther leaned over him, anxious to hear whatever Turnbuckle had to say.

"I'm right here, sir. Is there anything I can do to make you more comfortable?"

"Tell . . . tell . . ."

Turnbuckle had never been married and had no children, as far as Luther knew. But he must have other relatives, and surely there was some message, some dying words, that he wanted Luther to pass along to his family.

"Who do you want me to speak to, sir?"

Turnbuckle's eyelids fluttered. His eyes, bleary with pain, opened enough to focus on Luther's face.

"Tell Frank Morgan . . . I'm sorry I can't . . . help him."

Luther couldn't believe what he was hearing.

"You want me to go on to Buckskin, sir? After . . . after *this*?"

"Got a . . . client . . . client always . . . comes first." Turnbuckle lifted a hand. "Tell Morgan . . . delay case . . . get Stafford . . . You can . . . file a motion . . . for a delay . . . don't let . . . the client down . . ."

A long, rasping sigh came from Turnbuckle as his head fell back and his eyes closed again. Luther was sure the attorney was dead this time, but Turnbuckle's chest continued to rise and fall in a strained, ragged rhythm.

"Buckskin," Luther whispered. "He wants me to go on to Buckskin."

Turnbuckle was still alive when the conductor came through the car a few minutes later. Clearly shaken, with blood running down his face from a gash in his forehead where one of the outlaws had pistol-whipped him, he called for help and had the wounded lawyer carried into one of the Pullman cars by several porters. The passengers who had booked the compartment were forced to give it up. The fireman was also wounded, having put up a fight when several of the masked bandits stormed the locomotive's cab, and he was placed in another Pullman compartment while the conductor went to look for a doctor among the passengers.

Luther stayed by Turnbuckle's side, even though

there was nothing he could do to help the man. A short time later, the train jerked into motion again and finished its slow, laborious climb to the top of the pass.

The conductor came back into the compartment, accompanied by a beefy man with a white beard.

"This is Dr. Clemens," the conductor told Luther. "He's agreed to have a look at the wounded men while we get on to Carson City just as fast as we can."

"Do everything you can for him, Doctor," Luther told the physician. "Money is no object. This is Claudius Turnbuckle, the famous attorney."

Clemens grunted. "Never heard of him, young man, but I'll do everything I can for him anyway. Sort of swore an oath to that effect when I took up doctorin'."

Luther didn't really trust the man. Clemens didn't sound very educated, for one thing, and for another he had the faint scent of whiskey lingering about him. His hands seemed swift and competent enough, though, as he opened Turnbuckle's bloodstained clothes to reveal the two red-rimmed bullet holes in the lawyer's chest.

Clemens opened the bag he carried with him and took out a clean cloth and a bottle of something he used to swab blood away from the wounds. He leaned close to them and tilted his head in a listening attitude.

"Don't hear any whistlin'," he announced after a moment. "Means the slugs prob'ly missed the lungs. And they didn't get the heart or this fella'd already be dead."

"You mean he's going to survive?" Luther asked, astounded.

Clemens shook his head. "Oh, no, I didn't say that. He's lost a lot of blood and there's no tellin' what other damage that lead might've done in there. The fact that the shots missed his heart and lungs accounts for the fact that he's still alive, but I wouldn't hold out a lot o' hope, young fella. Is he your pa?"

"What?" Luther shook his head. "My father? No. He's my employer. I'm his law clerk."

"Well, I wouldn't count on him makin' it to Carson City. Even if he does, he prob'ly won't last much longer. Sorry. Nothin' I can do."

Luther was sitting on a stool next to the bunk where Turnbuckle had been placed by the porters. At the doctor's grim diagnosis, he closed his eyes and leaned back against the wall behind him.

He felt lost and unsure of what to do next. There wasn't really anything he *could* do until the train reached Carson City. Once there, he could wire Mr. Stafford in Los Angeles for instructions. He was sure that if Mr. Turnbuckle succumbed to his wounds, which seemed inevitable, the body would need to be prepared for burial and then shipped back to San Francisco for interment.

He was getting ahead of himself, he thought. Right now, Turnbuckle was still alive, and despite the doctor's dire prediction, there was no way of knowing for sure how long he would stay that way.

Clemens patted Luther on the shoulder and said, "I got to see about that fireman. He caught a slug, too, the conductor said."

"Yes, of course," Luther said. "Thank you, Doctor."

Clemens went into the next compartment, leaving Luther sitting there listening to the faint, ragged breathing that came from Turnbuckle.

The next few hours were some of the longest that Luther had ever spent in his life. It seemed to him that the train would never reach Carson City, that he would be stuck here for eternity, growing sick from the car's swaying and bumping as he sat there waiting for Claudius Turnbuckle to die.

Turnbuckle didn't die, though. His ragged breathing still continued as the train finally rolled into the station at Carson City. Ambulance wagons were sent for immediately, and Luther watched anxiously as attendants from the local hospital lifted Turnbuckle onto a stretcher, carried him off the train, and placed him in one of the wagons. The men allowed Luther to climb into the wagon, too, and let him ride along with them to the hospital.

When he got there, he spent another hour pacing back and forth nervously in a waiting room while Turnbuckle was examined again by other doctors. Finally one of the medicos, this one a tall, gaunt man with a black spade beard, came out and spoke to Luther.

"I regret to say that Mr. Turnbuckle's condition is quite grave," the doctor reported. "The loss of blood and the shock of his injuries might well have killed him already, but he continues to cling to life. I think it's only a matter of time until he succumbs to his wounds, however."

Luther blinked. "Are you talking about days, Doctor, or hours, or . . ."

"Impossible to say," the doctor replied in a brusque voice. "Could be days, could be a matter of minutes. I'd err on the side of hours, though."

"Can you keep him . . . comfortable?"

"Of course. We'll do everything we can for him.

And you never know, he might pull through. Miracles do occur from time to time, you know." His tone made it clear that he didn't expect that to happen in this case, though.

"Thank you. Thank you, Doctor," Luther mumbled. His hat was clutched in his hands. He turned it over a couple of times before he finally put it on and left the hospital.

There was a telegraph office at the train station, he recalled. He returned there, walking along the streets of Nevada's capital city. Those streets were paved, and light poles with gaslights on them were placed at regular intervals. Luther passed several brick buildings with multiple stories. Carson City was no longer the rough frontier town it had once been. While it was no San Francisco, it *was* an outpost of civilization, and Luther felt a little better for being here. The whole incident of the train robbery had begun to seem unreal to him.

But all he had to do was remember the terrible roar of the outlaw's guns and the sight of the blood welling from Turnbuckle's wounds and soaking his clothes, and it was all too real again.

When Luther reached the train station, he found that his bags, as well as Turnbuckle's, had been unloaded and left there. The train itself had moved on, of course, since it had a schedule to keep and the robbery already had delayed it. As soon as Luther had sent that wire to Stafford, letting him know what had happened to his partner, he inquired at the ticket counter as to when the next train for San Francisco would be leaving.

"There's one tonight, mister," the clerk said. "You want to buy a ticket on it?"

Luther opened his mouth and was about to say yes when he seemed to hear Claudius Turnbuckle's voice, once again instructing him to go to Buckskin and tell Frank Morgan what had happened. *The client always comes first,* Turnbuckle had said. He had lived by that philosophy for many years. Now Luther had to struggle with that same philosophy.

"Mister?" the clerk prodded. "You want a ticket for San Francisco?"

Luther could barely believe the words were coming out of his mouth as he said, "Could . . . could you tell me if there's a stagecoach or some other sort of transportation that runs from here to a town called Buckskin?"

"Buckskin? Sure. Stage runs down there twice a week. Is that where you need to go?"

"Yes." Luther swallowed hard. "I'm afraid that Buckskin is exactly where I need to go."

Chapter 10

Frank Morgan's life, full of violence and tragedy as it had been, had taught him to be thankful for small favors. To appreciate the peaceful times when nobody was trying to kill him or anyone else he cared about.

That was why he was more than willing to accept the respite that followed the gunfight with the Johnson brothers and the arrival of the telegram from Claudius Turnbuckle. Dex Brighton appeared to be lying low for the time being, waiting for the circuit judge to arrive, and Tip Woodford was content to wait for the lawyer that Frank had sent for. Nobody else stirred up any trouble. No more would-be fast guns showed up looking for a reputation. There weren't even any brawls between bored, drunken miners in the saloons.

So naturally, Frank started to worry. That old saying about things being *too* quiet sometimes had a lot of truth to it.

He and Catamount Jack were sitting in ladder-back chairs on the porch in front of the marshal's office a couple of days after the shootout in the Silver Baron. Frank's boots were propped on the railing along the front of the porch. Jack was doing the same thing, only he had his chair tipped back and was rocking it as he also rolled a quirly. The stagecoach was due to come in pretty soon, and the two lawmen were swapping lies to pass the time until its arrival.

"Ever fight any Comanches while you were down there in Texas as a younker?" Jack asked. He knew that Frank had been born on a spread near Weatherford, Texas, and had grown up in that area.

"Yeah, right after the war, while I was cowboying. We had to take some cows to a ranch up in the Panhandle. That was some years before Mackenzie broke the Comanches' spirits by destroying their horse herd at Palo Duro Canyon, so the boys who were going on the drive knew we might run into trouble."

Jack spilled tobacco from his pouch into the brown paper he cradled in his other hand. "That didn't stop you, though, did it?"

"Of course not," Frank said with a grin. "We were young and full of piss and vinegar. We were actually looking forward to the idea that we might wind up in an Indian fight. I reckon we thought we were going to live forever, the way most kids do."

"Just out o' curiosity, you know how many of that bunch is still alive?"

A faraway look stole into Frank's eyes. "Out of the dozen who went along on that drive . . . two, I think. Counting me."

"Ain't hardly forever, is it?"

Frank shook his head. "Nothing is."

Jack licked the paper and sealed it, then twisted

the ends of the quirly. "You were sayin', about the Comanches . . ."

"Yeah, we were southwest of Amarillo, not that far really from the spread we were going to, when they jumped us. Came out of nowhere like they sprouted from the ground, them and their horses, too. To this day I don't know where they were hidden. But there they were, and they were whooping and hollering so that the three hundred head we were driving stampeded. One of the fellas got caught in front and couldn't get out of the way. His horse went down and we lost him then and there. The rest of us managed to make it to a draw where we forted up."

"What about that stampedin' stock?"

"We let it stampede," Frank said. "Figured it was more important to save our hair first."

Jack nodded. "Reckon that makes sense. Them Injuns charge you?"

"Six or seven times," Frank said. "We lost another man and had a couple wounded, but they lost a dozen or more and finally decided that it was going to cost them too much to roust us out of there. So they took half a dozen of the cows and rode off."

Jack swiped a match into life on the seat of his pants and held it to the tip of his cigarette. When he had it going, he said, "So they killed two o' you cowboys and lost a dozen o' their own men, all for six cows?"

"That's right," Frank said. "They were kind of scrawny critters, too."

"Now tell me how in the hell six cows is worth all that killin' and dyin'?"

"They're not. What was worth the killing and

dying to them was the fact that we were there to start with, and they didn't want us there."

"And how about to you and the fellas with you?"

"We were young and stupid," Frank said. "That was enough."

"What'd you do, bury the boys you lost and then round up the cows and go on?"

"That's exactly what we did. That's what we were being paid to do."

A companionable silence fell on the porch. Both of these men could have told dozens of similar stories, tales of death and sacrifice, often for no good reason, or at least no reason that would have made sense to anyone who hadn't been there. He and Jack were fast becoming relics, Frank thought. They had been to see the elephant, but these days, most folks didn't even know where the elephant was anymore.

Frank was just as glad when he heard the rumble of hoofbeats and the creaking of wheels, because those sounds meant that the stagecoach was coming into town. He lowered his boots from the railing and stood up. Jack did, too, although he nearly tipped his chair over in the process.

"You still expectin' that lawyer fella on today's stage?"

"I haven't heard any different since that telegram he sent me," Frank said.

They walked along the street toward the stage station, and as they approached they could see the cloud of dust boiling up from the hooves of the team and the wheels of the coach as it reached the edge of town. The jehu hauled back on the reins and brought the vehicle to a perfect stop in front of the station. The coach, still painted a fading red and yellow from its days of service with the Butterfield line, swayed back and forth slightly on the broad leather thoroughbraces that ran underneath it.

Catamount Jack lounged against a hitch rail while Frank planted his feet, squared his shoulders, and waited for the passengers to climb out of the coach. The driver and shotgun guard leaped down from the box, and the guard reached underneath the seat to pull the mail pouch out of the compartment there. A little frown appeared on Frank's face as the doors of the coach remained closed and no one emerged from it.

"No passengers this run?" he asked the driver.

The grizzled jehu laughed. "Oh, there's a passenger in there, all right. I reckon he's feelin' a mite poorly, though. Didn't take to all the bouncin' on the trail. Had to hang his head out the window a few times between here and Carson City."

Frank walked over to the coach and grasped the handle on one of the doors. He twisted it and pulled the door open. Slumped on the forward-facing seat inside the coach was a man in a dusty brown suit and hat. "Mr. Turnbuckle?" Frank said.

The passenger groaned and turned a pasty, washed-out face toward the sound of Frank's voice. He was much younger than Frank expected, with spectacles on his nose and a thatch of sandy hair under the expensive hat.

Frank leaned toward him. "You need a hand?"

"I . . . I need . . ." The man groaned again and closed his eyes.

Frank turned and motioned to his deputy. "Give me a hand here, Jack. Mr. Turnbuckle doesn't appear to feel too good."

They reached into the coach, got hold of the new arrival, and helped him out onto the street. Frank tried to be careful about it, but there was no way to avoid some jostling. Still, Turnbuckle seemed to feel a little better once he got his feet back on solid ground. He leaned against the hitch rail, took off his hat, and used a bandanna he pulled from his pocket to mop his sweat-drenched face.

"That's the worst ordeal I've ever endured," he announced. His voice was still weak. "Every bone in my body aches, and I think all my teeth have been shaken loose."

"Yeah, that stagecoach road's a mite rough, all right," Jack said. "You'll get used to it, I reckon."

Turnbuckle shook his head. "No. Not in a million years."

Worry had begun to gnaw at Frank. Not only was this fella younger than he'd expected, but he didn't strike Frank as the sort of man who would be a famous, high-powered lawyer either. Of course, lawyering was sort of like being a gunfighter, he reminded himself. The only thing that really counted was the result of a showdown, whether it was in the middle of a dusty street at high noon or in a courtroom.

"Listen, you *are* Claudius Turnbuckle, aren't you?" he asked. He couldn't afford to make a mistake, not with the future of his friend Tip Woodford perhaps on the line.

"I'm . . . I'm . . ." The young man took a deep breath, closed his eyes, and nodded. "Yes. I'm Claudius Turnbuckle."

Frank grasped Turnbuckle's limp hand and shook it, saying, "I'm Frank Morgan. I'm the fella who sent for you, Mr. Turnbuckle, but in this case, I'm not your client. If you'll come with me, I'll introduce you to him." Frank added to the deputy, "Jack, can you see about getting Mr. Turnbuckle checked into the hotel and have his bags taken over there?"

Jack nodded. "Sure. Don't worry about a thing, Marshal."

Frank took hold of Turnbuckle's arm and steered the lawyer's unsteady steps toward the office of the Lucky Lizard Mining Company. Earlier in the day he had told Tip Woodford that he expected Turnbuckle to arrive on today's stage, and Tip had promised to stay around town rather than riding out to the mine as he usually did. Frank wanted to get the two of them together as soon as possible so that they could start working out their strategy for the court case.

"I told you in my telegram that this business concerns a mining claim," Frank said, "but not one that belongs to the Browning Mining Syndicate. It's the Lucky Lizard Mine. My friend Thomas Woodford owns it, and his claim to it is under attack from an hombre I suspect is a crook of some sort."

"Lucky Lizard," Turnbuckle muttered. The man still seemed a mite disoriented, Frank thought.

"That's right. Tip's office is right up here, and he can tell you all about it. That's what they called Woodford."

Turnbuckle scrubbed a hand over his face. "Let me get this straight. You want me to help a man . . . who owns a rival mine?"

"I reckon there's plenty of silver in these mountains for all of us," Frank said with a smile.

"That's . . . an unusual attitude . . . in business."

"My son Conrad would agree with you. He'd heard rumors that there was a potential problem with one of the mining claims in this area and came up here to make sure it wasn't the Crown Royal. That's the Browning mine."

Turnbuckle nodded. "Yes, I know."

"Anyway, when he found out that the trouble didn't have anything to do with our mine, he thought we ought to just stay out of it."

"That seems like a sound business decision."

"Problem is, I'm not much of a businessman and never have been," Frank said. "But I *am* Tip Woodford's friend, and I wasn't going to let him face this alone. Anyway, I've run across skunks like this hombre Brighton before. If he gets away with stealing the Lucky Lizard out from under Tip, he's liable to get greedy and go after one of the other mines next. And it might be the Crown Royal he sets his sights on."

"You want to stop him now, before he can try to hurt anyone else," Turnbuckle muttered.

"You don't stand around watching a rattlesnake to see if he's going to strike at somebody *before* you shoot him. You know he's going to sooner or later, and then an innocent person is going to get hurt."

The lawyer shrugged. "I don't suppose I can argue with that."

Something else occurred to Frank. "You want a drink or maybe a cup of coffee, or something to eat, before you talk to Tip?"

A shudder ran through Turnbuckle. "Perhaps some coffee later on. But right now . . . nothing."

"All right. Here's the Lucky Lizard office."

They stepped onto the porch in front of the office

and Frank opened the door. He ushered Turnbuckle inside. There were two desks in the office. Tip sat at one of them, Diana at the other. Both of them stood up as Frank and Turnbuckle entered.

"Here he is," Frank said. "The famous Claudius Turnbuckle."

Woodford and Diana looked surprised, and Frank knew what they were thinking. They had been expecting an older, more impressive individual than the man who had gotten off the stage. But Tip cleared his throat and came around the desk to extend his hand to the newcomer.

"Welcome to Buckskin, Mr. Turnbuckle," he said. "Frank here tells me you're one of the best lawyers west o' the Mississippi." He pumped Turnbuckle's hand and went on. "You'll need to be, because that fella Brighton is smart and dangerous. Reckon it'll take all your legal expertise to give him his comeuppance."

Turnbuckle gave a weak nod. "Tell me all about it, Mr. Woodford."

Chapter 11

What the hell *do you think you're doing?*

A shrill voice screamed those words in the back of Luther Galloway's brain. It wasn't bad enough that he hadn't corrected Frank Morgan's mistake when Morgan took him for Mr. Turnbuckle. Now he was allowing the ridiculous charade to continue, even to the point of sitting down to discuss the case with the man on whose behalf Morgan had summoned him.

The problem was that he had felt so bad when the stage arrived in Buckskin, had been so sick and disoriented, that he wasn't even fully aware of what was going on at first. Then, Morgan had shaken his hand and seemed to be so glad to see him, and no one had really acted that way around Luther before, certainly not a man as famous as Frank Morgan . . .

For God's sake, Luther had read dime novels about this man! And *Morgan* was welcoming *him* . . .

Surely it wouldn't hurt anything if he waited a few minutes to correct Morgan's mistake, Luther had thought. Surely not. After everything he had gone through to get here . . . the terrible violence on the train, then the hellish bouncing and swaying of the stagecoach, not to mention the choking dust . . . after all that misery he deserved something, he decided, and the scorn that Morgan would surely heap on a lowly law clerk wasn't it.

Even so, he had intended to tell Morgan who he really was while they were walking down the street to the offices of the Lucky Lizard Mine. But then Morgan had begun telling him about the case and despite the fact that he still felt terrible, Luther found himself getting interested. The idea that a man would summon his own lawyer to assist a business rival seemed quite odd to Luther, but clearly Frank Morgan was not the sort of man they usually dealt with in San Francisco. He had a power about him, a compelling way of speaking and carrying himself, and Luther didn't want to disappoint him.

Of course, it was impossible for him to continue this masquerade for much longer. He would have to tell Morgan the truth, along with this man Woodford and his daughter.

But he could at least listen to the details of the case first and perhaps give them some advice. He *had* studied law, after all, even if he hadn't been able to pass the bar examination so far, and he had spent two years working for Mr. Turnbuckle and Mr. Stafford, two of the keenest legal minds in the country.

"Here's the story," Tip Woodford said as they all sat down. "This fella Dex Brighton showed up in Buckskin a while back and said that he was the rightful owner of my mine. He said that his pa and the fella I bought the claim from were partners and they had an agreement sayin' they could only sell out to each other, not to anybody else."

Woodford continued with the explanation until Luther felt that he had the whole thing straight in his mind. When Woodford paused, he asked what seemed to him to be the most logical question.

"Have you actually seen this so-called partnership agreement?"

Woodford shook his head. "Brighton's playin' his cards close to the vest. He won't show anybody the document. Says he'll produce it for the judge, but not until then."

"That's his right, although I might be able to file a motion as soon as the judge gets here compelling Brighton to produce his evidence. Litigants in a civil suit have more leeway about such things than, say, the prosecution in a criminal proceeding, but still, the judge might see things our way."

What was he saying? He was talking as if he were going to proceed with the case! That was completely out of the question. He lacked the experience for such a thing, not to mention the fact that representing himself as an attorney was fraudulent. He would be risking not only Woodford's case, but his own future as an attorney. He would never be admitted to the bar if his deception was discovered.

But what if he won the case? The question prodded his mind. If he won the case, disposed of Brighton's claim, and went back to San Francisco, the people in this frontier town might never know the difference. It was possible that someone would hear later about Turnbuckle's death, but if they read that he was killed during a train robbery, they would probably think that it happened while he was returning to San Francisco, not on the way to Buckskin.

"Do you really think you can win?" Diana Woodford asked.

Luther turned to look at her. He had been struck by the young blonde's beauty as soon as he walked into the office with Morgan, and now he had an excuse to look directly at her. Her blue eyes seemed huge, and he could tell she was worried about her father's future. Nor did she seem to have a great deal of faith in Luther's ability to help.

What would the real Claudius Turnbuckle do in this situation? Even as Luther asked himself that question, he knew the answer. Turnbuckle never doubted his abilities. The lawyer's brash self-confidence bordered on arrogance.

Luther clenched his right hand into a fist and thumped it on his knee. "Of course we can win!" he declared. "I can tell already that this man Brighton has no real case other than his word and a mysterious document that will probably turn out to be a complete fake. Once I've demonstrated that to the judge, Brighton will be exposed as a swindler who's trying to cash in on all the hard work you and your father have done to turn the Lucky Lizard Mine into the highly successful operation that it is, Miss Woodford."

There, he thought. That little speech must have raised her opinion of him. If he was actually going to continue his audacious pose as the real Claudius Turnbuckle, he would have to keep in mind at all times the way Turnbuckle would behave in these situations. He wasn't as physically imposing as the real Turnbuckle, so he couldn't match the lawyer's domineering presence, but he could imitate Turnbuckle's attitude.

Luther found himself on his feet. "In fact," he said, "I think I should pay a visit to this man Brighton right now, just to let him know that he's in for a fight." Luther summoned up a laugh. "Who knows, perhaps when he sees the sort of opponent that he's up against now, he'll decide not to pursue his spurious claim at all. He might just abandon the idea and leave Buckskin."

Tip Woodford looked up at him, clearly impressed. "You really think he might light a shuck?"

Luther frowned briefly in confusion, until Frank Morgan leaned forward and said, "Leave town, like you were talking about, Mr. Turnbuckle."

"Oh," Luther said, nodding in understanding. "Yes, I think there is indeed a chance that Mr. Brighton might . . . light a shuck. We won't know until we try, will we?"

Morgan stood up. "Brighton's got a room over at the hotel. We'll see if he's there."

"You plan to accompany me, Mr. Morgan?"

"Yeah, I think that'd be a good idea."

"Very well then." Luther had taken off his hat when they came into the room. He placed it firmly on his head now, trying not to wince as he did so. He still had a bit of an ache behind his eyes from the bumpy, dusty ride on the stagecoach. "Let's go confront Mr. Brighton. Mr. Woodford, Miss Woodford, don't worry about a thing. Claudius Turnbuckle is on the case."

"I feel better already," Woodford said.

So did Luther . . . except for the part of his brain

that was still trying to convince him he had gone totally, irrevocably mad.

Frank didn't know what to make of Claudius Turnbuckle. When he'd first seen the lawyer in the stagecoach, Turnbuckle had seemed to be one of the most miserable, unimpressive specimens of humanity he'd ever seen, not to mention being way too young. Frank's opinion hadn't risen any during the first few minutes of talking to Turnbuckle. The man looked totally lost, completely out of his element, as well as being downright sick.

Turnbuckle had started to get more animated, though, as they walked down the street to Tip Woodford's office and discussed the case, and he had perked right up when he entered the office, met Tip and Diana, and started getting the details of the job that had brought him here.

Some men were only at their best when they were working, and Frank thought that maybe Claudius Turnbuckle was one of them. Turnbuckle certainly seemed to have a new spring in his step as they left the Lucky Lizard office and started toward the hotel to confront Brighton . . . assuming that Brighton was in his room. The lawyer's features were still pale and showed lines of strain, but he was stronger now. He was throwing off the effects of the stagecoach journey.

"Is this man Brighton dangerous?" Turnbuckle asked. "Physically dangerous, I mean?"

Frank nodded. "I've got a hunch he can be. He and Tip got in a pretty bad ruckus a few days ago. Tip's a tough old bird, but I think Brighton would have hurt him pretty bad if I hadn't stepped in to put a stop to it. To make things worse, I had to arrest Tip, because Brighton filed a charge of assault against him."

"I can defend him against that charge as well," Turnbuckle said without hesitation.

Frank chuckled and said, "You'll lose if you do. A lot of people saw him throw the first punch. I'm not saying that he wasn't provoked, but he started the ball. Reckon the judge will probably fine him, maybe sentence him to a night or two in jail. Tip can handle that." Frank grew more solemn. "This business about who really owns the Lucky Lizard is the real case. That's where we need your help."

"And you shall have it," Turnbuckle promised. "To the best of my ability."

"Nobody can ask for any more than that," Frank said.

Turnbuckle rubbed his jaw, and for a second a look of doubt and worry passed across his face. It disappeared quickly, though, and Frank didn't think anything of it. Everybody had those moments, even someone as supremely self-confident as Claudius Turnbuckle seemed to be.

When they reached the hotel and went into the lobby, Frank spoke to the desk clerk. "Mr. Brighton in his room?"

The man checked the key rack, then turned back to Frank and Turnbuckle and nodded. "His key's not here, so I assume he is, Marshal. Room Twenty-seven."

Frank nodded. "Much obliged." He put a hand on Turnbuckle's shoulder and steered the lawyer toward the staircase.

A few moments later, Frank knocked on the door

of Brighton's room. He glanced over at Turnbuckle as he did so, and again he saw a flash of nervousness on the lawyer's face. It disappeared as soon as the door was opened, though.

Dex Brighton stood there with his coat off and his collar loosened. He had a drink in his hand, and when Frank looked past him he saw the bottle on the table next to the bed. Brighton wasn't drunk, though. His gaze was too keen for that.

"Hello, Marshal," he said. "What brings you here?" He gave Turnbuckle a dismissive glance. "And who's this?"

"I'll tell you who I am, sir," Turnbuckle said without giving Frank a chance to answer Brighton's question. "I am Claudius Turnbuckle, attorney at law, and I've come to Buckskin to expose your scheme to obtain the Lucky Lizard Mine through fraudulent means."

Turnbuckle might look a mite mousy, but he obviously believed in putting his cards on the table, Frank thought. Turnbuckle stared defiantly at Brighton and waited to see how the man was going to react.

If Brighton was surprised, he didn't show it. He lifted his glass to his lips and casually tossed off the rest of the whiskey in it. "Is that so?" he said as he lowered the glass.

"Yes, sir, it is."

Brighton looked at Frank again. "So this is that bulldog of a lawyer you called in, Morgan. I've got to say that he's a little smaller and younger than I expected."

Frank didn't let on that he'd had the same reaction when he first saw Turnbuckle. "I don't reckon it matters how big you are or how old you are in court, as long as you've got the facts on your side."

"You're awfully quick to assume that I don't," Brighton snapped.

"If the partnership agreement you have is genuine," Turnbuckle said, "why don't you go ahead and produce it? Why didn't you show it to Thomas Woodford as soon as you came to Buckskin? The two of you might have been able to settle this matter without ever taking it to court."

"I offered to settle with Woodford. He threw me out of his office."

"You didn't show him the document."

"That paper is staying in a safe place until I'm good and ready to use it," Brighton said. "Anyway, if Woodford wouldn't take my word to start with, why would he believe the partnership agreement was real? He would've just claimed it was a fake, like he's saying now."

"Am I to understand that you intend to prove in court the document *isn't* a fake?"

Brighton smiled coldly. "I don't give a damn what you understand or don't understand, Turnbuckle. And I'm sure as hell not going to tell you what I intend to do. What kind of fool do you take me for?"

"A greedy one, sir, who has overreached with this scheme to steal the Lucky Lizard Mine from its rightful owner."

Brighton's face darkened, and his hand closed more tightly around the empty glass. Frank kept a close eye on the man, ready to step in if he needed to. He had been content for the moment to stand back and watch Brighton and Turnbuckle spar verbally with each other, but if it came down to a real fight, Frank didn't figure the lawyer would stand a chance.

Brighton reined in his anger, though, and forced a smile back onto his face with a visible effort. "And you'll have to prove *that* in court, Turnbuckle. Until that time comes, I don't think you and I have anything else to say to each other. If you came here hoping to arrange a settlement, you failed miserably."

"I would never advise a client to settle with a thief," Turnbuckle shot back. "Good day, sir."

He turned and stalked off down the hall toward the stairs.

Frank lingered for a second, and Brighton said, "Where'd you find that little banty rooster, Morgan? He's not going to stand a chance once *my* lawyer gets through with him."

This was the first time Brighton had mentioned an attorney of his own, although Frank had assumed that the man intended to be represented by one when the judge arrived. He had figured as well that Brighton would bring in somebody from out of town. There were several lawyers practicing in Buckskin, but none of them were the sort Brighton would pick to handle a case like this, Frank thought.

"Just who is your lawyer?" Frank asked. He didn't know if Brighton would tell him or not, but the question was worth asking.

A smug smile spread over the man's face. "Desmond O'Hara."

"Don't reckon I've heard of him."

"You will have by the time this is over, Morgan. You will have."

Frank jerked his head in a curt nod and followed

Turnbuckle. The lawyer was already halfway down the stairs. Frank caught up to him in the hotel lobby.

"So that's our opponent, eh?" Turnbuckle mused. "I agree with you, Mr. Morgan. Brighton is a ruthless, dangerous man. You can see it in his eyes. But no man is bigger than the law. He'll be cut down to size once I get him in a courtroom."

For Tip Woodford's sake, Frank hoped that Turnbuckle was right about that.

Chapter 12

"Tell me everything you can remember about Jeremiah Fulton," Luther said to Tip Woodford that evening. "I want to know how you met him, anything he said about his background, how it came about that you bought his mining claim from him . . . You understand, Mr. Woodford, that any detail, no matter how small, may turn out to be the vital piece of evidence in our attempt to derail Brighton's claim." Luther shrugged. "Unless, of course, it turns out that the partnership agreement is blatantly false, in which case that will be all we need to bring this affair to a successful conclusion."

"Well, all right. I'll try to remember as much as I can, but that's been a while back. You want a cigar, maybe some brandy?"

The real Claudius Turnbuckle would never have refused such an offer, Luther thought. He nodded and said, "That sounds excellent, Mr. Woodford. Thank you."

"How about you, Frank?"

Morgan shook his head. "You know me, Tip. I'm

not much of a drinking man, and the most I smoke is a pipe now and then."

They were in Woodford's study in the big house on the outskirts of Buckskin where Woodford and Diana lived. Woodford had had the house built during the first silver boom, when the Lucky Lizard originally made him a rich man. The boom had collapsed, Woodford had lost his fortune, and his wife had taken their young daughter and gone back East to live, leaving Woodford to cling stubbornly to his faded hopes and dreams.

Then, a few years earlier, Diana's mother had passed away, and she had returned to Buckskin to live with her father. The big house had fallen into disrepair by then, although Woodford was still living in it. The discovery of a new silver vein had changed everything, and Woodford was once more a rich man. Diana had taken charge of the household and seen to it that things were put back in order. It was a grand place. Nothing to compare to the fine houses in San Francisco, of course, but certainly the most opulent dwelling in Buckskin. Probably in this entire part of Nevada.

Frank Morgan had told Luther about Tip Woodford's history that afternoon, after Luther had rested for a while in his hotel room. Morgan had come to the hotel to inform Luther that Woodford wanted both of them to have dinner at his house that evening. Even though Luther was still exhausted from the grueling trip from Carson City, he hadn't hesitated in accepting the invitation. It would give him a chance to discuss the case some more with Woodford, and it was exactly what Mr. Turnbuckle would have done in this position.

Besides, dining at the Woodford house meant that he would have the opportunity to spend more time with Diana Woodford, and that prospect was definitely appealing to Luther. He'd always had an eye for a pretty woman, and Diana had an elegance and grace about her, to go with her physical beauty, that Luther wouldn't have expected to find in a frontier settlement such as Buckskin.

She was a good cook, too, as she had demonstrated with the meal she'd prepared for them—steaks cooked in some sort of light, crispy breading the likes of which Luther had never encountered before, potatoes, gravy, incredibly light and fluffy biscuits . . . simple fare really, but Diana made all of it delicious.

They hadn't talked about the case during dinner. Diana had lived in St. Louis, so she was familiar with cities, but she had never been to San Francisco and wanted to know about it. Having grown up there, Luther knew all about it and was more than happy to spin tales about the city's history and describe its attractions. Morgan had been to San Francisco on numerous occasions and knew most of the places Luther talked about.

That made Luther appreciate even more the stroke of luck that had prevented Morgan from ever making Claudius Turnbuckle's acquaintance in the past. If the two men had ever met, Luther couldn't have even attempted this ruse.

That might have been better, the cautious part of him insisted. He had never been one to take a lot of chances.

Which was probably one reason why it felt so good to attempt something this daring. Despite his fears, he was beginning to enjoy playing this role.

Dinner was over now, and the men had withdrawn into Woodford's combined study, library, and office. Woodford took cigars from a humidor on his desk and handed one to Luther. Luther recalled seeing Mr. Turnbuckle trim his cigars before lighting them, and Woodford was doing the same thing. He took a penknife from his pocket and followed suit, then puffed the fat cylinder of tobacco into life as Woodford held a match for him.

The smoke was harsh in Luther's lungs, but even though he choked a little, he managed not to cough. Sipping the brandy from the snifter Woodford handed him helped. Luther might not have ever smoked an expensive cigar before, but he'd had brandy on numerous occasions.

Woodford had donned a suit and vest and cravat this evening, and he actually looked a little like a businessman instead of a hardrock miner, although his attitude was still somewhat rough around the edges. Case in point. He said, "I met Jeremiah Fulton in a Virginia City whorehouse."

Luther couldn't stop his eyebrows from rising.

Woodford looked around the room, as if to make sure that Diana hadn't slipped in while he wasn't looking, and went on. "I ain't proud of some of the things I've done, Mr. Turnbuckle, but I won't deny 'em either. I'm as human as the next fella and always have been. But I don't want to hurt Diana's feelin's."

"Don't worry, sir," Luther said. "I won't share any details with your charming daughter except the ones that are absolutely necessary."

"Anyway," Woodford went on, "I ran into Fulton in the bar of this sportin' house, and since we were both prospectors we got to talkin'. You know, tellin' each other about places where we'd looked for gold and silver, places where we'd had a little luck and them where we hadn't had any."

Luther puffed on the cigar and nodded. "Of course."

"Fulton told me about this spot that he swore was a natural for silver. He'd had a mite of education and said all the signs were there, the right kinds o' rocks and stratification and such like. But he'd sunk a couple of shafts and hadn't found a thing, so he'd decided that he was wrong about it and was wastin' his time."

"This was the claim that turned out to be the Lucky Lizard?"

Woodford nodded. "That's right. Fulton had filed on it with the land recorder, all properlike, and he said he'd sell me the claim if I was interested in givin' it a try."

Morgan said, "Why would you be interested in prospecting a claim that hadn't panned out?"

"You know the answer to that, Frank," Woodford said with a smile. "Fellas like me, and ol' Jeremiah Fulton, too, for that matter, always think that we're luckier than the next fella, that fate's gonna smile on us and we're gonna be the ones to find the strike. Anyway, Fulton sounded like he knew what he was talkin' about with all that talk about geology and such, so I decided to take a chance. He sold me the claim for twenty dollars."

"Such a small amount?" Luther asked in surprise.

"Well . . . Fulton was flat broke. He'd just spent his last coin on a drink. And twenty bucks would buy quite a bit of what the place we were in had to sell, if you know what I mean. That was all Fulton was interested in right then."

Frank chuckled. "So he was really just trying to promote enough dinero to take one of the girls upstairs."

"Yep. And I came out of it with a claim that made me a rich man, not once but twice."

Luther asked, "At any time during this conversation you had with Fulton, did he make any mention of having a partner in this claim?"

Woodford shook his head firmly and emphatically. "He didn't say a blessed word about that. He didn't mention anybody named Chester Brighton."

"You remember that clearly, even though it's been years since the conversation took place?"

"A fella tends to remember things that have a big effect on his life. Nothin's ever had a bigger effect on mine than buyin' that claim."

"What about finding the silver on the claim? How did that come about?"

Woodford grinned. "That's the best part of the story. I had just about as much luck as Fulton did at first, namely none at all. I was about to give up on the claim, too. I didn't figure I could even sell it to some other poor deluded fool and get my twenty bucks back. Then I saw this little lizard run up into a crack in the rocks, and for no real reason, I looked to see where he'd gone."

"And *that's* where you found the silver vein!" Luther guessed.

"Yep. It come up almost to the ground. It was pure luck I followed that lizard to it, though, so when it came time to name the mine, I knew what I was gonna call it."

Luther couldn't help but laugh. It was a colorful,

amusing story, and he didn't doubt the veracity of it. But whether or not it would help them win the case . . . well, that he didn't know yet.

"Thank you, Mr. Woodford. You've given me several ideas for approaches we may take in our legal efforts. I'm still confident that we're going to emerge from this affair victorious."

"I sure hope so. I've lost one fortune already, Mr. Turnbuckle. Don't reckon I could stand to lose another one. Especially not for Diana's sake."

"Miss Woodford doesn't need to worry. Claudius Turnbuckle won't let either of you down."

Luther didn't even have to remind himself this time that when he spoke of Claudius Turnbuckle, he meant himself. *He* wasn't going to let them down.

Especially not Diana Woodford . . .

Dex Brighton stepped out of the Top-Notch Saloon and turned toward the hotel. The Top-Notch wasn't as fancy as the Silver Baron, but it would do since he couldn't very well patronize his enemy's place of business. He had played poker for a couple of hours this evening and come out almost a hundred dollars ahead. And since none of the other players had been very good, he hadn't even had to resort to any of the tricks he had learned back in his cardsharp days, when he'd had to settle for little payoffs.

He was on the trail of a big payoff now, and he wasn't going to let anything stop him from getting his hands on it.

He was passing the mouth of an alley when he heard a hiss from the shadows. "Boss! Hey, Boss!"

Brighton recognized Cy Stample's voice. Anger

welled up inside him. Stample wasn't supposed to be here in Buckskin. He and the rest of the gunmen who were working with Brighton were supposed to stay out of sight for now, which meant not straying far from the old abandoned mine they were using as a hideout.

Quickly, Brighton glanced around and saw that no one on the street was watching him. He stepped into the darkness of the alley and whispered, "Damn it, Stample, what are you doing here?"

"I just wanted to let you know that all the boys finally got here except for Deuce Dooley, and he ain't gonna make it." A callous chuckle came from Stample. "He come down with a bad case o' lead poisonin' over in El Paso. Damn fool tried to draw on Falcon McAllister. Asa Perkins told me about when he rode in this evenin'." Stample paused. "So I reckon we're ready to grab that mine whenever you give the word. There's eighteen of us, all good men. That's more'n enough to handle a bunch o' damn miners."

Stample was a deadly fighter and was fiercely loyal to whoever was paying him, but he was as dumb as a rock, Brighton thought. Suppressing the impatience he felt, he said, "I told you, Stample, we're not going to attack the mine and take it over that way. Only as a last resort. I still think I can convince Woodford to sign it over to me peacefully."

Brighton heard a faint rasping sound in the darkness, and realized it was Stample's fingertips rubbing over the beard stubble on his jaw. "I dunno about that, Boss. Old-timers like this fella Woodford are usually pretty damn stubborn."

"He'll come around to my way of thinking,"

Brighton insisted, "especially when he doesn't have Frank Morgan as an ally anymore. I want you to draw Morgan out of town so that you and your men can get rid of him." Brighton thought about the problem for a moment, then went on. "Maybe some trouble at the Crown Royal would do it. Morgan and his son own that mine. Take care of that before you deal with the judge coming into town on that stagecoach next week."

"Sure, we can handle that," Stample said. "Morgan's gonna die this time. I guarantee it."

"I hope you're right. Once Morgan has been dealt with, there'll be just one more thing I need you to do. Woodford has a lawyer now, a man that Morgan brought in from San Francisco. He doesn't look like much, but he has quite a reputation." Brighton nodded, sure now that he was on the right track and even glad that Stample had come into Buckskin so that they could talk about how to proceed.

It was simple really.

"Yes, once Frank Morgan is dead," Brighton told the leader of his crew of gun-wolves, "I want you to kill Claudius Turnbuckle."

Chapter 13

Garrett Claiborne had brought the latest mining techniques with him when he began supervising the operation of the Crown Royal Mine, and as a result it had become quite profitable. When Tip Woodford's discovery of a new vein in the Lucky Lizard had prompted Conrad Browning to order that the Crown Royal be reopened and explored more extensively, Conrad had hoped for a modest success. Claiborne had delivered much more than that, locating a particularly rich vein deep in the mine. The ore coming out of the Crown Royal these days assayed just as much silver per ton as that from the Lucky Lizard—and a little better than what the Alhambra Mine was producing.

Conrad was pleased, and although he wasn't one to heap extensive amounts of praise on his employees, he didn't mind telling Claiborne as much. The two men sat in Claiborne's office at the mine, going over the assay reports for the past month. Rebel was back in Buckskin; Conrad had driven out here alone in the buggy early this morning while the dew was still on the grass.

"You've done good work here, Garrett," Conrad said as he placed the sheaf of papers back on Claiborne's desk. "Excellent work."

"Thank you, sir."

"Clearly, I made the right decision when I hired you to be the Crown Royal's superintendent. How long do you think the mine will continue at this level of production?"

Claiborne shook his head. "That's impossible to say, Mr. Browning. The vein could run out tomorrow, for all we know. I will say this, though . . . at this point the vein shows no signs of ending. It's as solid as ever."

"That's a good, honest answer," Conrad said with a nod. "Stay with it as long as you can . . . and when it *does* run out, we'll see if we can find another one."

The men grinned at each other. Claiborne asked, "Would you like a drink before you head back to town, sir?"

Conrad pulled a gold turnip watch from his pocket and opened it to check the time before he answered. "It's late enough, I suppose. I wouldn't mind."

Claiborne got up and went to a filing cabinet, opening the bottom drawer to take out a bottle of whiskey and a couple of glasses. He splashed a couple of inches of the amber liquid into each glass and handed one to Conrad.

"To the Crown Royal's continued success," Conrad said as he lifted his glass.

"Indeed," Claiborne responded. They drank, and the mining engineer went on. "When do you plan to head back East?"

"I don't really know. I'd thought that we might

start back before now, but Mrs. Browning seems to be enjoying herself out here so much that I hate to ruin her fun."

"She's originally from . . . New Mexico Territory, is it?"

Conrad nodded, thinking of the dangerous adventure during which he and Rebel had met. She was a Western girl through and through, and he had to wonder if he was stifling her by insisting that they live in Boston. She had adjusted to life there, or so she claimed, and seemed happy enough most of the time, but he had seen with his own eyes how she had blossomed during their sojourn out here in the West.

Maybe it was time to start thinking about moving the headquarters of his business ventures to Denver, say, or possibly San Francisco. With all the modern advances in telegraphic communications and the speed and efficiency of the postal system, it was possible to run a company from almost anywhere these days.

"Well, I hope you'll stay out here as long as you want to," Claiborne was saying. "I know that Mr. Morgan enjoys your visits."

"He does, does he?" Conrad murmured. Even though he and his father had grown closer over the past couple of years, he was still leery about fully accepting their relationship. It was difficult to forget all the things Frank Morgan had done in the past, all the men he had killed . . .

The sudden crash of gunshots somewhere outside made both men jerk their heads up in surprise.

"What the devil!" Claiborne exclaimed.

They started for the doorway at the same time. Conrad was closer, so he reached it first. When he stepped outside onto the porch, another shot blasted out. The bullet whipped past him to chew splinters from the doorjamb. He felt their sting on the back of his neck and cursed in pain.

Claiborne had followed closely behind him. As another slug thudded into the wall of the office building, the mining engineer grabbed Conrad's collar and hauled him backward. The two men stumbled into the office. Claiborne kicked the door closed.

"Sorry about handling you so roughly, Mr. Browning," Claiborne said as he hurried over to a gun rack on the wall and reached for a Winchester.

Conrad rubbed the back of his neck, which was still smarting from the splinters. He would have to get someone to dig out the ones that were still stuck in his skin, which wasn't a pleasant prospect.

But it beat actually getting shot all to hell, and he said, "No apologies necessary, Garrett. I was a damned fool for running out there like that before I knew what was going on, and you probably saved my life. Could you tell what was happening?"

"I didn't get much of a look, but from what I saw and heard, several men are firing from the trees downslope, just spraying lead around wildly. It sounds like they're still at it."

As a matter of fact, the ragged volley of rifle fire had picked up in intensity. A few of the bullets struck the log walls of the office building, but didn't penetrate them. The gunmen were probably shooting at the stamp mill and the mine entrance, too, judging by the amount of powder they were burning.

Claiborne went to one of the windows and pushed up the pane, crouching low so as to keep out of the line of fire as much as possible. Conrad started to follow him, but Claiborne motioned him back.

"I'll see if I can get a shot, sir."

Claiborne edged the Winchester's barrel over the windowsill and risked a look. Then he swiftly brought the rifle butt to his shoulder, nestled his cheek against the smooth wood of the stock, and began firing. Three shots crashed out as fast as he could work the Winchester's loading lever. He had to duck back down as a bullet shattered the windowpane and sprayed glass over him.

"I seem to have drawn their attention," he said with a wry grin as he crouched among the shards and splinters of glass. "But the men in the stamp mill are returning their fire, too. I don't know what those bushwhackers hope to accomplish. If they're trying to waltz in here and take over, they're going to have a big fight on their hands."

Claiborne waited a moment and then rose up and opened fire again, sending several more shots toward the places in the trees where he had spotted powder smoke rising. This time there wasn't any response. Claiborne ceased fire and waited.

After a few moments, he said, "They seem to have called off the attack. The only shooting is coming from the stamp mill now."

"Do you think it's safe to go outside?" Conrad asked.

"Better wait a few minutes just to be sure. Those varmints could be trying to trick us."

That sounded just like something his father would say, Conrad thought. Spending all that time around Frank Morgan must have rubbed off on Claiborne.

Gradually, the firing from the stamp mill died away, too, and the eerie silence that always followed a gun battle hung over the mine headquarters. Claiborne stood up, said, "Wait in here, sir," and pushed the door open with the barrel of his rifle.

When there were no shots, he stepped outside. Conrad followed far enough to see the stamp mill and saw men armed with rifles emerging from that building, too. Claiborne hustled over to join them. A short time later, a group of men headed for the trees to see what they could find.

Conrad watched with interest. The searchers returned a short time later and spoke to Claiborne, who then returned to the office.

"The bushwhackers lit a shuck, all right," Claiborne reported. "The men who went out there found shell casings and the tracks of their horses, but if any of the riflemen were wounded or killed by our fire, the others took them with them when they pulled out." Claiborne shook his head. "That's about what I expected. They wouldn't want to leave anyone behind to possibly be identified."

"Who could they have been?" Conrad asked. "Indians perhaps?"

"Not around here," Claiborne stated with certainty. "The Utes and Paiutes who live in the area have all been pacified and haven't cause any trouble for quite a while."

"Outlaws then. Maybe they thought you had a payroll on hand and intended to steal it."

"Then they would have tried to get to the office here and take us by surprise." Claiborne shook his head. "No, it doesn't make any sense. It was like they started shooting willy-nilly, just trying to shake us up and do whatever damage they could."

"Well, whatever they were up to, I know someone who can probably figure it out," Conrad said.

Claiborne nodded. "I was just thinking the same thing. We need to go tell Mr. Morgan what happened."

Luther Galloway understood fully now what the old saying about waiting for the other shoe to drop meant. He was astounded that his masquerade as Claudius Turnbuckle had continued unchallenged for a couple of days. He kept waiting for someone to tell him that he was too young and too incompetent to possibly be the esteemed attorney from San Francisco.

In the meantime, though, he was enjoying getting to know Diana Woodford, who had proven to be as charming as she was beautiful. He was getting a considerable amount of satisfaction out of preparing Tip Woodford's case for trial, too. He had always enjoying doing the legal research that Mr. Turnbuckle called on him to do, and he had assisted in the writing of enough briefs so that he had no trouble getting the facts of the case down in clear, logical fashion.

He and Woodford had gone over the story several more times while waiting for the circuit judge to arrive, until Luther was confident that he knew it backward and forward. He had devised a possible angle of attack, but the first step in it would be to force Dex Brighton to produce that so-called partnership agreement between his father and Jeremiah

Fulton. Luther's course of action after that would depend on whether or not he was successful in persuading the judge to order Brighton to produce the document immediately . . . and if so, what he found in it.

And in addition to all that, Luther found that the clear mountain air seemed to have put some extra spring in his step. It certainly wasn't like the dank, oppressive atmosphere to be found in San Francisco most of the time.

When he left the hotel on Monday morning, the day before the judge was due to arrive on the stagecoach, Luther found Frank Morgan waiting for him on the porch.

"Had breakfast yet?" Morgan asked.

"As a matter of fact, I haven't, Marshal."

Morgan grinned. "Come on over to the café with me then," he invited. "Best flapjacks you'll find anywhere in these parts."

"Well, that sounds . . . appetizing, I suppose."

"Wait'll you wrap your gums around them. You'll think you've died and gone to heaven."

Luther couldn't imagine being quite so impressed with a stack of flapjacks that he would consider them divine, but he supposed he should reserve judgment. He walked down the street with Morgan, cutting across its dusty width diagonally to reach the café.

They went inside the neatly kept establishment, which was doing a brisk business. A couple of tables covered with red-checked tablecloths were empty, though, and Luther and Morgan took one of them. A young, blond woman, a little plump but still extremely pretty in a gingham dress and white apron, came over to them and greeted them with a smile.

"What can I get you and your friend, Marshal?" she asked.

Morgan glanced at Luther. "You have any preferences?"

"Whatever you think is good," Luther replied with a shake of his head.

Morgan smiled. "All right." He turned to the young woman. "Big stack of flapjacks, hash browns, and plenty of bacon, for both of us. And a pot of coffee."

"Strong enough to get up and walk off under its own power?" the waitress asked.

"You bet," Morgan told her.

The blonde went back to the kitchen. Luther saw two other women working there, one of them a redhead with a ready smile and a slight Southern drawl, the other a brunette who was a few years older. Like the blonde, both of the other women were very attractive, Luther noted, and he commented on that fact to Morgan.

The marshal nodded. "Lauren and Becky and Ginnie used to work in one of the houses in Virginia City, before they came here. I'm not sure where all they'd been before that, but I'm glad they decided to settle down in Buckskin. They're hard workers, and this place has the best food you'll find in these parts."

Luther frowned. "You say they worked in a . . . house?"

"That's right."

Luther lowered his voice to a whisper. "You mean a house of ill repute?"

"Yep. And you don't have to whisper. Just about everybody in town knows about it."

"And yet they . . . they continued to patronize this establishment?"

"Why wouldn't they?" Morgan asked with what appeared to be genuine puzzlement.

"But . . . but those women used to be—"

"Lots of people used to be lots of things," Morgan said, breaking in. "Out here folks don't care all that much what somebody *used* to be. They care more about what a fella or a gal is *now*. That's all that really matters, isn't it?"

"Yes, I suppose so," Luther said, somewhat abashed. Morgan's voice had been quiet and friendly, without even a hint of scolding to it, and yet Luther felt that he had just been reprimanded.

And he felt more than ever like a fraud, too. For a second, he wished he could just tell Frank Morgan who he really was and what had happened to Mr. Turnbuckle. It would be nice to put an end to this charade, even though he had enjoyed certain aspects of it.

It was too late for that now. Things had gone too far. He had no choice except to keep pretending that he was Claudius Turnbuckle.

Besides, he was beginning to think that he could actually win this case for Tip Woodford. If that happened, he could return to San Francisco and no one there would ever have to be the wiser, but at the same time Luther would go back with renewed confidence in his abilities and the knowledge that he could be a good lawyer, no matter what the results of the bar exam had said so far.

Their breakfast arrived, the plates weighted down with food being carried to their table by the blond Ginnie Carlson. Morgan introduced Luther to her, and he managed a polite smile, even though he couldn't quite banish thoughts of her previous profession from his mind. The redhead was Becky Humphries, Morgan informed him, and the pretty, dignified brunette was Lauren Stillman.

The food was as good as Morgan claimed, which came as a bit of a surprise to Luther. In fact, it was as good as anything he had ever had in San Francisco, a city known for its fine restaurants. The two men ate with gusto and then lingered over cups of coffee, which was as strong as Ginnie had promised and quite bracing.

"How's the case coming along?" Morgan asked, and Luther wondered if that was the real reason the marshal had invited him to breakfast this morning.

"Quite well, I think," he replied. "Mr. Woodford and I have spent a lot of time going over the details, and I have an idea about how to prove that Brighton's claim on the Lucky Lizard is a phony."

"How's that?"

Luther hesitated. He trusted Frank Morgan— after all, the man was one of the law firm's most important clients—but he wasn't sure that he wanted to share his strategy until he knew more about whether it was going to develop the way he hoped.

He was saved from having to decide one way or the other by a sudden commotion from the street outside. The swift rataplan of hoofbeats made him and Morgan both glance toward the café's front window, and they saw a buggy race past the place.

"That was Conrad's buggy," Morgan said as he came quickly to his feet. "Something must be wrong for him to be running those horses like that. I'd better see what's going on."

He started for the door, lifting a hand in farewell to the three young women who ran the café, and he called out to the brunette, "I'll be back to settle up with you later, Lauren."

"No hurry, Frank," she told him. "I reckon you're good for it."

Morgan threw a grin in her direction, and then he was gone.

He hadn't even looked back to see if Luther was following him.

For some reason, that bothered Luther. He got to his feet hurriedly and left the café, too. If more trouble was about to descend on Buckskin, then maybe he could help.

After all, he was a famous lawyer . . . wasn't he?

Chapter 14

By the time Frank got outside, Conrad had brought the buggy to a stop in front of the marshal's office. Catamount Jack, who had been in the office while Frank was having breakfast with Claudius Turnbuckle, came out to see what the ruckus was about. He was talking to Conrad as Frank strode up, and Frank saw now that Garrett Claiborne was perched on the buggy seat, too, holding a Winchester. Frank knew from talking to Conrad the night before that his son had intended to visit the Crown Royal Mine this morning. Obviously, something had happened out there that was bad enough to bring Conrad and Claiborne racing into town.

"Looking for me, Conrad?" Frank asked.

Conrad and Claiborne both climbed down from the buggy. "There was an attack on the mine," Conrad said.

"An attack?" Frank repeated with a frown.

Claiborne nodded. "Several men opened fire on the buildings and the tunnel entrance from the cover of the trees. We put up a fight, of course, and after a few minutes the gunmen fled."

"Did you see who they were?"

"I never got a look at them, just saw their powder smoke," Claiborne replied with a shake of his head. "I asked the rest of the men, and they never saw them either."

Frank looked at his son. "How about you?"

"I'm sorry, Frank. I don't have any idea who they were or why they attacked the mine."

"It doesn't make any sense," Claiborne said. "Only one man was wounded, and that was by a ricochet. Several miners were out in the open when the shooting started, and if the bushwhackers wanted to kill them, they could have without much trouble."

Before Frank could ask any more questions, Diana Woodford came hurrying along the street, almost running. "Garrett, are you all right?" she asked as she came up to them. "Someone told me that you and Mr. Browning were in that buggy that raced by, and I thought there might be trouble."

Claiborne smiled and told her, "I'm fine, Diana. Puzzled by what happened but unhurt."

She put her arms around him and hugged him. "Thank goodness. My first thought was that there had been a cave-in or something like that out at the mine."

"No, it wasn't a natural disaster at all," Claiborne told her, his expression becoming serious again. "Somebody took some potshots at us instead."

Diana stepped back to stare at him. "Somebody tried to *kill* you?"

"That's what we were just talking about," Frank said. "It sounds to me more like they were trying to throw a scare into you, Garrett."

Claiborne nodded. "Maybe. But if that was their goal, they failed. We put up enough of a fight to send them packing in a hurry."

"I'll ride out there and take a look around," Frank said. "Might be able to find something to tell me who they were or what they were really after."

He hadn't forgotten about that mysterious attempt on his own life a few days earlier. He had no real reason to think that this attack on the Crown Royal Mine had any connection to the earlier incident . . . but two unexplained acts of violence in less than a week made Frank curious.

"I'll go with you," Catamount Jack said.

Frank shook his head. "No, I need you to hold down the fort here, Jack."

"Seems like that dang fort needs lots o' holdin' down these days," the old-timer grumbled. "Blamed thing must be light as a feather."

Frank chuckled but didn't change his orders. Buckskin was relatively peaceful right now, but peace was a fragile thing on the frontier. And despite the inexorable advance of civilization these days, this part of Nevada still qualified as frontier.

"Why don't I go with you, Marshal?" Claudius Turnbuckle suggested.

Frank glanced at the lawyer in surprise. He had known Turnbuckle for only a few days, but the man didn't strike him as the sort of hombre who'd want to go gallivanting across the countryside looking for bushwhackers.

"I don't know if that's such a good idea . . ." he began.

"I'd like to see some more of the area around

here," Turnbuckle said. "This seems like a perfect opportunity to do so."

"This won't be a sightseeing jaunt," Frank pointed out. "It could be dangerous."

"I don't mind," Turnbuckle said. "I promise to be careful, though, since I still have to represent Mr. Woodford in court and crush Brighton's fraudulent claim." He gave Diana an encouraging smile.

"Well, if you're bound and determined . . . You'll have to have a horse, though. I reckon Amos Hillman would be glad to rent you a mount and saddle."

"Excellent!"

"Can you handle a gun?"

That question appeared to take Turnbuckle a little by surprise, as if he hadn't quite thought this all the way through. If Frank was able to pick up the trail of the bushwhackers, he might run them to ground, and if that happened it was likely there would be shooting.

But then steely resolve glittered in Turnbuckle's eyes, and Frank remembered that the lawyer had a pretty combative reputation, at least in the courtroom. Maybe that carried over into other areas as well.

"I'm an adequate shot with a rifle," Turnbuckle said.

"Let's hope that's good enough." If Frank couldn't scare Turnbuckle off with the possibility of getting mixed up in a corpse-and-cartridge session, then he wasn't going to waste any more time arguing with the man. "We'll go see about getting you a horse."

"I'll pick up a mount at the livery stable, too," Garrett Claiborne said. "That way Mr. Browning won't have to take his buggy back out there."

Diana hugged the mining engineer again. "Be careful, Garrett," she told him.

Frank might have been wrong about it, but he thought he saw something flash in Claudius Turnbuckle's eyes when Diana embraced Claiborne. That would explain why Turnbuckle was suddenly so anxious to help him track down those bushwhackers. The hombre wanted to impress Diana!

This might be trouble in the making, Frank thought. Now he not only had to try to track down those bushwhackers, but he also had to ride herd on a young man who wanted to make an impression on a gal who was interested in somebody else.

That just might prove to be the most dangerous part of the job.

He was getting in the habit of making impulsive, downright foolish, and potentially lethal decisions, Luther Galloway thought as he contemplated the horse standing in front of him. It looked big enough to kill him, not to mention that a fall from its back would probably prove to be fatal, too.

Then don't fall off, he told himself. That was simple enough.

"Here you go," Catamount Jack said as he shoved a rifle into some sort of leather scabbard attached to the saddle. "Got fifteen rounds in her, so you ought to have plenty o' ammunition."

Luther swallowed. "Thank you, Deputy."

"No offense, Mr. Turnbuckle, but I wish I was goin' with the marshal instead o' you. It's been too blasted long since I got to swap lead with any ringtailed hellions."

Was the man making fun of him, or trying to scare him? From the twinkle in Jack's eyes, Luther thought that both were possible, even likely. But it didn't change anything, so screwing up his courage, he grasped the reins and the saddle horn, put his left foot in the stirrup, and swung up onto the horse's back.

Amos Hillman, the livery stable's proprietor, had saddled and led out the big brown horse, claiming that it was one of his best and not too rough for a relative novice to ride. Luther knew that Westerners sometimes liked to play tricks on people they considered "tenderfeet," and he certainly fell into that category. Frank Morgan had nodded in approval of Hillman's choice, though, and Luther didn't think Morgan would allow such trickery under the circumstances.

Luther had barely settled himself in the saddle, and tried not to gasp at how high off the ground he was, when Morgan rode out of the stable on a big gelding whose hide had a peculiar golden sheen. Garrett Claiborne followed on another mount rented from Amos Hillman.

When Luther looked at Claiborne, he felt a mixture of anger and jealousy. It was obvious that Diana Woodford cared a great deal for Claiborne. Luther had been unaware of the relationship between them until today—and he didn't like it. When he saw them embracing, the thought occurred to him that Diana might like it if he helped Morgan track down whoever was responsible for the attack on the mine, and the words popped out of his mouth before he knew what he was doing.

Once the offer was made, though, it certainly

couldn't be taken back. Luckily, he'd been able to persuade Morgan to take him along. Or perhaps unluckily, depending on how you wanted to look at it.

Either way, they were ready to ride.

"You sit a saddle like you've done it before," Morgan commented as the three men swung into Buckskin's main street and headed out of the settlement.

"I ride in one of the parks in San Francisco," Luther said. That was true, as far as it went. He had ridden only a few times, most recently about six months earlier. He knew enough about it, though, to stay in the saddle without a great deal of awkward bouncing.

He had about the same level of experience with firearms. He had been on a few hunting trips as a young man, and he had gone target shooting a couple of times. He knew which end of the gun the bullet came out of, as the old saying went, and he was confident that in the event of trouble he wouldn't be a total liability.

He hoped that would be the case anyway.

He hoped even more that the situation wouldn't come up. If Morgan failed to find the bushwhackers' trail, it wouldn't be any reflection on him, Luther told himself. All Diana would remember was that he had volunteered without any hesitation to go along on what might turn out to be a dangerous mission.

They left the town behind and headed toward the Crown Royal Mine. Luther had never been out there and had only a vague idea of where it was located. He had seen it on a map that was pinned to the wall of Tip Woodford's office, but since he had never been in the area before, the landmarks shown on the map didn't mean much to him.

"You think Jessica Munro might be trying to stir up some trouble between the Crown Royal and the Alhambra again?" Claiborne asked as the men rode along, following a fairly well-defined trail.

Morgan frowned in thought for a moment before answering. Then he shook his head and said, "I doubt it. She wouldn't have anything to gain from it, and anyway, she's not the type. If her husband wanted something, *he* might've sent a crew of gunnies to get it, but Hamish Munro's dead. I think Mrs. Munro's probably content just to sit back and let the Alhambra earn however much it will before the silver peters out."

"As it likely will sooner or later," Claiborne observed.

Morgan shrugged. "Good or bad, most things come to an end."

That was true, Luther thought. Sooner or later, the role he was playing would have to end. But not until after he had shown everyone that he was a decent lawyer, he hoped.

It took about an hour of riding to reach the Crown Royal, and by that time Luther's muscles were beginning to ache from being in the saddle. He didn't say anything about the discomfort, though, remaining stoic instead.

"There's the stand of trees where the bushwhackers were hidden," Garrett Claiborne said, pointing out a thick growth of pines about a hundred yards from the mine office. The stamp mill was clearly visible off to one side, and so was the entrance to the mine tunnel, a short distance up the hill.

Morgan nodded. "Yeah, they were close enough to have ventilated some of the hombres working here if they wanted to." He turned the gold-colored horse toward the trees. "Let's see what we can find."

Luther and Claiborne followed him. Luther hoped that the mining engineer wasn't planning on staying with them the whole time. That wouldn't help him impress Diana Woodford. Surely, Claiborne had duties here at the Crown Royal that required his presence.

When the three men reached the trees, Morgan dismounted and led his horse into the pines. Claiborne followed suit, so Luther had no choice except to do likewise. Morgan pointed out several sets of hoofprints, and even hunkered down to study the marks more closely.

"Sometimes a horseshoe will have something distinctive about it that makes the prints it leaves easy to identify," he told Luther. "That's not really the case here." He looked around and suddenly called sharply, "Dog!"

A wolf leaped out of the brush, startling Luther and sending fear coursing along his veins. He reached for his rifle, thinking that the massive beast might attack Morgan and try to rip out his throat.

Instead, the big, shaggy, gray animal bounded up to Morgan's side with his tongue lolling out of his mouth in what appeared to be a grin. "What in the world!" Luther said.

"That's Dog," Claiborne explained with a grin. "He was with us all the time. Didn't you see him?"

Luther had to shake his head. "No, I didn't. I thought it was a wild animal, a wolf."

"Part wolf maybe," Morgan said as he scratched

behind the beast's ears. "I've never asked him, and he hasn't volunteered the information." He leaned closer to the big cur. "Dog, search."

Dog lowered his muzzle to the ground and started sniffing around the prints left by the horses. After a few moments he stiffened, and a growl came from him as his hackles rose. That just make him look even more fearsome as far as Luther was concerned.

"I thought he might pick up a familiar scent," Morgan said. "Those hoofprints may not be all that distinctive, but Dog never forgets something once he's smelled it."

"He knows these horses?"

"Or the man who was riding one of them," Morgan replied, his expression growing hard and grim. "The same fella took a couple of shots at me almost a week ago, when Conrad and Rebel and I were heading for Buckskin."

Claiborne said, "You're talking about the ambush you believe was set up after somebody stole that letter you sent me?"

Morgan nodded. "Yeah, the letter you never got. Somebody saw it, recognized my name on it, and snagged it in hopes of finding out when I was going to be arriving in Buckskin. Somebody who didn't want me to get there alive."

One possibility burst on Luther's brain like a rocket. "Dex Brighton!" he exclaimed.

Frank looked over at him and nodded. "Could be, but there's no way of knowing for sure—yet. Brighton didn't try to ambush me himself, or else Dog would have caught his scent in town, as much as Brighton has been around. But he could have hired somebody to kill me, and he could have hired the same hombre and some partners of his to carry out this attack on the mine."

"But why?" Claiborne said. "I suppose Brighton might not want you around because he's trying to bully the Lucky Lizard away from Tip Woodford and he knows that you and Tip are friends. But what does the Crown Royal have to do with any of that? This mine isn't connected to the Lucky Lizard case at all."

Morgan rubbed his jaw in thought and then said, "There's one connection . . . me."

Luther was thinking the same thing. And as those thoughts went through his head, he happened to glance up at a rocky knob some three hundred yards behind Morgan. The sun struck a bright, almost blinding reflection off something up there . . .

"Look out, Marshal!" Luther cried as he leaped toward Morgan. All he was trying to do was to get the man to move. He certainly didn't intend to get in the way of a would-be murderer's bullet.

But as something struck him a heavy blow and knocked him backward so that he sprawled on the ground, he realized to his horror that was exactly what he had done.

Chapter 15

Frank heard Claudius Turnbuckle's shout at the same time as the distant crack of a rifle sounded. A shaved fraction of a second later something buzzed past his ear, and he knew it was a bullet. He had shifted a little, though, as Turnbuckle leaped toward him, so in that instant he knew that the attorney had probably just saved his life.

Turnbuckle cried out in pain as the slug knocked him backward. Frank caught a glimpse of blood spurting from the lawyer's arm. He whirled around since the shot had come from behind him. In the same motion he reached for the butt of the Winchester that stuck up from the saddle boot strapped to Goldy. His fingers closed around the rifle's stock. He pulled the weapon from its sheath as he called to Claiborne, "Garrett! Get Turnbuckle out of here!"

Frank didn't have time to see if the mining engineer followed the order. His keen eyes had already spotted a thin curl of powder smoke coming from a rocky knoll a few hundred yards away. He had been able to tell from the sound of the first shot that the bushwhacker was too far away for a handgun to do any good; that was why he had grabbed for the Winchester right away.

He saw a spurt of orange flame from the muzzle of a gun as the sound of another shot came to his ears. The bullet smacked into the trunk of a pine tree about five feet to his right. Frank knew the rifleman would try to correct his aim, so he darted toward the spot where the previous shot had struck. Sure enough, the next bullet screamed through the air to his left. He ducked behind the thick trunk, braced the Winchester's barrel against it, and opened fire.

Frank heard more shots coming from behind him and glanced over his shoulder to see that Claiborne had dragged Turnbuckle behind some of the trees and rocks, then gotten his own rifle and was joining in the fight. Together they poured lead toward the knob where the bushwhacker was hidden. A couple of return shots struck the tree Frank was using for cover, but after that the rifleman must have given it up as a bad job. Frank didn't hear any more shots coming from up there, nor did he see any tendrils of powder smoke climbing into the clear air above the knoll.

"Hold your fire, Garrett," he called to Claiborne. "I think the varmint's gone."

"How can you be sure?" Claiborne asked.

"Can't. That's why we're going to wait right here for a few minutes, just in case he's trying to trick us." Frank paused. "How's Turnbuckle?"

"Hurting like blazes, but I don't think he's hit too bad. It looked like the slug just creased his arm. He looked pretty shook up, though. Guess he's not used to getting shot."

Frank gave a grim chuckle. "Nobody ever gets used to that, I reckon." He watched the knob where the would-be assassin had hidden and saw no sign of movement. He thought he heard the sound of hoofbeats, though, coming faintly from a distance.

Claiborne heard them, too. "You think that's our man?"

"Likely," Frank said. "Give it a few more minutes."

He didn't want to wait too long before checking on Turnbuckle's injury himself, so when his instincts told him it was safe to move, he said to Claiborne, "Cover me. I'm going to see if I can get Turnbuckle back on his horse."

"Let me do that," Claiborne suggested. "If anybody needs covering, you're a better shot than I am, Frank."

After a second's thought, Frank nodded. "Go ahead. I'll keep an eye on those rocks where the hombre was hiding."

Claiborne leaned his rifle against the tree he was using for cover and ran back to the spot where he had left Turnbuckle. Frank heard the lawyer groaning in pain as Claiborne lifted him to his feet and then half-carried, half-dragged him toward their mounts. The horses had drifted back deeper into the trees when the shooting started, so they had remained relatively safe.

Nobody tried to take any more shots at Claiborne and Turnbuckle. After a moment, Claiborne called, "I've got him in the saddle, Frank!"

"Head for the mine office!" Frank told him. "I'll bring up the rear."

As he began withdrawing, he grabbed up Claiborne's rifle and tucked it under his arm while still holding his own Winchester ready to fire. A low whistle came from his lips, and Goldy trotted to him, meeting him halfway. Frank put his rifle into the saddle boot, then holding Claiborne's weapon, swung up onto the gelding's back and sent it loping after the horses carrying his two companions.

In a matter of minutes, they reached the building that housed the Crown Royal's office. Frank had caught up to Claiborne and Turnbuckle by then, so he dismounted quickly and helped Claiborne get the wounded lawyer out of the saddle. Turnbuckle still seemed a little stunned, and his face was drained of color from the shock of being shot. Frank saw a crimson stain on the sleeve of Turnbuckle's coat, but it didn't look like the wound on his arm had bled a dangerous amount.

With Frank on one side of him and Claiborne on the other, they didn't waste any time getting Turnbuckle into the office. Turnbuckle groaned again as they lowered him into the chair behind Claiborne's desk.

Heavy footsteps sounded on the porch. Frank wheeled around, his hand going to the Colt on his hip, but it was only a couple of the miners who crowded into the office. He recognized both of them from their visits to Buckskin.

"We heard shots, Mr. Claiborne," one of the men said. "Are you all right?"

"Fine," Claiborne replied, "but Mr. Turnbuckle here got creased."

"Who was doing the shooting?" the second man asked.

"We don't know. He was hidden in the rocks on that big knoll to the northeast."

"Want us to go take a look around up there, Boss?"

Claiborne looked at Frank, deferring the decision to him. Frank said, "No, boys, just steer clear of there for now, if you would. I'll go check it out later, once I've seen to Mr. Turnbuckle's wound."

That prompted Turnbuckle to mutter, "Need . . . need a doctor . . ."

"We'll get you some medical attention back in Buckskin," Frank promised. "Right now, though, we need to make sure we get the bleeding stopped in that arm."

"I think my arm . . . was shot off . . ."

Frank managed not to chuckle. He was sure that Turnbuckle was in a great deal of pain. "Your arm's not shot off. That first bullet just nicked it. Likely would've blown my brains out, though, if you hadn't yelled and jumped at me. It came that close to my head before it hit you."

Turnbuckle nodded, but Frank wasn't sure if the lawyer really understood what he was saying or not. He worked Turnbuckle's suit coat off, then ripped the shirt sleeve down to expose the wound. As Claiborne had guessed, the slug had ripped a shallow furrow along the outside of Turnbuckle's upper left arm. Blood had run down to his elbow.

Frank glanced at Claiborne. "You've got a bottle of whiskey in that filing cabinet, don't you, Garrett?"

"I do."

"Get it and a clean cloth, if you've got one."

"Of course."

Claiborne fetched the whiskey and the cloth, and Frank used them to clean away the blood around the wound. Turnbuckle winced and whimpered as some of the fiery liquor touched raw flesh.

"Sorry to have to tell you this, Mr. Turnbuckle," Frank said, "but it's going to burn a lot worse before it gets any better."

"Just . . . warn me . . . first," Turnbuckle said between gritted teeth.

"Sure," Frank said, and then with no warning at all poured the whiskey over the bullet crease.

Turnbuckle opened his mouth like he was going to scream, but no sound came out. After a moment, his head fell back.

"He's passed out," Claiborne muttered.

"Probably a good thing," Frank said. "That wound's not bleeding bad. We'll tie it up, and he'll be fine until I can get him back to Buckskin."

"You won't be taking him back there alone," Claiborne said. The mining engineer's face was grim. "I'll be going with you, and so will some of the men. That bushwhacker was after you, Frank. Somebody tried to kill you . . . again."

Frank nodded and said, "Sure looked like it, all right."

"The attack on the mine earlier was just to lure you out here so that the killer could make another try for you," Claiborne went on, a tone of bitterness coming into his voice. "And I played right into his hands by running straight to Buckskin to tell you what happened."

"You didn't have much choice in the matter," Frank said. "And you weren't alone either. Conrad was with you."

"Yes, but this mine is my responsibility, and I almost got you killed by going to you for help."

Frank put a hand on Claiborne's shoulder. "Don't start thinking like that, Garrett. There's only one person to blame for Turnbuckle being wounded and me nearly getting ventilated, and that's the son of a buck who pulled the trigger."

"Well, you're right about that, I suppose," Claiborne admitted. "Still, I don't like being used that way."

"Don't blame you a bit for feeling that way."

Turnbuckle moaned and started trying to sit up.

"He's coming around," Frank said. As Turnbuckle's eyes flickered open, Frank lifted the whiskey bottle and held it to his lips. "Take a slug of this, Mr. Turnbuckle."

The lawyer complied, not really seeming to know what he was doing. His eyes opened wide, though, as the whiskey burned its way down his gullet and landed in his stomach. Turnbuckle opened his mouth, too, and gasped.

"My God! What . . . what was that?"

"Whiskey," Frank said with a chuckle. "Strictly for medicinal purposes, you know."

Some of Turnbuckle's strength seemed to have returned. He even reached for the bottle. Frank let him take another long swallow from it.

"Arm doesn't . . . hurt quite so bad now. Must be . . . good medicine."

"Think you're up to riding back to Buckskin."

"Of course. I can make it. I'll be fine."

Claiborne turned to the miners who had come to the office to find out what was going on. "I want six men, armed with rifles and mounted on saddle horses, back here in ten minutes."

"I appreciate the thought, Garrett," Frank said, "but I don't need an escort back to town. I've been taking care of myself for a long time, you know."

"Of course you have, but now you have Mr. Turnbuckle to look after, too. Whoever that bushwhacker was, he'll be less likely to try another shot at you if you're surrounded by me and my men."

"I still own half of this mine, you know . . . and I'm the marshal of Buckskin."

"Yes, but with all due respect, sir, your jurisdiction as a lawman runs out at the edge of the settlement. And I've always had the authority to assign whatever tasks I saw fit to the men who work here at the mine."

Frank didn't want to waste time arguing the point, and he figured Turnbuckle wouldn't want him to either. So he just nodded and said, "All right. I'm much obliged for the help. I want to take a look up on that knoll before we start back to town, though."

"Shall I come with you?"

Frank shook his head. "No, stay here with Turnbuckle. I'll have Dog with me. He'll be enough company right now."

He left the office and found Dog waiting outside with the horses. "Come on," he said to the big cur as he swung up into the saddle. He pulled his Winchester from the boot again as he turned Goldy toward the rocky knob where the bushwhacker had lurked, waiting for his target to show up after being summoned from Buckskin by Conrad and Claiborne.

There was no doubt in Frank's mind now about the motivation of the earlier attack. The only explanation that made any sense was the gunmen had been baiting a trap for him by shooting up the mine.

He was lucky that only one of them had stayed behind to wait for his arrival and then try to kill him.

They might not make that same mistake again. The whole bunch might come after him next time. He was going to have to be more watchful from here on out . . . not that he had ever been all that careless. He wouldn't have lived as long as he had if he'd been in the habit of taking foolish chances.

Frank sent Dog on ahead to make sure no one was hiding on the knoll. The big cur bounded away eagerly, happy to be on the hunt again. No man could have asked for a more dependable trail partner. When Dog came loping back, his tongue lolling from his mouth, Frank knew that the coast was clear. The bushwhacker really was gone.

Approaching the knob from this side, the slope was too steep for Goldy to ascend it comfortably, so Frank dismounted and went the rest of the way on foot, carrying the rifle with him. When he got to the top and looked around in the rocks, he found a few scuff marks that he assumed had been left by the bushwhacker's boots. Dog confirmed that by sniffing at the ground and growling.

"Same hombre, eh, boy? We'll cross trails with him again and settle up the score one of these days."

The slope was gentler on this side. Frank walked down into a grove of aspen and found where the rifleman had left his horse. The freshness of the droppings on the ground there were proof enough of that. Again, there was nothing distinctive about the few hoofprints Frank found.

He paused at the top of the knoll and surveyed the field of fire that the unknown gunman had had. It was a long shot from here to where Frank, Claiborne, and

Turnbuckle had been standing, but certainly within range for a man who was good with a Winchester. The bushwhacker had been good. He had come too blasted close with all of his shots. That told Frank he was a professional. Frank had dodged two attempts by the man to kill him. How much longer, he had to wonder, could that sort of luck hold out?

Of course, he wasn't going to leave it to luck. He was going to find out for sure who was trying to kill him, and why. He knew a good starting place.

Dex Brighton.

Frank rode back down to the mine office. The armed men Claiborne had sent for were gathered there, along with horses. These were miners, not professional fighting men, but they were tough and canny and as Frank looked around at them, he knew they would be good allies.

Claiborne helped Turnbuckle out of the office. The lawyer was steadier on his feet now than he had been right after he was wounded, but he swayed a little and looked rather bleary-eyed as Claiborne helped him across the porch. Frank guessed that Turnbuckle had had a few more slugs from that whiskey bottle.

"Find anything?" Claiborne asked.

Frank shook his head. "No more than we did before, when we were looking at the sign those other gunmen left."

"You agree that it was just a scheme to get at you, Mr. Morgan?"

"That's the only thing that makes sense," Frank agreed. "So I reckon I'm obliged for the company on the way back to town."

"We're glad to go with you. Some of you men give me a hand with Mr. Turnbuckle here."

Turnbuckle looked around owlishly and announced, "I've been shot."

"Yes, sir, you sure have," Frank said, trying not to grin. "But you'll be just fine."

Turnbuckle reached over with his right hand to clutch his injured left arm. "Badge of honor," he said.

Frank didn't see anything particularly honorable about getting shot by a bushwhacker, but if Turnbuckle wanted to think there was, then Frank supposed that was all right. With help from several of the miners, Turnbuckle climbed up into his saddle.

"Sorry I wasn't . . . any more help," Turnbuckle said as the group of riders started toward Buckskin.

"You were plenty of help," Frank told him. "There's a good chance I'd be dead now if not for what you did."

"Really?" Turnbuckle looked like he was having trouble grasping that. "Wouldn't think . . . somebody like me . . . could do something like that . . . would you?"

Frank wasn't quite sure what Turnbuckle meant by that. The man had a long record of accomplishments as a lawyer and had helped a lot of people.

"Just take it easy," Frank said. "We'll have you back to Buckskin before you know it, and then the doctor can take a look at that arm."

Turnbuckle didn't seem particularly worried about his wound anymore, though.

In fact, he looked downright happy.

Chapter 16

Luther had never before experienced this disconcerting blend of pain, shock, and giddiness. The pain and shock came from his wounded arm, of course. The giddiness was the result of the whiskey he had slugged down from the bottle in Garrett Claiborne's office. The loss of blood might have had something to do with it, too.

But mainly, he kept thinking that Diana Woodford had to be impressed with him now. He had saved the life of the famous Frank Morgan. Morgan himself had said so. He, Luther Galloway, law clerk and failed law student, was a hero.

Unfortunately, Diana didn't even know who Luther Galloway was. She believed he was Claudius Turnbuckle, the successful attorney from San Francisco.

When they got back to Buckskin, Luther thought as he swayed slightly in the saddle, he ought to tell Diana the truth about who he really was. If she was going to like him, he wanted her to like him for himself.

The problem with that idea was that when she learned what a big liar he was, she was bound to hate him. His only hope was to make her fall so in love with him that she wouldn't be able to hate him when she finally found out the truth, as she inevitably would.

So, like it or not, the masquerade had to continue, Luther decided.

Morgan rode beside him on his left, with Garrett Claiborne on his right. The miners from the Crown Royal were ranged around them, rifles held ready across their saddles in case they ran into trouble.

Although Luther was having a little trouble thinking straight because of the whiskey, the attempts on Morgan's life kept cropping up in his mind. If Dex Brighton was behind those attempts, he must have wanted to get Morgan out of the way so that his chances of stealing Tip Woodford's mine would improve. Likewise, if Brighton regarded Morgan as a threat because the marshal was Woodford's friend, then how would Brighton feel about the man who had been brought in to plead Woodford's case in court . . . ?

Luther suddenly sobered a little as he put that chain of thought together. He seemed to feel a cold spot right in the middle of his back, and it took him a moment to figure out what it was.

The bull's-eye on a target—because that's what he would be wearing as long as Brighton was trying to steal the Lucky Lizard out from under Tip Woodford.

Sunk in thought, Luther started slightly as Morgan spoke to him. "How're you doing, Mr. Turnbuckle?"

Luther swallowed. "I . . . I'm fine. My arm hurts, of course, but I suppose that's to be expected when you've been shot."

"Always hurt when I got shot," Morgan said with a wry chuckle.

"Have you been . . . wounded in battle often?"

Morgan nodded. "More than I like to think about. I've got bullet scars all over, and a few from knives and tomahawks, too. I was shot up so bad one time it took me several months to recover."

"And yet you come back for more," Luther said with an amazed shake of his head.

"Life hasn't given me much choice in the matter," Morgan said heavily. "One reason I drifted around so much over the years was that I was looking for a place where I might find some lasting peace and quiet. It took me a long time before I realized that probably wasn't going to happen. Buckskin has come closer to that for me than most places, and even here it seems like a week doesn't go by without somebody shooting at me."

"What a terrible thing to have following you around and hanging over your head," Luther murmured. "To always travel in the shadow of death."

Morgan's face was grim as he nodded. "That's about the size of it. It's not going to change any time soon either, at least not as long as Brighton is around trying to steal the Lucky Lizard."

"Well, the judge will be here in a few days, and we ought to be able to move pretty quickly with the case. Once Brighton has lost, do you think he'll slink away with his tail between his legs?"

"No telling. I've got a feeling he's not going to be a gracious loser, though . . . assuming that the judge doesn't rule in his favor."

"He won't," Luther declared. "I'm going to destroy his claim, especially if I can send some wires from Carson City and get the replies back in time."

"Write out the messages," Morgan said. "I'll see to it that they get sent. There are several fellas in town I can trust to take the wires to Carson City and then wait for the replies."

Not long after that, the group of riders reached Buckskin. At the edge of town, Morgan thanked Claiborne and the miners, and the men turned their mounts around and headed back to the Crown Royal. Luther and Morgan headed their mounts on down the street toward the office of Dr. William Garland.

Diana must have been watching for them, because she hurried out of the mining company office and met them in the road. Her father followed her out of the office.

Luther was still coatless, and the bloodstain on his torn shirt sleeve was clearly visible, as was the makeshift bandage tied around his arm. When Diana saw those things, she exclaimed, "Oh, no! You're hurt, Mr. Turnbuckle!"

"Call me . . . Claudius," Luther said. He had started to use his real name and had caught himself just in time. He didn't think anyone had noticed his hesitation, though. Diana and Woodford were too surprised and upset by the fact that he was wounded.

Diana looked at Morgan. "How bad is it, Frank?"

"Not too bad," he assured her. "The bullet just creased Mr. Turnbuckle's arm. I would have been a lot worse off if he hadn't acted when he did, though. He spoiled a bushwhacker's play for me."

"Really?"

Luther glowed warmly inside at the look in Diana's

eyes. He saw worry there, of course, but also admiration. Just as he had hoped. Not that he had *wanted* to get shot when he rode out with Morgan . . . but if he had to suffer a wound, this one was just about perfect.

Quickly, Morgan filled in Diana and her father about what had happened at the Crown Royal, then concluded by saying, "Mr. Turnbuckle and I are on our way down to Doc Garland's office so the doctor can take a look at that crease."

"Do you need any help?" Diana asked.

"We'll be fine," Morgan answered before Luther could say that it might be a good idea for Diana to come along. That way she could see how brave he was while the doctor was tending to his injured arm. But since he'd been a little too slow to get the words out, all he could do now was nod in agreement with Morgan's reply.

"Yes, don't worry about me, Miss Woodford," he managed to say. "I've suffered much worse than this in the pursuit of justice."

Tip Woodford said, "I'll bet a hat Brighton had something to do with the attack on the mine and that dry-gulch attempt on you, Frank."

Morgan nodded and said, "That's what Mr. Turnbuckle and I think, too, and Garrett Claiborne goes along with it."

"How is Garrett?" Diana asked. "He wasn't hurt, was he?"

"No, Claudius here is the only one who got elected. I heard the nomination speech, though, when that slug went right past my ear."

Morgan heeled his horse into motion again. He had the reins of Luther's mount, so Luther had no choice but to go with him. And as a matter of fact, his arm *was* starting to hurt a little worse, so he thought it would be a good idea for the doctor to look at it. Luther turned slightly in his saddle and lifted his good arm in a small wave of farewell to Diana and her father.

"This doctor of yours," he said to Morgan, "he knows what he's doing?"

"Yeah, he's a good sawbones. He'll be able to patch you up better than I could. Your arm should be fine, providing that you don't get blood poisoning."

"That sounds bad."

"It would be, if you wanted to keep that arm, which I reckon you do."

"Of course." Luther paused. "I imagine that having the arm in a sling will look fairly dashing, though. Might make a good impression on a jury, if it ever comes to that."

Frank chuckled. "Yeah, Counselor, you're a lawyer, all right."

Luther was starting to think there might be some truth to that.

At one fairly recent point in the settlement's existence, Professor Henry Burton was the closest thing to a doctor that Buckskin had. When the town began to grow as news of the silver spread, Dr. Garland had arrived and hung out his shingle. He was young, not that long out of medical school, but he had proven to be a good physician and was tougher than his rather mild appearance indicated.

While Frank looked on, Garland carefully removed the bandage from Claudius Turnbuckle's arm, using a wet sponge to soak away the dried blood that made the cloth want to cling to the wound. Turnbuckle turned pale again at this fresh pain, but he didn't moan or cry out. Frank could tell by the tense set of the lawyer's jaw that he was gritting his teeth.

"You did a good job, Marshal," Dr. Garland told Frank. "I think it would be a good idea, though, to clean out the wound a little better and take some stitches in it before I bandage it again."

"Stitches," Turnbuckle repeated. "That will leave a scar, won't it?"

"A small one," Garland said. "But your sleeve will cover it."

Turnbuckle nodded. "All right, Doctor. Do whatever needs to be done."

"Well, first off, I'm going to give you a dose of laudanum."

"Is that absolutely necessary?" Turnbuckle asked with a frown.

"I think you'll be a lot more comfortable if I do."

Turnbuckle still looked leery of the idea, but after a moment he nodded. "All right, Doctor. Go ahead."

Garland took a small brown bottle from a cabinet and poured a dose of laudanum from it. Frank didn't like the sickly sweet smell of the stuff and was glad when Turnbuckle downed it.

Within moments, a sleepy glaze came over Turnbuckle's eyes. Frank and Garland stretched him out on the examination table, and Garland went to work cleaning and stitching up the wound in his arm.

Turnbuckle began muttering as he drifted into semi-consciousness under the influence of the laudanum. Frank asked, "What's he saying?"

"I don't know," Dr. Garland replied. "I've learned

not to pay any attention to what patients say after they've been given an opiate. It usually doesn't make any sense."

Frank leaned closer anyway, trying to make out the words the lawyer was slurring. He thought he heard "Turnbuckle" several times, along with either the name "Luther" or the word "loser." He wasn't sure which. Finally, shaking his head, Frank gave up on the effort. Turnbuckle seemed more asleep than awake now anyway.

It didn't take long for Garland to finish with his efforts. As he tied the bandage around Turnbuckle's arm in place, he said, "I'll fix up a sling for him to wear on that arm, so he can keep it still."

Frank smiled. "He'll be glad to hear that. He thought a sling would look dashing. I expect black silk would be best."

"I think I can manage that," Garland replied with a laugh. "I also think it would be a good idea for him to stay here for a while, at least until that laudanum wears off."

"That's fine. I appreciate what you've done for him, Doctor. I think I should warn you, though . . . There's a possibility that whoever took those shots at us may make another try on Mr. Turnbuckle here."

Garland's eyebrows rose in surprise. "Really? No offense, Marshal, but I just assumed that you were the target and Mr. Turnbuckle was hit by accident."

"That's what I figured at first, too, but that might not be the case. Are you sure you want him to stay here?"

"No one's going to bother him in the middle of town," Garland declared. "Besides, I have a medical responsibility, and I'm not going to shirk it."

"All right, Doctor. I just wanted you to know. I'll be back by to check on him later."

"If you don't mind my asking, Marshal, does this have something to do with that man who claims he owns Mayor Woodford's mine?"

"That's what I'm going to try to find out right now," Frank said.

Chapter 17

Frank knew that Dex Brighton was usually in his hotel room or at the Top-Notch Saloon. He checked at the hotel first and was told that Brighton wasn't there. So he headed for the Top-Notch.

Catamount Jack intercepted him on the way. "I heard about what happened out there, Frank," the deputy said. "Are you all right?"

Frank nodded. "I'm fine."

"That lawyer fella got hit, though?"

"Yes, but he should be all right, too. He'll be laid up for a short time, but he'll still be able to handle the court case when it comes up next week."

"Brighton," Jack said, glaring. "Got to be."

"That's what I thought, too. I'm looking for him now, to see what he's got to say for himself."

Jack snorted. "Nothin' good, I'll bet. I'm comin' with you."

"Glad for the company," Frank said.

When they entered the Top-Notch, which was a narrow, dingy establishment that didn't really live up to its name, Frank looked around the place and didn't see Brighton. A balding man named Mason was behind the bar, wearing a dirty apron. He had a prominent Adam's apple, and it bobbed up and down nervously as Frank and Catamount Jack approached the bar.

"Howdy, Marshal," he said, nodding and trying to look friendly. "Deputy. You fellas want a drink? It's on the house."

"No, thanks," Frank said, ignoring the way Jack licked his lips in anticipation. "We're looking for Dex Brighton."

Mason shook his head. "Haven't seen him, Marshal. Sorry."

"Your eyesight's not very good, Mason." The drawling words came from a man who was sitting alone at one of the felt-covered poker tables, dealing a hand of solitaire. Frank turned to look at him and recognized him as a gambler called Winston. The man had been around Buckskin for a while, and even though Frank suspected he was no more honest than he had to be, Winston hadn't caused any trouble that Frank knew of.

"What do you mean by that, Winston?" Frank asked.

"Brighton was in here until about forty-five minutes ago," the gambler said. "About the same time you and that lawyer fellow arrived to such commotion, in fact. Someone came in here talking about how you and Turnbuckle had been shot at out at the Crown Royal Mine, and how Turnbuckle was wounded. Brighton left right after that." Winston looked at the bartender. "I don't see how you missed that, Mason."

"I was busy, all right?" Mason replied in a surly voice. To Frank he said, "Sorry, Marshal, but I can't be expected to keep up with the comin's and goin's of everybody who comes in here. I got work to do."

Frank nodded. "Sure, Mason. I understand."

He did understand. Mason was either afraid of Dex Brighton, or else Brighton had paid him off to keep quiet about his whereabouts.

Frank went over to the table where Winston sat. "I don't suppose you heard Brighton say where he was going."

Winston shook his head. "He didn't say anything about it, at least not in my hearing."

"Why are you being helpful, Winston? You and Brighton have some trouble between you?"

"I wouldn't call it trouble. He's won more than his share of poker hands since he's been in town, though."

"You think he's cheating?"

Winston gave a curt laugh. "No, he's winning fair and square. That's even more annoying. I don't mind losing, but I hate losing to an honest man."

Frank chuckled, too. "All right. I'm obliged. And I figure I should tell you, when word of this gets to Brighton, you're liable to have made an enemy of him."

"I'll worry about that tomorrow . . . if I get around to it."

As Frank and Jack left the saloon, the deputy said, "Brighton lit a shuck when he heard that the ambush he set up didn't do for you, Frank."

"That's the way it sounds to me, too."

"You reckon he'll be back, or has he left Buckskin for good?"

"Oh, I think we can count on him being back," Frank said. "He's not going to let us off that easy."

* * *

Brighton seethed as he rode toward the abandoned mine that his men were using as a hideout. Things had been on the verge of working out perfectly. In a lucky break, the lawyer Turnbuckle had ridden out to the Crown Royal with Morgan, and Stample had had a chance to get rid of both men. If he had been able to handle that simple chore, then kill the circuit judge a few days hence, then Tip Woodford would have been left without any powerful friends or any legal recourse. He could have been pressured into accepting Brighton's claim on the Lucky Lizard. Probably, all it would have taken was a subtle threat to his daughter's safety.

Instead, Morgan and Turnbuckle had escaped from the ambush attempt, even though Turnbuckle had been slightly wounded, according to what Brighton had heard. With the two men still alive to help him, Woodford would remain stubborn. Worse still, Morgan would be on the alert now, more so than ever after two attempts on his life in the past week or so. The man was no fool.

Brighton was still several hundred yards away from the mouth of the abandoned mine when a voice called out from behind a boulder beside the trail. "Hold it right there, mister!" The command was punctuated by the unmistakable sound of a Winchester being cocked.

Brighton reined to a halt. His right hand moved toward the butt of the pistol he carried in a shoulder rig under his coat.

"Don't try it!" the voice warned. "Who are you, and what do you want out here?"

Brighton realized that this unseen gunman must be a guard that Stample had posted. That meant he was one of the hired killers recruited by Stample.

"You damned fool," Brighton bit off, too irritated by everything that had happened to be careful about what he said. "I'm the man you're drawing your pay from."

The sentry stepped out from behind the boulder. He was lean and unshaven, with dull eyes that indicated he wasn't too bright. His big hands cradled the Winchester with natural ease, though. A man didn't have to be smart to be an efficient killer . . . even though it often helped, as Dex Brighton knew from experience.

"I don't know you, mister," the man said, "and I ain't takin' no chances."

"Go tell Stample that I'm here. My name is Brighton."

The guard looked like he might be disposed to argue the matter some more, but at that moment both of them heard the pounding of hoofbeats. Brighton looked toward the old mine and saw a figure fogging it toward them on horseback. As the rider came closer, Brighton recognized him as Cy Stample.

"You blamed lunkhead!" Stample yelled at the guard a few moments later as he reined his mount to a halt. "This is the boss."

The scrawny gunman looked offended. "Nobody ever said nothin' to me about the boss comin' out here. I figured you met up with him in town, Stample."

"I do when I have to," Stample snapped. "Now get back behind that rock and keep your eyes open for somebody who's *not* supposed to be here." To Brighton he said, "Come on into camp, Boss."

The two of them rode toward the mine. Brighton said, "I'm sure you can guess why I'm here, Stample."

"Morgan," Stample said with a bitter edge to his voice. "He got away again."

"And so did that lawyer, Claudius Turnbuckle. You had a shot at both of them."

"I would've got 'em, too, if Morgan hadn't moved just as I squeezed off my first shot," Stample said, defending himself. "That's when the lawyer got hit, I reckon. Is he dead?"

Brighton snorted in disgust. "He's just wounded. A bullet crease on his arm."

Stample leaned over in the saddle and spat. "If it wasn't for bad luck, I wouldn't have no luck at all, I reckon. If I had to miss Morgan, I should've at least got the lawyer."

"Yes," Brighton agreed, "you should have."

"If I'd got Morgan with my first shot, it wouldn't have been any problem to pick off Turnbuckle. Chances are he would've started runnin' around like a chicken with its head cut off."

"We'll never know," Brighton said. They had reached the tunnel mouth. He saw several hard-faced, roughly dressed men lounging around the mine entrance. All of them were heavily armed, and their cold-eyed gazes told Brighton they were killers.

He knew that because he had seen the same look in his shaving mirror often enough.

Stample introduced Brighton to the men. He didn't bother trying to remember any of their names. They didn't mean anything to him. They were just tools, like a gun or a deck of cards.

Brighton refused Stample's offer of a drink. "Morgan's going to be on the lookout now," he said. "Two attempts on his life will have warned him that something is going on. Chances are he'll blame it on me, too."

"Well . . . you're payin' for it, ain't you?"

"Yes, but he can't prove that," Brighton said. "I'm counting on things staying that way, too. I don't give a damn what Morgan suspects as long as he doesn't have any evidence to link me to those bushwhack tries."

"We'll go after him again, the whole bunch of us this time," Stample promised. "We'll get him for you, Boss."

Brighton shook his head. "Not now. I want you to lie low until that stagecoach holdup we spoke about. Get rid of the judge, and then we'll deal with Morgan and Turnbuckle later."

"You sure?" Stample asked with a frown.

"I'm certain. I want to lull Morgan into forgetting those shots you took at him."

"You really reckon that's gonna happen with a gunfighter like him?"

"Maybe not, but we're going to try." Brighton gave the leader of his crew of gun-wolves a hard look. "Just don't foul up the job with the judge."

"He's as good as dead," Stample promised.

A check at Amos Hillman's stable told Frank that Brighton had picked up the horse he was renting and ridden out of town earlier in the afternoon, shortly after he'd left the Top-Notch, according to the gambler called Winston. Frank didn't see any point in trying to trail Brighton; Buckskin was a busy place these days, and there was no way to pick out the tracks of his horse from the hundreds of others in the street near the livery stable.

Instead, he kept his eyes open for Brighton's return to the settlement, and that effort was rewarded late in the afternoon when Frank saw Brighton ride into town and head for the livery stable. By the time Brighton dismounted and strolled back out of the barn, Frank was there waiting for him.

Brighton's face didn't show any expression except polite disinterest as he muttered, "Marshal," and started to go on past.

"Hold on a minute, Brighton," Frank said. "Where have you been this afternoon?"

Brighton stopped and gave Frank a cool stare. "What business is that of the law's?"

"It was more in the nature of a personal question."

"In that case, I don't see any reason for me to answer it."

"Humor me," Frank said in a hard voice.

After a second, Brighton shrugged. "All right. It doesn't really matter anyway. I was just out taking a ride in the countryside. It's good exercise, you know."

"You hear that somebody tried to kill Mr. Turnbuckle and me while we were out at the Crown Royal Mine earlier today?"

"As a matter of fact, I did. Or rather, I heard that someone took a shot at you. I didn't know the lawyer was involved. And frankly, shouldn't you be used to people trying to kill you by now, Morgan? You've been a gunman practically all your life, from what I've heard. You've lost more than one wife to bullets meant for you, haven't you?"

Frank's breath hissed between his teeth. Vivian and Dixie had been too good to even be mentioned by a snake the likes of Dex Brighton. It was all he could do not to plant a fist in the middle of the man's smug face. Brighton grinned as he reached inside his coat pocket and took out a cheroot. He put it in his mouth, lit a match, and puffed the thin cigar into life, seemingly unaware of just how close he had come to provoking Frank into violence.

Or maybe that was just what the bastard wanted, Frank told himself. Brighton had goaded Tip Woodford into a fight, and now Tip would be facing assault charges when the judge arrived. He would be found guilty, too, just as Frank would have been if he had hauled off and walloped Brighton like he wanted to.

"You think you're so damn smart," Frank grated, "coming in here and claiming things that aren't yours, thinking you can push folks around and get everything you want. You're going to find out that the law doesn't work that way."

Brighton's teeth clamped down on the cheroot and he said around it, "You're a fine one to talk about the law, Morgan. You pin on a badge and you think it can wipe out all the things you've done, all the men you've gunned down. You're just a hired killer. That's all you've ever been."

"I never hired out my gun. Not like that."

"Tell that to all the dead men whose blood is on your hands."

Frank turned away, struggling to control himself. He knew that Brighton was wrong about him; his conscience was clear, or as clear as that of any man who was prey to human frailties could be, and that was all that really mattered. Well, that and the opinion of his friends and loved ones, and the folks here in Buckskin knew what kind of man he was. Conrad was in the process of figuring that out, despite the rough patches they'd had in the past.

"Things are going to be different around here when I'm the owner of the Lucky Lizard, Morgan," Brighton called after him. "Then I'll be the most powerful man in these parts, and you'll be out of a job. You'll have to go back to being a drifting killer with no place to call home."

Frank tried to shove the arrogant words out of his mind.

But they haunted him all the way back to the marshal's office.

Chapter 18

Claudius Turnbuckle did indeed look dashing in the black silk sling, Frank supposed, and he seemed to thoroughly enjoy having Diana Woodford fussing over him for the next couple of days. Diana visited him and brought him his meals while Turnbuckle was still at Doc Garland's place, and she continued doing that once he was strong enough in the doctor's opinion to move back to his room in the hotel.

Frank tried to keep an eye on Turnbuckle, too. He didn't believe that Brighton's hired killers would attempt to assassinate the lawyer right there in the middle of town, as Doc had said, but when dealing with a tricky varmint like Brighton, it was wise not to put *anything* past him.

Because of that, Frank found himself entering the hotel dining room on Monday evening, making one of his regular checks to be sure that Turnbuckle was all right. Turnbuckle had taken his midday meal in the dining room, and he was there for supper, too, joined by Diana Woodford.

Diana wasn't the only one at the table with

Turnbuckle, though. Garrett Claiborne was there, too, and the mining engineer didn't look happy.

Frank knew there was a budding romance between Diana and Claiborne; he knew because he had engineered it himself, Cupid with a Colt rather than that silly little bow and arrow, in order to divert Diana's interest from him. He and Tip were roughly the same age, after all, which meant he was old enough to be Diana's father.

Now Diana seemed to be quite taken with Claudius Turnbuckle. Maybe that was just because Turnbuckle was helping her father defend the Lucky Lizard from Brighton's claim, or because Turnbuckle was from San Francisco, or maybe being a lawyer was just a more glamorous profession than being a mining engineer. Whatever the cause, Frank saw there was a romantic triangle in the making . . . and that could spell even more trouble.

He took his hat off as he approached the table. Diana was talking animatedly to Turnbuckle, who sat there with a smile on his face while Claiborne looked on with a slight frown. Diana broke off with whatever she was talking about and looked up to greet Frank.

"Oh, hello, Frank," she said. "We were about to have supper. Would you like to join us?"

Since three was already a crowd, Frank didn't figure four could be much worse. In fact, it might even be a small improvement. He hung his hat on the back of the empty chair and smiled.

"Thanks, Diana. Don't mind if I do."

The food here in the hotel dining room wasn't as good as what Lauren, Ginnie, and Becky dished up at their café, but it was passable, about the same as the

Chinaman's. The other three had already ordered. When an apron-clad waitress came over, Frank told her to bring him the usual steak and potatoes with all the trimmings, and coffee, of course.

"We were just talking about the court case," Diana said. "I guess the circuit judge is still supposed to arrive on tomorrow's stage?"

"I haven't heard any different," Frank replied.

"Have there been any replies to the telegrams I sent?" Turnbuckle asked.

Frank shook his head. "Not yet." He had sent Phil Noonan to Carson City with a handful of sealed messages that Phil was supposed to turn over to the telegrapher in the Western Union office there. Then Phil was to wait for the replies before he came back to Buckskin. Frank guessed that it was taking longer for those replies than either he or Turnbuckle had hoped.

Either that or something had happened to Phil, and that possibility worried Frank. He had sent word through Catamount Jack that he wanted to talk to Phil, then met with the messenger in the alley behind the marshal's office at night, when the shadows were thick. For all Frank knew, Dex Brighton had spies keeping an eye on him, and if Brighton suspected that Phil was carrying messages that might hurt his case in court, Brighton might send gunmen after him.

Frank had made sure that Phil understood the possible danger before he took the job. Phil had laughed it off.

"Don't worry, Marshal. I'll slip out of town without anybody knowing about it. Besides, that pony of mine is pretty fast. I can outrun most trouble."

"I'd go to Carson City myself, Phil," Frank had

said quietly, "but I've got to keep an eye on things here so that they don't boil over."

"You just tend to your job, Marshal. I'll be back with the replies to those wires just as soon as I can."

Frank had faith in Noonan's abilities, and in fact he had begun to consider suggesting to the town council that they hire him as a part-time deputy, to give him and Jack some relief. Phil's cough had subsided some, and his health seemed to improve the longer he stayed out of the mine. Some hombres just weren't cut out to work underground, but they could handle other tough chores just fine.

"I really need the information that I sent for," Turnbuckle went on with a frown. "If I don't get it, I may have to ask for a continuance."

Diana asked, "How likely is it that the judge would grant one?"

"Not very, I'm afraid. A circuit judge has to adhere to a fairly strict schedule. If I'm not ready to present our case, the entire affair might have to be postponed until the judge comes around again."

"Sounds to me like you should have prepared a little faster," Claiborne said.

Turnbuckle's face darkened. "I was busy getting shot at and saving Marshal Morgan's life."

"I was there, remember?"

"There's still time," Frank said, cutting in, trying to head off a squabble between the other two men. "The stagecoach won't get here until the middle of the day, and the judge probably won't want to hold court until the next morning. So there's no need to worry about it just yet."

"I suppose not," Turnbuckle said with a shrug.

The food arrived then, and for the next little

while everyone was busy eating. The atmosphere of tension that hung around the table dissipated a little. Steak and potatoes had a way of doing that, Frank thought with a mental chuckle.

As they were finishing up the meal and sipping from cups of coffee, Frank suddenly straightened in his chair as he saw Dex Brighton appear in the arched entrance to the dining room. Brighton looked as smug as ever. He had a tall, stiff-backed man with him. The stranger wore an expensive suit, had iron-gray hair and a brush of a mustache. Brighton saw Frank, Diana, Turnbuckle, and Claiborne sitting at the table and pointed them out to his companion.

Then the two men started across the dining room toward the table, which came as no surprise to Frank. Brighton had been lying low since their confrontation a couple of days earlier, but now with the court date looming on the horizon, it was time for the man to start stirring up trouble again.

Turnbuckle leaned toward Frank and asked, "What do we do, Marshal?"

"Just take it easy," Frank advised. "Brighton's not going to try anything here in the hotel dining room. I'm sort of curious who that fella with him is, too."

He figured he would find out soon enough, and he was right. Brighton and the other man came up to the table, and Brighton gave the four people sitting there what appeared to be a friendly nod. His eyes remained as cold and flinty as ever, though.

"Good evening," Brighton said. "Turnbuckle, I thought you might like to meet the man who's going to destroy you in court. This is my attorney, the esteemed Colonel Desmond O'Hara, from Chicago."

O'Hara gave them a curt nod and said, "Hello, Turnbuckle. I've heard of you. Always nice to meet a fellow counselor-at-law, even though we'll be opponents in the courtroom."

Turnbuckle stood up and extended his uninjured right arm. "It's good to meet you, too, Colonel," he said as he shook hands with the man. "When did you get into town? The stagecoach doesn't arrive until tomorrow."

"Oh, I have my own transportation," O'Hara replied vaguely with a wave of his hand. He turned to the others and gave Diana a chilly smile. "Since no one had introduced us, my dear, I'll take care of that myself. Colonel Desmond O'Hara, at your service. You're Miss Woodford?"

"That's right," Diana said.

"I assure you, I bear no ill will toward you or your father. When the trial begins I'll simply be representing my client to the best of my ability, as is my duty."

"Of course."

A faint sneer curled O'Hara's lip as he looked at Frank. "And you'd be the famous gunman, I suppose? I've heard a great deal about *you*, Morgan."

"Can't say as I've *ever* heard of you, Colonel," Frank replied, unable to resist the temptation to prick O'Hara's vanity.

Sure enough, the man's face flushed a little. He turned back to Turnbuckle and asked, "Are you acquainted with the judge we'll be facing in this case, sir?"

"All I know is his name," Turnbuckle replied. "Judge Grampis. I've never appeared before him."

"Nor have I, so we'll be on equal footing there."

"Let's go, Colonel," Brighton said to O'Hara. "I'll buy you a drink, and we can talk about the case."

"All right. I'd like to get some of the details straight in my mind." O'Hara glanced around the table. "Good evening. I'll see you in court, Turnbuckle."

"I'll be looking forward to it," Turnbuckle said.

When Brighton and O'Hara were gone, Diana said in a worried voice, "The colonel seemed confident of victory, Mr. Turnbuckle."

The lawyer tried to wave away her concern. "No more than I am."

"And, well, no offense . . . but he's considerably older than you, too."

"Age doesn't necessarily mean wisdom or legal skills. More importantly, we have the facts of the case on our side. We'll prevail no matter what Brighton throws at us, Diana."

"I hope so," she said. "It would destroy my father to lose the Lucky Lizard."

"That will never happen," Turnbuckle vowed.

Frank took a sip of his coffee and hoped that the lawyer would be able to keep that promise.

When they left the hotel, Brighton and Colonel O'Hara turned toward the Top-Notch. "I thought that went quite well," O'Hara declared.

Brighton didn't sound as confident as he said, "You might've thrown a little scare into Turnbuckle. Not Morgan, though."

O'Hara made a slashing motion with his hand.

"Morgan is nothing but a cheap gunman. If we have the law on our side—"

Brighton's scornful laugh cut into the other man's pompous voice.

"Don't start spouting that stuff at me, O'Hara. I know you're not a real lawyer *or* a colonel. You're just a cheap actor and con man."

"Now see here," O'Hara began angrily.

"No, you listen to me. Don't start thinking that this case will ever really go to trial. I don't want to risk it. That's why Stample and his men are going to take care of the judge tomorrow. The delay that will cause ought to be enough to give them a chance to get rid of Morgan and Turnbuckle, too. With all of Woodford's allies gone, and facing a formidable legal opponent like you, he won't have any choice but to give in. Then we'll all collect our payoff."

"I've actually had a considerable amount of legal training, you know," O'Hara muttered. "I've played attorneys on numerous occasions."

"In numerous swindles, you mean."

"A role is a role," O'Hara said with a scowl.

"That's right," Brighton said. "Just play your part, O'Hara. Play your part, and leave the rest of it to me."

Judge Theodore Grampis was a bandy-legged man with deeply pitted eyes, a white brush of a beard, and long white hair that was seldom tamed, just jammed down under a bowler hat. If he had been dressed differently, in overalls instead of a sober brown tweed suit, he would have looked more like a prospector or a stagecoach driver than a distinguished jurist. He rode inside the coach that swayed along the rough trail, though, not on the jehu's seat.

Grampis had been a circuit judge for many years

here in Nevada and was used to rough transportation and rougher characters. He carried an old cap-and-ball pistol under his coat and knew how to use it if he had to. His gnarled hand made an instinctive move toward the butt of that pistol as the driver called out, "Uh-oh. Looks like trouble up ahead, Judge."

Since Grampis was the only passenger today, he would have known the warning was directed toward him even if the driver hadn't added his title. He took his hat off and placed it on the seat beside him, then stuck his head out the window. The wind plucked at his long white hair as he said, "What is it? Highwaymen?"

"Looks like it. They got the trail blocked in front of us."

The stagecoach was going down a hill. The trail was relatively narrow, with high banks on either side, so there was no way the vehicle could turn around. It had to go straight ahead until it reached the bottom of the slope.

And waiting down there, Grampis saw, were close to a dozen armed, masked men on horseback. Stagecoach robbers!

The driver had begun to slow down. Grampis called, "Plow right through 'em! Can't turn back, so we might as well go straight ahead!"

The driver and shotgun guard exchanged worried looks. The guard said, "Judge, there's too many of 'em. They'd shoot us to pieces."

"Oh, all right," the judge grumbled. "Although it galls me to give in to lawlessness. Better to turn over the mail pouch and our valuables and get on to Buckskin with our lives, I suppose."

The driver hauled back on the reins even more

as the stagecoach approached the bottom of the slope. The outlaws spread out so that their horses completely blocked the trail. As the stage rocked to a halt, one of the masked men bellowed, "Stand and deliver!"

"Take it easy, mister," the driver called back. "Don't go gettin' trigger-happy. We're gonna cooperate."

"That's bein' smart," the man, who was evidently the leader of the gang, said. "Toss down the pouch. Anything in the boot?"

"Just the judge's bag."

"Judge?" the boss outlaw exclaimed.

"That's right!" Grampis said as he swung the coach door open and hopped out with a nimble spryness that belied his age. "I'm Judge Theodore Grampis, and if you varmints know what's good for you, you'll turn around and hightail it out of here right now!"

"Sorry, Judge," the leader said with a chuckle, "but I ain't afraid of you. He moved his horse forward. "We'll have your money and your watch and anything else you got in your pockets that's valuable."

"You damned thief! You'll pay for your lawlessness—if not now, then someday!"

"Hand it over, hand it over," the outlaw snapped as he rode even closer.

Grampis pulled his coat back and started to reach for an inside pocket where he kept his wallet.

At that moment, the leader of the masked men shouted, "Look out! He's got a gun!" The heavy revolver in his hand started to swing up.

Grampis gaped up at him. It was true that the butt of the cap-and-ball pistol was visible as it jutted up from the holster where the judge wore it, but he wasn't reaching for the gun. He was cooperating, about to hand over his wallet.

The outlaw's Colt crashed, flame spewing from its muzzle. The bullet slammed into the judge's body and knocked him back a step. Several of the other outlaws opened fire as well, and Grampis was driven against the side of the stagecoach by the series of stunning hammer blows as the lead struck him. Blood welled from his mouth, staining his white beard crimson as he tried to shout at the crazy bastards that he wasn't reaching for his gun.

It was too late. The words wouldn't come, and the strength had flowed from the judge's muscles along with his blood. Death claimed him as he folded up and collapsed beside the stagecoach.

The driver and shotgun guard hadn't moved. They sat there on the box, stunned by the unexpected horror of Judge Grampis's murder.

"Old coot tried to grab his gun!" the leader of the outlaws cried. He swung his gun toward the driver and guard. "I reckon we better kill them, too."

The two men on the box threw down their guns. "Hold it, mister!" the guard said. "Don't shoot! For God's sake, please don't shoot!"

Their fates hung in the balance for a second, and then the boss outlaw jerked his head in a nod. "All right, boys," he told the other robbers. "We won't kill 'em. Get the mail pouch, and then cut the leaders free so it'll take 'em a while to get where they're goin'."

The masked man swung down from the saddle and pawed through the pockets of the dead judge, removing his wallet and watch. He opened the boot and took Grampis's carpetbag as well, tying it on behind his saddle to go through for valuables later. Meanwhile, two of his men cut the lead horses free.

Then the leader of the gang hefted the judge's blood-soaked body and slung it back into the coach. Grampis's corpse sprawled on the floor between the seats as the outlaw slammed the door. Then he mounted up as his men moved their horses to the side so that the trail was open again.

With whoops and shouts and shots fired over the heads of the terrified driver and guard, the outlaws sent the stagecoach on its way toward Buckskin. Under the bandanna mask tied around the lower half of his face, Cy Stample's brutal mouth curved in a grin.

That old pelican of a judge had played right into his hands by having a gun under his coat. The driver and guard hadn't been able to see exactly what happened from the box, so for all they knew Grampis really had tried to draw his gun and gotten ventilated for his trouble. It really did seem like a stagecoach robbery turned murderous, instead of the outright assassination that it was. Once those two got to Buckskin and told their story, nobody would be able to connect the judge's shooting to Dex Brighton.

And that was exactly the way Brighton would want it, Stample thought as he and his men headed for the abandoned mine. Stample knew the boss was upset with him because Frank Morgan and that lawyer, Turnbuckle, were still alive. But Brighton would see that this was a good day's work. Yes, sir, a good day's work indeed.

Morgan and Turnbuckle wouldn't be alive for much longer either. Stample was damned sure of that.

Chapter 19

Frank had never liked waiting around for something to happen, and Tuesday brought a couple of those instances. Phil Noonan still hadn't returned from Carson City with the replies to Turnbuckle's telegrams, and as morning turned to midday and then stretched into afternoon, the stagecoach carrying the circuit judge didn't show up on schedule.

Of course, there could be any number of reasonable, innocent explanations for that, Frank told himself as he sat on the porch in front of the marshal's office, waiting. Catamount Jack sat with him.

"Stagecoach should'a been here by now," the grizzled deputy said.

Frank nodded. "Yeah, I know."

"Could've had a wheel come off or lock up. Might've even broke an axle."

"I suppose."

"Every so often you get an avalanche that blocks the trail, too, and then the coach has got to find some other way to go around. That'll throw it behind schedule."

"Sure will," Frank agreed in a mild, seemingly unworried voice.

He wasn't that calm inside, though. His instincts told him that something serious was wrong. If the stagecoach didn't show up soon, he was going to have to saddle up either Stormy or Goldy and take Dog and go looking for it.

Tip Woodford came along the street and stepped up onto the porch. "Stage ain't here yet?" he asked, even though he could see for himself that the street in front of the stage station was empty.

"Haven't seen it," Frank said.

"It should've rolled in about an hour ago, shouldn't it?"

Frank nodded.

"I think it must've busted an axle," Catamount Jack said.

"Yeah, you're probably right," Tip agreed.

A few minutes later, Diana walked up with Claudius Turnbuckle, whose arm was still in the black sling. "The stage is late, isn't it?" the lawyer asked.

Frank reined in the annoyance he felt. These folks were sure good at noticing, and stating, the obvious.

"Let's give it a little longer," he said. "If it still doesn't come in, then I'll ride up the trail toward Carson City and see if I can find out what happened to it."

"Brighton's men might try to ambush you again," Turnbuckle warned.

The same possibility had already occurred to Frank. Even though he had no proof that the gunmen who had attacked the Crown Royal worked for Dex Brighton, he knew it in his bones, and he knew that those gun-wolves might have stopped the stage to lure him out of town so they could try to bushwhack him again.

He wasn't going to ride blindly into a trap, but he couldn't just ignore the fact that the stagecoach was late either.

A sudden flurry of surprised shouts from the end of Main Street caught his attention. He stood up and stepped over to the railing along the front of the porch so he could lean out and look in that direction. So did the others who were waiting with him.

"Son of a gun!" Catamount Jack exclaimed. "Looks like they run into trouble, all right!"

The stagecoach rolled slowly into town, pulled by only two horses instead of the usual four. Frank knew that cutting the leaders free and running them off was a common tactic used by stagecoach bandits to delay a coach from getting to town and spreading the word of the robbery. Not as common as it once was, of course, because there were fewer and fewer stagecoaches these days and therefore fewer stagecoach holdups, but Frank still recognized immediately what he was seeing.

He stepped down from the porch and moved at a fast walk toward the stage station, followed by Catamount Jack, Woodford, Turnbuckle, and Diana. The driver and shotgun guard didn't appear to be hurt as they clambered down from the box. As Frank came up, the driver turned toward him and said, "Bad news, Marshal. We were held up about ten miles north of here."

Frank leaned over to look through the windows into the coach, but he didn't see the judge who was supposed to arrive. "Anybody hurt?"

"That's the even worse news." The driver jerked a

thumb over his shoulder toward the coach. "Judge Grampis is in there. The outlaws killed him."

"Old Grumbler Grampis, dead!" Tip said. "Lord help us. I've known him for years."

Woodford reached for the coach door, then stopped and said over his shoulder, "Take Diana back to the office, would you, Mr. Turnbuckle? This is liable to be pretty bad."

"It sure is," the driver said. "They blasted him plumb to pieces."

Diana looked like she wanted to argue about being sent away, but she was pale and didn't put up a fuss as Turnbuckle took her arm and said, "Come along, Diana. There are some things women shouldn't be forced to see."

Once she was gone, Frank, Woodford, and Catamount Jack stood by the opened door and looked into the coach at the bullet-riddled body of the elderly jurist. Frank felt rage boiling up inside him. He hadn't known Judge Grampis all that well, but he liked the old-timer. No one deserved to be savagely murdered like that.

"Tell me what happened," he said to the driver and shotgun guard.

The two men explained about the masked outlaws lying in wait for them at a spot in the trail where the stagecoach couldn't turn around and flee. "The judge wanted me to try to bull on through 'em," the driver said. "We convinced him it'd be loco to pull a stunt like that, though. The polecats had us outgunned."

"So you stopped," Frank said. He couldn't blame the men for that, under the circumstances they had described. "What happened then?"

"The outlaws told us to stand and deliver. I started to throw the mail pouch down when Judge Grampis got out of the coach. The fella who seemed to be the boss of the gang told him to hand over his valuables, and then he yelled out that the judge was goin' for a gun and all hell broke loose."

The shotgun guard put in, "Must've been at least half a dozen of those bastards plugged the judge. Then they said they were gonna kill us, too, but they decided not to."

Frank leaned into the coach to take a closer look at Judge Grampis's body. He lifted the judge's coat and saw the butt of the old pistol.

"That was a mighty foolish play, trying to draw on that many men who already had their guns out and ready," Frank commented.

The driver took off his hat and wiped a bandanna over his bald head. "You didn't hear the judge when he was yellin' for us to bust right through 'em, Marshal. That old pelican was just spoilin' for a fight."

Tip Woodford nodded. "Grumbler was like that, Frank. Never one to stand aside or take anything from anybody. Not a bit of back-up in him. He was as fair and honest as the day is long. I knew he wouldn't give me any favors in the court case with Brighton, but I knew Brighton wouldn't stand a chance in hell of buyin' him off either. He would have decided things accordin' to the law, and nothin' else."

"Well, he won't decide anything now," Frank said. "You know what that means, don't you, Tip? There won't be any trial tomorrow. You'll still have Brighton's claim hanging over your head."

Woodford rubbed his jaw. "Yeah. That's mighty

bad luck. I don't see how you can blame this on Brighton, though, Frank. The stagecoach got held up, which ain't all that common but ain't unheard of either, and Judge Grampis made the mistake of tryin' to fight back. Seems pretty simple to me."

"Yeah, it does," Frank agreed as he nodded.

But he had learned not to believe that anything was as simple as it might appear at first.

"There's only one thing to do now," he went on. "We'll have to send word to Carson City and get another judge sent out."

"That could take weeks."

"Maybe, maybe not. The governor's liable to appoint a special judge to take Grampis's place, given the circumstances of his death and the seriousness of the case that was waiting for him here in Buckskin. There's one thing I'm sure of, though."

"What's that?" Catamount Jack asked.

"I'm going to see to it personal-like that the next judge gets here safe and sound," Frank said.

In Dex Brighton's hotel room, Brighton smiled tightly as O'Hara reported what he had just overheard on the street.

"It sounds like your man Stample succeeded admirably this time," O'Hara was saying. "The judge is dead, the case is delayed, and everyone is completely convinced that the tragedy occurred during a simple stagecoach robbery that had nothing to do with you."

"I wouldn't be so sure that Morgan is convinced," Brighton replied. "He wouldn't have lived as long as he has if he wasn't fairly smart. But as far as everyone else is concerned there's no connection between us and the judge's death, and that's all that matters."

"Perhaps this would be a good time to approach Woodford with another settlement offer," O'Hara suggested. "Say, you allow him to retain a ten per cent interest in the Lucky Lizard."

Brighton mulled it over for a few moments, then said, "All right. It won't hurt anything to try. Maybe we can avoid any more killing, at least for now. Of course, Woodford won't actually get ten per cent. I suspect that he'll meet with an unfortunate accident before *that* ever happens."

A wolfish grin stretched across O'Hara's face. "If such a tragedy were to take place, his share in the mine would go to his lovely daughter, I'm sure."

"That's right." An intriguing possibility occurred to Brighton. "In that case, Diana Woodford would need a friend and protector, wouldn't she? I'm sure the notion would appall her right now, but under different circumstances?" A cynical chuckle came from him. "A woman will do what she has to in order to survive, my friend. Whatever that may be."

Luther Galloway paced back and forth in the offices of the Lucky Lizard Mining Company. His wounded arm still troubled him from time to time, but not nearly as much as this new development did.

Tip Woodford and Diana sat there looking dispirited, and Luther wished he could think of something to tell them that might make them feel better. They had been hoping that this whole mess might be over soon, but now, with the death of Judge

Grampis, everything would be pushed back that much longer.

"Marshal Morgan is correct," Luther finally said. "The governor will probably appoint a special judge to take Judge Grampis's place, and under the circumstances should see to it that the replacement is sent to Buckskin as quickly as possible. Another week, perhaps, but that should be all."

Woodford sighed and shook his head. "I don't know, Mr. Turnbuckle. It's startin' to seem to me like I'm jinxed. Maybe Brighton's been right all along and I'm in the wrong. Jeremiah Fulton could've lied to me about not havin' a partner. Maybe Brighton's claim is the real thing."

"No!" Luther startled himself by the vehemence of his response. "You can't give up. We can beat Brighton. I know we can."

Actually, Luther wasn't as convinced of that as he was trying to sound. His strategy depended largely on the information he was expecting in response to the wires he had sent. If he didn't get that information in time, or if it turned out to be different than what he expected, then it was going to be Woodford's word against Brighton's, for the most part . . . and in a case like that, there was no way of knowing for sure how a judge would rule.

Before they could discuss the matter any further, the door opened. Luther turned around to see Colonel Desmond O'Hara coming into the office. The Chicago lawyer took his hat off and nodded politely to Diana.

"Miss Woodford," he said. "Delightful to see you again. And you, too, Mr. Woodford."

Luther noticed that O'Hara didn't have a polite

greeting for him. He said, "What do you want, Colonel?"

"I've just heard the tragic news concerning Judge Grampis. It seems to me that these changed circumstances warrant further discussion."

"The circumstances haven't changed," Luther snapped. "Another judge will be sent out, and the case will proceed as planned."

"Eventually, yes," O'Hara said. "But this continued controversy does no one any good, Counselor. The matter needs to be settled, once and for all, so that it's not hanging over everyone's head. Therefore, my client has decided to extend an olive branch to your client and offer him a percentage of the mine in exchange for acknowledgment of the validity of the partnership agreement between Jeremiah Fulton and Chester Brighton."

"He did that before, right at first," Woodford said. "What's he offerin' now?"

"Five per cent of the mine's profits," O'Hara said.

Woodford's face purpled. "Five per cent o' my own mine?" He came to his feet, not looking defeated any longer. "By the Lord Harry—"

O'Hara held up a hand, palm out. "Please, sir. Control yourself."

"This is my office! I'll control myself if I damned well please!"

"I told him." O'Hara shook his head. "I told Mr. Brighton that such an offer was insulting, but he insisted that I make it. However . . . at my urging, he agreed that if you refused the initial offer, I had the authority to double it."

Luther said, "That's still only ten per cent."

"Ten per cent of the profits that your client has

no legal right to whatever, Counselor," O'Hara said. "It seems like a fair offer to me."

Woodford shook his head. "Not to me. The Lucky Lizard is mine."

"But if the judge who eventually hears the case doesn't agree with you, sir, you'll be left with nothing. Not only that, but the judge might even rule that Mr. Brighton is entitled to all the profits that have been realized from the mine up to this point."

Luther went cold inside. Up until now, they had been wrangling over who would own the silver that came from the Lucky Lizard in the future. It hadn't even occurred to him that Dex Brighton might also have his sights set on the fortune that Tip Woodford had already made from the mine.

Judging from the stunned look on Woodford's face, that possibility hadn't occurred to him either. "A lot of that money went right back into the mine to expand it," he said. "It's not like I've got the cash in the bank."

"Well . . . that wouldn't be Mr. Brighton's problem, now would it?" O'Hara asked with a bland smile.

Woodford scrubbed a hand over his face and looked worried again. *I should have seen this coming*, Luther thought. The real Claudius Turnbuckle would have. Not only that, but the real Turnbuckle would have already thought of a way to combat Brighton's latest maneuver.

Woodford looked at his daughter. "What do you think, Diana?"

She appeared to be worried, too, but she said, "I don't think you should make any decisions, Pa, without talking to Frank first. And you need to talk it over with Mr. Turnbuckle here, too."

In the absence of a real strategy, boldness sometimes had to suffice, Luther told himself. He swung around toward O'Hara so sharply that a twinge of pain went through his wounded arm as it shifted in the sling.

"My advice to my client, Colonel, is to flatly reject Brighton's flimsy offer. There will no settlement because no settlement is called for. My client is completely in the right and his claim will soon be vindicated in court. The best course of action for your client would be abandon this charade and leave Buckskin as soon as possible."

O'Hara's jaw tightened and his eyes flashed with anger. He didn't respond directly to Luther, though, turning to Woodford instead.

"Your attorney's fiery speech is very impressive, sir, but the decision rests with you, not him. You've heard what he has to say; now, what do *you* say? Will you accept my client's generous offer, or *not*?"

Woodford took a deep breath, and for a second Luther thought he was going to surrender rather than risk being completely ruined. But then he shook his head and said, "Tell Brighton the Lucky Lizard is mine. Always has been, ever since I bought it from Jeremiah Fulton, and always will be unless I decide to sell it to somebody myself, which ain't likely to happen."

"That's your last word on the matter?" O'Hara prodded.

"Yes, sir, it is. If it's a fight Brighton wants, then it's a fight he'll get, right to the bitter end."

O'Hara sighed. "Very well. I'll convey your decision to Mr. Brighton. I must say, though, that I believe you're making a grave error."

"It's my mistake to make," Woodford snapped. "So long, Colonel. I don't reckon there's any need for you to pay us another visit. The answer's still gonna be the same."

Luther's spirits soared as he saw that Woodford's combative nature had finally come to the forefront again. The man had almost gotten discouraged enough to quit . . . but not quite.

"In other words, Colonel," Luther told O'Hara with a cool smile, "we'll see you in court."

Chapter 20

About an hour after the stagecoach arrived in Buckskin carrying the body of Judge Theodore "Grumbler" Grampis, a knock sounded on the back door of the marshal's office. Frank was inside, pouring himself a cup of coffee from the pot that was usually simmering on the old stove, when he heard the quiet rapping. He set the coffee aside and put his hand on the butt of his Colt as he moved over to the door.

"Who is it?" he called through the panel, then took a step to the side in case his visitor tried to blast through the door with a shotgun.

"Phil Noonan, Marshal," the answer came back.

Frank felt relief go through him. Still, he was cautious and kept his hand near his gun as he swung the door open. Somebody could have figured out that Phil was working with him, grabbed him, and brought him here at gunpoint to get Frank to open the door unsuspectingly.

Frank saw that his wariness wasn't necessary, at least in this case. Phil was alone. He grinned as he came into the office and reached under his shirt to pull out a packet of papers.

"Here are all the replies to those telegrams you had me send, Marshal," he said. "Sorry it took me so long to get back here with 'em. The last one didn't come until late yesterday afternoon, too late to start back then. As important as you made this whole thing sound, I figured it'd be better to wait until today rather than spendin' a night on the trail and takin' a chance on something happenin' to 'em."

Frank took the bundle of messages, which were tied together with string. Judging by the thickness of the bundle, Claudius Turnbuckle had received a reply to every wire he had sent out, and some of them must have been lengthy.

"You did the right thing, Phil," Frank assured the messenger. "I don't know what-all is in here, but Mr. Turnbuckle is expecting some mighty important information for that court case of his."

"Did I get back in time for the trial?" Phil asked. "I worried about that. The judge was supposed to get here today, wasn't he?"

Frank's face took on a grim cast. "You haven't heard what happened?"

"I came straight here, so I haven't heard anything." Phil started to look worried. "What's wrong, Marshal?"

"The stagecoach carrying the judge arrived today, all right . . . but Judge Grampis was dead. He was killed in a holdup while the stage was on its way down here from Carson City."

"Dead!" Phil exclaimed. "Good Lord, Marshal! What's that mean for Tip Woodford's court case?"

"It's been postponed until another judge can get here."

"Got any idea when that's gonna be?"

"Not yet . . . but I'm going to ride to Carson City and bring back the next one myself, just to make sure that nothing happens to *him*." That brought up another point, and even though Frank hadn't discussed it with Tip Woodford or the other members of the town council, he decided to go ahead and broach the subject with Phil. "I know the last time I left town for a while Catamount Jack took care of things by himself, but I'm not sure that's such a good idea. I could use an extra deputy, Phil. Are you interested in the job?"

The man's eyes widened in surprise. "You'd trust me to be a deputy, Mr. Morgan, when I couldn't make it as a miner?"

"Some men are good at some things, other men are good at different things. You've done a fine job helping me out now and then, like delivering those messages and bringing back the replies. Your health is better now, and I know that you used to be good in a scrap because I remember you getting mixed up in the occasional saloon brawl. Can you handle a gun?"

"Well . . . not like you. I ain't Smoke Jensen or Falcon McAllister, and I reckon they're probably the only fellas as slick on the draw as you are, Mr. Morgan." Phil put his hand on the butt of his old Colt. "But I can get this hogleg out without too much trouble, and I generally hit what I aim at if I don't rush too much."

Frank nodded. "That's good enough for me. I can't make any promises about wages yet because

I haven't talked to the mayor or the town council, but I reckon there's a good chance they'll go along with whatever I suggest."

"Hell, if you need an extra deputy, I'd do it without any wages! Buckskin owes you a lot, Marshal. This probably wouldn't be a fit place to live if it wasn't for you. It's not just a boomtown anymore; it's a *real* town, with law and order and everything, thanks to you."

"I appreciate that sentiment, Phil." Frank clapped a hand on Noonan's shoulder. "Consider yourself hired. Come on over here to the desk. I think I've got an extra badge."

He found the badge in a drawer and handed it to Phil, who pinned it to his vest almost reverently. "Never gave any thought to being a lawman," he said.

"I believe you'll make a good one."

"I hope so." A look of worry suddenly crossed Phil's face. "But I've got a family, Marshal. Maybe I shouldn't take such a dangerous job."

"Swinging a pick or working with blasting powder down in a mine is just as dangerous," Frank pointed out. "You won't find anything in this world that's completely safe."

Phil rubbed his jaw. "Well, no, I reckon that's true." Abruptly, he thrust out his hand. "You've got yourself a deputy, Mr. Morgan."

"Since we're going to be working together, you'd better call me Frank."

That brought a grin to Phil's face. "All right, Frank."

Lifting the packet of telegrams, Frank said, "Now, I reckon I'd better get these over to Mr. Turnbuckle. I know he's been anxious to see what they have to say."

* * *

Frank found Turnbuckle in the office of the Lucky Lizard Mining Company, as he thought he might. Woodford and Diana were there, too, and all of them seemed upset about something.

Turnbuckle explained about Colonel O'Hara's visit and the settlement offer that the colonel had made. "It was rejected out of hand, of course," Turnbuckle said. "There's no need for a settlement since we're going to win in court."

"Well, I got to admit that I thought about it for a second," Tip said. "No offense to you, Mr. Turnbuckle, and don't think for a second that I'm doubtin' you. It just seems like everything keeps goin' wrong, and I thought maybe it was time to start considerin' a settlement."

Frank held out the bundle of telegrams. "Maybe this will make a difference," he said. "I just got these back from Carson City."

Turnbuckle sprang forward eagerly to take them. Since his wounded arm was still in the sling and he had only one good hand at the moment, he fumbled awkwardly with the messages for a second before Diana came to help him.

"Let me get that," she said as she took the bundle and began to untie the string around it.

When she had the string undone she placed the stack of telegrams on the desk and handed the first one to Turnbuckle, who was able to unfold the message form and read what was printed on it. Frank saw his eyes light up as he did so.

"Let me see the next one," Turnbuckle said as he set that wire aside and held out his hand.

For several minutes, with Diana's assistance, Turnbuckle read the replies, and the grin on his face got bigger and more excited with each one. Finally he said, "Yes! That's exactly what I needed to know!"

"Good news, I reckon," Frank said with a wry chuckle.

"It certainly is. My theory has been confirmed."

"What theory?" Woodford asked.

Turnbuckle opened his mouth as if he were about to answer, then stopped short. He shook his head. "I don't have everything worked out yet," he said, "and there's more information that I may not find out until the trial, so I'd prefer to keep this to myself for the time being. You understand, I hope."

"Well, not really," Woodford said with a frown. "But you're the lawyer, I reckon, so I'll go along with what you say. I figure you know what you're doing."

Frank hoped that Tip was right about that. So far Turnbuckle seemed to be smart enough, and a fighter to boot. But there had been a few moments when Frank had experienced a twinge of doubt about the man. Right from the start, Turnbuckle hadn't really met his expectations of an attorney with such a sterling reputation.

In the end, though, results were what mattered. Frank was willing to give Turnbuckle a chance and see what results the lawyer achieved.

"With any luck you won't have to wait very long," Frank said. "I'm leaving for Carson City this afternoon."

The three of them turned surprised faces toward him. "Leaving?" Turnbuckle repeated. "Why?"

"I'm going there to get a new judge and bring him back."

"I assumed you'd just send a messenger to the governor—"

Frank shook his head. "There's no way of proving it right now, but I've got a hunch Brighton might've had something to do with that so-called stagecoach robbery."

Turnbuckle's eyebrows rose. "You think he had Judge Grampis *assassinated*?"

"We can't rule it out, can we?"

Woodford clenched a fist and thumped it on the desk. "That low-down skunk! You're right, Frank. Ol' Grumbler gettin' killed like that was one of the things that almost made me want to give up. I didn't like the idea of waitin' for another judge to show up. Could be that Brighton was countin' on that."

Frank nodded and said, "That's what I thought, too. Brighton's tried to kill me and the counselor here to put you in a deeper hole, Tip. I'm convinced of that. Delaying the trial does the same thing. He's been trying to pile so much on you that you collapse under the weight."

"That's not gonna happen," Woodford declared. "I'll keep fightin'."

"And so will I," Turnbuckle added. "What you say makes a great deal of sense, Frank. But if you leave town, won't that just give Brighton the opportunity to send his hired killers after you again?"

"Maybe. I'll try to slip out without anybody noticing, though, and I reckon I can trust you folks not to tell anybody that I'm gone."

"Of course," Turnbuckle said.

Diana pointed out, "People will notice that you're not around town, Frank."

"Maybe not until I'm gone, though. Jack can

pretend like I'm still here, and so can Phil Noonan. I just signed him up as an extra deputy."

Woodford grunted in approval. "Noonan's a good man. Not cut out to be a miner, but that don't mean he won't be a good deputy."

"That's how I saw it, too."

Diana came over to Frank and laid a hand on his arm. "You'll have to be careful, Frank. We need all the allies we can get if we're going to keep Brighton from taking over the mine."

He smiled at her. "Don't worry, I know that." He looked at Woodford and Turnbuckle. "If anything happens while I'm gone, find Jack or Phil. Any other wires you need sent from Carson City, Claudius?"

Turnbuckle shook his head and tapped a finger on the stack of telegrams on the desk. "This is all I need, providing that everything works out at the trial . . . which I hope will be soon."

"You and me both, Counselor," Frank said. "You and me both."

Frank got Catamount Jack and Phil Noonan together in his office and explained his plan to them, after informing Jack that Phil was now a deputy, too.

"But I'll be in charge while you're gone, right, Marshal?" Jack asked.

Phil held up his hands before Frank could even answer. "I wouldn't want it any other way, Jack," he declared. "You've been working with Frank and wearing a badge for quite a while. I don't really have any idea how to be a deputy, so I'll be lookin' to you to take charge."

"Well, all right then," the old-timer said. "Didn't mean to sound proddy. I just wanted to know where we stand."

"Now you know," Frank said. "Anyway, I don't intend to be gone any longer than I have to. I'll ride as long as I can before it gets too dark to travel, then start out again in the morning at first light. Ought to reach Carson City by midday. If I can get in to see the governor right away and convince him to appoint a new judge to replace Judge Grampis, maybe we can start the next morning. That'll put us back here day after tomorrow."

"Assumin' you don't run into any trouble," Jack said. "Like more o' them no-good bushwhackers tryin' to kill you."

"I'm hoping I can get out of town without Brighton finding out about it right away. If I've got a good enough start, Brighton's gunnies won't be able to catch up to me."

Jack squinted in thought. "No, but once they figure out that you're gone, they can lay for you on your way back."

That same dangerous possibility had occurred to Frank, but there was nothing he could do about it. "I reckon the judge and I will just have to take our chances."

"You could take a bunch of heavily armed men with you," Phil suggested. "You have plenty of friends here in Buckskin who would be glad to help out, Marshal."

"And I won't put any of them at risk if I don't have to," Frank answered without hesitation. "Besides, one or two men can move faster and be harder to trail than a whole bunch."

Jack grunted. "Yeah, I reckon that's true, all right."

Frank packed a few supplies for the journey. As he did, he told his deputies, "I've talked to Mr. Turnbuckle and told him to stay here in town, with lots of people around. I'm convinced that Brighton would like to see him dead, too. That would be one more threat to his plan eliminated. But he can't afford to have Turnbuckle bushwhacked right out in the open. Keep an eye on him, though, just in case."

Jack and Phil nodded. The older deputy said, "Don't worry, Frank. We won't let anything happen to the little fella."

With that taken care of, Frank sent Jack down to the livery stable with instructions for Amos Hillman to saddle up Stormy and bring him to the back of the marshal's office and jail in half an hour. Goldy was younger and perhaps stronger, but on a possibly perilous trek like the one he was facing, Frank wanted the more reliable Stormy as his mount. Stormy had never let him down during times of trouble and never would.

Frank had the two deputies out watching for any signs of Brighton, O'Hara, or anybody else who looked suspicious when Hillman delivered Stormy in the alley behind the jail. Dog was with them, and the big cur didn't seem bothered by anything, which Frank took as a good sign. He hung the bag of provisions and ammunition from the saddle, shook hands quickly with the liveryman, and said, "Thanks, Amos," then swung up onto Stormy's back. He lifted the reins and sent the big stallion cantering toward the trees at the edge of the settlement.

With Dog trotting alongside him, Frank rode west from Buckskin. Leaving town in that direction was a pretty transparent attempt at subterfuge, he thought, but it *might* work to throw off anybody who saw him heading that way. He didn't start circling back to the north until he was several miles out of town. This would make the trip longer, but possibly safer.

Coming back would be a different story. If he could convince the governor to appoint a new judge—and if he could convince that new judge to risk his neck by coming down here—then Frank intended to hustle back to Buckskin by the shortest, fastest route possible.

As he rode through the rugged but beautiful Nevada landscape, it was easy to forget the seriousness of the chore he had taken on and just enjoy the spectacular scenery. Slopes covered with the deep, dark green of pine forests rose around him, and towering over them were the craggy, snow-capped peaks of the mountains. Icy, fast-flowing streams cut deep ravines through the hills. Flowers dotted lushly grassed mountain meadows. Frank saw several moose loping across one of those meadows, and he spotted a bear poking its paw into the rotten trunk of a fallen pine. An eagle wheeled through the blue sky overhead.

Yes, it was easy to forget why he was here and what he was doing, Frank thought—but he didn't allow himself to do so. That would be risking not only his own life but the futures of Tip and Diana Woodford, and possibly the life of Claudius Turnbuckle. Dex Brighton had committed himself to his effort to take over the Lucky Lizard, and Frank knew he wasn't going to stop at anything to get what he wanted. Frank had run into men like that plenty of times before, and sooner or later it nearly always came down to gunplay and killing.

This time, there was a chance that things might be settled in court instead of with powder smoke. Frank was going to hold on to that hope . . .

But every instinct in his body told him that the guns hadn't fallen silent for good.

Chapter 21

Dex Brighton was sitting in an armchair in his hotel room, smoking a cheroot, when a soft knock sounded on the door. He slipped his hand inside his coat and curled his fingers around the butt of the little pistol he carried there as he called out, "Come in."

He relaxed and let go of the gun as the door opened and Desmond O'Hara strolled in. The phony lawyer was trying to look nonchalant, Brighton thought, but worry lurked in his eyes.

"What's wrong?"

"You read me too well, my friend," O'Hara said. "Frank Morgan is gone."

Brighton sat up straighter. "Gone? What do you mean?"

"Just what I said," O'Hara replied, spreading his hands. "I was talking to Mason in the Top-Notch a short time ago, and he said that someone told him Amos Hillman delivered Morgan's horse to him in the alley behind the jail this afternoon. That alarmed me, so I started asking around. It turns out no one has seen Morgan since that time."

Brighton slammed a fist down on the little table beside the chair. "Damn it! He's stolen a march on us."

"Maybe he just left town and doesn't intend to come back."

Brighton shook his head. "Not Morgan. Not that stubborn son of a bitch." The wheels of his brain were turning over rapidly. "He's gone to Carson City to bring back another judge."

Brighton gave voice to the conclusion even as he reached it, but as soon as he heard his own words he knew they were right. That was just the sort of thing Morgan would do. In the normal course of events, the death of Judge Grampis would have delayed the trial a couple of weeks, perhaps even longer. But with Morgan taking a direct hand like this, he might be back from Carson City in a matter of days.

A glance out the window told Brighton that night had fallen. "When did Morgan leave?"

O'Hara shrugged and said, "All I know for sure is what Mason told me. Hillman took Morgan's horse over to the jail around four o'clock."

"That means he's had several hours' head start." Brighton shook his head. "Morgan's been a hunted man for most of his life. He'll know all the tricks of throwing off pursuit. Sending Stample and the others after him now would be a waste of time. They'd never catch him."

"If Morgan plans to fetch another judge," O'Hara observed, "he'll have to come back to Buckskin for the ploy to do any good."

Brighton jerked his head in a nod. "Exactly. And that will be our chance to stop him. I'll have men watching all the trails into Buckskin, just in case

Morgan tries to circle around and come in from another direction."

"Do you have that many men?"

A cold, thin smile curved Brighton's lips. "I told Stample several days ago to send for reinforcements. They'll be coming from all over, as soon as the word gets around. With any luck, by the end of the week, I'll have between thirty and forty men working for me."

"And just how do you intend to pay them?" O'Hara asked. "I'm willing to work on a percentage basis, because I've seen you pull off audacious schemes before, Dex. But not all of those gunmen will know you as well as I do."

"They know Stample, though, and they trust him," Brighton replied. "As much as men like that trust anybody, I mean." He lifted his almost forgotten cheroot to his lips and puffed on it. "Don't worry, Desmond. When the big payoff comes, there'll be enough loot to go around. You have my word on that."

"And in the meantime . . . ?"

"In the meantime, since we can't do anything about Morgan until he tries to return to Buckskin, we'll rid ourselves of another obstacle." Brighton's fingers tightened on the cheroot. "We're going to do something about Claudius Turnbuckle."

It was difficult for Luther not to share the reasons for his excitement with Woodford and Diana after he went through the replies to his telegrams, but he didn't want to get their hopes up too much just yet. There were still too many things that could go wrong with his strategy . . . such as the fact that a great deal of it depended on information he would have to uncover during the trial. If that didn't work out . . .

Luther preferred not to think about that.

Taking the telegrams with him, he returned to the hotel and closed himself up in his room to go over them again. He sat at the small table in the room with some paper and a pencil and began making notes for the brief he would submit to the judge. That was assuming, of course, that Frank Morgan would be successful in his attempt to return to Buckskin in fairly short order with a jurist to hear the case.

Luther was so caught up in his work that he didn't really notice time passing until the rumbling of his stomach reminded him that he hadn't eaten for quite a while. He glanced out the window and saw that night had fallen. Morgan should be well on his way to Carson City by now.

With a sigh, Luther pushed his penciled notes away from him and stretched in the hard wooden chair. He stood up and reached for his hat. He would go downstairs, get a bite to eat in the dining room, and then come back up here to work some more on his trial preparations.

His fingers were cramping a little from the writing he had scrawled across several sheets of paper. Because of that, his hat slipped out of his grasp and fell to the floor beside his chair. He bent to retrieve it.

At that same moment, something crashed through the window, spraying glass over the floor and the foot of the bed. Even with that racket, Luther heard what sounded like a whisper just above his head. He had been in this frontier settlement long enough to realize that a bullet had almost parted his hair just now.

Some of the unbroken glass in the window shattered as another bullet punched through it. Luther was still moving, though, so the second slug missed, too. In a continuation of the move that had saved his life, he threw himself to the floor, crying out as the jolting impact sent pain shooting through his injured arm.

The blasted thing would never heal up if people kept shooting at him, he thought wildly.

He rolled over a couple of times, putting the bed between himself and the window. More shots slammed, somewhere in the night. Luther thought they sounded like they were coming from a Winchester, but he was hardly an expert in such things. Anyway, he couldn't hear the shots that clearly, since his own pulse was hammering in his head like a thunderstorm.

Plaster showered down from the wall in a couple of places where it was stuck by bullets, and then the lamp suddenly shattered. Blazing kerosene sprayed across the table. As the flames licked out hungrily toward the piles of telegrams and notes Luther had left there, he cried, "No!" and lunged to his feet without even thinking about the fact that he was exposing himself once more to the person who was trying to kill him. The information in the telegrams could be replaced, and the notes could be recreated, but Luther wasn't thinking about that at the moment. All he saw was his case going up in flames.

He was reminded of the danger a second later when a bullet tugged at the tail of his coat as it passed close by his hip. He was moving too fast to stop, though. He threw himself at the table and grabbed the papers. A couple of them were already burning around the edges. He slapped out the flames.

The garish, madly leaping light from the fire was probably what saved him, making it difficult for the ambusher to draw an accurate bead on him. Another slug whistled past Luther's head as he gathered up the papers. By now, the wall behind the table and the table itself were burning. Smoke began to fill the room, stinging his nose and throat and half-blinding him. Luther used both arms, ignoring the pain in the wounded one, to clutch the precious documents to his chest as he stumbled toward the door. After what seemed like an eternity of fumbling with the knob, he finally managed to throw the door open and half-lunged, half-fell out into the corridor, yelling hoarsely, "Fire! Fire!"

No cry struck as much fear into the hearts of Westerners, who had heard all the stories about entire towns burning to the ground. Some of them had lived through such disasters. Several hotel guests had already smelled the smoke and now came hurrying out of their rooms. They took up the cry of alarm.

Luther tripped and went to one knee, then struggled back to his feet and stumbled toward the stairs. He still had belongings in the burning room, but nothing as important as what he carried with him. People crowded around him as the other frightened guests tried to escape the blaze, too.

He felt a sudden pain in his side and nearly fell again. A man caught hold of his arm and steadied him. "You all right, mister?" the man asked as they reached the staircase.

"No," Luther managed to say. "Can . . . can you give me a hand down to the lobby?"

"Sure. Folks got to stick together when all hell breaks loose."

With the man's help, Luther managed to get downstairs, where he stumbled outside with the other fleeing guests. Buckskin had a volunteer fire-fighting company. Its members were rushing into the hotel as the terrified guests were rushing out. A crowd of hotel guests and onlookers gathered in the street to watch as the firemen tried to save the place. A horse-drawn wagon filled with barrels of water careened to a halt in front of the hotel, and a bucket brigade was soon set up. Other volunteers used buckets to refill the barrels from the creek at the edge of town. The line of them stretched all along the street.

Luther's head spun dizzily. He shoved the papers he had saved from the fire into his sling, then pressed his hand against his side where the pain had struck. When he pulled it away, he saw that his palm was coated with blood. It looked even more crimson than usual in the light from the fire. For a second, Luther thought he was going to pass out as he realized that he had been wounded again. He struggled to hang on to consciousness.

"Mr. Turnbuckle!"

The voice made Luther look around. He recognized Tip Woodford. Close behind Woodford were Catamount Jack and another man wearing a deputy's badge. That must be Phil Noonan, Morgan's new deputy, Luther recalled.

Woodford gripped his arm. "Are you all right, Mr. Turnbuckle?"

Luther shook his head and held up his blood-covered hand. "No, I . . . I don't think I am," he said. "In fact, I seem to be—"

That was all he got out before his knees buckled and he felt himself falling.

"Son of a gun!" Catamount Jack exclaimed as Claudius Turnbuckle crumpled to the street in front of him. He knelt beside the lawyer and pulled back his coat, revealing a large bloodstain on Turnbuckle's shirt. "This hombre's hurt! We better carry him down to Doc Garland's."

He was about to grab Turnbuckle under the arms and tell Phil Noonan to get the lawyer's feet when Turnbuckle roused enough to clutch at his sleeve. "J-Jack," Turnbuckle muttered. "Jack . . . listen to me . . ."

Jack leaned closer. "I'm right here, Mr. Turnbuckle. What're you tryin' to tell me?"

"Somebody . . . shot at me . . . through the window . . . tried to . . . kill me . . ."

Jack had to struggle to make out the words over all the commotion going on, but he heard them clearly enough to understand what Turnbuckle was saying. The words didn't come as all that much of a surprise either, considering the violence that had plagued Buckskin and the surrounding area recently. Ever since the arrival of Dex Brighton, in fact.

"Bullet broke . . . the lamp . . ." Turnbuckle was saying. His voice was getting weaker, though, as consciousness kept trying to slip away from him.

Jack glanced toward the hotel. He didn't know if the firefighting company would be able to save the building or not, but they were already doing all they could and didn't particularly need his help. There was something else he could do, though.

He could try to find the bushwhacking son of a bitch who'd taken those shots at Turnbuckle and accidentally started the fire.

"Tip, grab hold of Mr. Turnbuckle here. You, too, Phil. Take him down to the doc's and have Garland see how bad he's hurt. From the sounds of what he told me, he may be shot again."

"Shot?" Woodford said. "You mean Brighton actually tried to kill him right here in town?"

Jack straightened from his crouch and put his hand on the butt of the big revolver at his waist. "That's what I figure on findin' out."

Tip and Phil got hold of Turnbuckle and carefully lifted him, then started off toward the doctor's office with the wounded man between them. Jack turned to study the hotel. He knew which room was Turnbuckle's, and when he studied the window now he saw that the glass in it was shattered. That could have been caused by heat from the fire.

But it could have been caused by shots being fired through it, too, before the blaze ever broke out.

Jack turned his head to look across the street. Directly opposite the hotel was Patterson's Hardware Store, a one-story building with a false front. It was closed at this time of night, which meant that somebody could have climbed onto its roof, hidden behind that false front, and shot almost straight into Turnbuckle's room. Jack grated a curse. He had promised Frank Morgan that he would look after the lawyer, and then he'd let Turnbuckle sit up there like a target in a shooting gallery.

Maybe he could make up for that mistake by finding the man who had done the bushwhacking.

Catamount Jack drew his gun as he trotted into the dark passage next to the hardware store. He had the revolver ready as he rounded the rear corner of the building, just in case the bushwhacker was still lurking back there.

He didn't see or hear anything, though, not that he could see much in the gloom. Jack stood there, listening intently, and decided after a moment that the rifleman was long gone, if he had even used the hardware store as a shooting platform.

Jack started forward, but had gone only a few steps before he nearly tripped over something. Catching his balance, he knelt and felt around with his free hand. His fingers brushed what felt like a ladder.

He fished a lucifer out of his shirt pocket and snapped it into life with his thumbnail. The glare from the match revealed that his guess was right. A ladder lay crookedly on the ground at his feet, as if it had been propped against the building and then toppled over. Jack's eyes narrowed as he noticed that one of the rungs was broken, as if it had cracked clean in two under somebody's weight. He took hold of the ladder, raised it from its current position, and leaned it against the rear wall of the store. The broken rung was three down from the top.

The bushwhacker had been on top of the hardware store. Jack was sure of it now. The man had taken his shots at Claudius Turnbuckle, then start to descend hurriedly on the ladder when the fire broke out in the hotel room.

But that rung had snapped under his foot, and he had probably fallen the rest of the way to the alley, bringing the ladder down with him. Jack could see the scene in his head as clearly as if he had witnessed it with his own eyes . . . except for the identity of the would-be killer, of course. He didn't know that.

But he was going to find out. He lit another match and found fresh footprints in the dirt and dust of the alley. Not many people came back here, so there wasn't the welter of prints there would have been in the street. In addition to that, the prints looked like the fella who'd made them had been dragging one leg. That fit right in with Jack's idea about the ladder rung breaking and the bushwhacker falling. The hombre had hurt his leg.

He began following the tracks along the alley, lighting a fresh match each time one burned out. At one time in his long life he had done some scouting for the army, and he still knew a thing or two about trailing. He was able to follow this trail all the way to the back door of the Top Notch Saloon, a considerable distance down the street from the hotel.

Jack tried the knob and found the door unlocked. He eased it open and stepped inside. He was in a darkened storeroom. He could hear a few voices coming from the front of the place, along with the clink of glasses. Making his way carefully through the storeroom, he found the door that led into the main part of the saloon.

Jack opened the door just enough to put his eye to the crack and peer through. In the narrow slice of barroom he could see from here, he spotted Mason, one of the regular bartenders, leaning on the hardwood and breathing heavily. He wasn't wearing his apron, and one of the other drink jugglers was also behind the bar. Only a couple of customers were left in the saloon because all the others had hurried out to watch the fire being fought in the hotel.

Jack's gaze went to a Winchester lying on a shelf underneath the bar. He'd be willing to bet a hat that if he sniffed the barrel of that rifle, he would find that it had been fired recently.

"Gimme a drink," Mason croaked to the other bartender. He straightened and took a step toward the man, who started to draw a beer. As Mason moved, he winced in pain. He had a pronounced limp, too.

Jack didn't need to see any more than that. He pulled the door open, stepped into the saloon, and pointed his gun at Mason, who was reaching for the mug of beer the other bartender had filled.

"Enjoy that beer, Mason," Jack said. "Reckon you won't be gettin' any behind bars."

Chapter 22

Mason jerked around, his mouth gaping open and his prominent Adam's apple bobbing in his scrawny neck. His hand moved instinctively toward the Winchester.

"I wouldn't," Jack said.

"Wh-what do you want, Deputy?" Mason demanded, trying to look and sound outraged. "You can't just come in here wavin' a gun around—"

"You're under arrest," Jack interrupted him. "That's why I've got this gun on you."

"Under arrest? What for?"

"For tryin' to kill Mr. Claudius Turnbuckle and maybe for burnin' down the hotel. We'll have to wait and see about that one, I reckon."

"Why, you crazy old coot! I didn't shoot at anybody, and I sure didn't try to burn down the hotel!"

"No? Then how'd you hurt your leg?"

Mason shook his head. "My leg's fine."

"Really? Let's see you dance a jig then."

Jack shifted the barrel of his gun so that it

pointed at Mason's feet, and it was obvious that he was about to start shooting.

Mason thrust the palms of his hands toward the deputy. "Wait!" he cried. "We were unloadin' some barrels of beer earlier, and one of 'em fell on my foot. That's all that happened, I swear." He looked at the other bartender. "Ain't that right, Smithy?"

The man hesitated, and it was clear to Catamount Jack that he didn't want to back up Mason's story by lying. Jack let the fella off the hook by saying, "Anyway, Mason, if you didn't have anything to do with what happened to Turnbuckle, how in blazes did you know somebody *shot* at him? I just said somebody tried to kill him."

Mason's eyes were bugging out now, and he looked like a trapped animal. He licked his lips and said, "Lemme have that beer. You said I could have it."

Jack made a motion with the barrel of his gun. "Go ahead."

Mason turned and reached out to take the mug from Smithy. As soon as he had it in his hand, though, he whirled and flung the full mug at Jack's head. Jack cursed and ducked and almost pulled the trigger, but Smithy stood right behind Mason and if his shot missed, it might hit the other bartender.

Then Mason grabbed the Winchester and swung it up, and Jack didn't have any choice. The heavy revolver bucked and roared in his hand.

The Winchester went off, too, but the bullet plowed harmlessly into the floor between Jack and Mason as the bullet from the deputy's gun shattered Mason's right shoulder. He slumped back against the bar and groaned. Blood welled between the fingers of his left hand as he used it to clutch the wounded shoulder.

Jack held his fire as he squinted against the haze of powder smoke that had erupted from the guns.

"Don't try nothin', Smithy," he grated.

The other bartender backed off, hands raised to shoulder level.

"This is none o' my business, Deputy," Smithy insisted. "Whatever Mason did, I didn't have anything to do with it. We just work here together in the saloon."

"You didn't see him talkin' to anybody tonight?" Jack asked, hoping that Smithy would testify that he had witnessed Mason being hired by Dex Brighton to kill Turnbuckle. Jack's gut told him that was exactly what had happened.

"Hell, no. He was off work tonight. I didn't even see him until he came limpin' in, out of breath, with that rifle. He told me to keep my trap shut and act like he'd been here all evening, and I knew right then that he'd been up to something no good."

Jack grunted. It didn't take a damn professor to figure that one out, he thought.

Mason whimpered as he leaned against the bar. Jack stepped forward and grasped his uninjured shoulder.

"Come on, you blasted bushwhacker," the deputy ordered. "We'll get the doc to patch you up, then I'm gonna *lock* you up until the marshal gets back. Frank Morgan'll know what to do with you."

Mason gasped and cursed as Jack steered him toward the door, his injured leg still making him limp heavily. They moved through the batwings onto the porch.

"I'm gonna bleed to death," Mason moaned. "You've killed me."

"No, you ain't," Jack told him. "You're gonna stay alive to tell me the name o' the varmint who paid you to get rid of Turnbuckle—"

Flame suddenly spewed from the shadows at the corner of the building. Jack heard the thud of lead striking flesh, then a bullet sizzled past his ear. He let go of Mason and twisted around, flinging himself to the planks of the boardwalk as more shots erupted. He triggered twice, aiming at the spot where he had seen the muzzle flashes.

As the echoes of the shots faded, Jack caught the sound of rapid footsteps. He surged upright and ran to the corner, stopping just short of it and pressing his back against the wall of the building. Then he darted around the corner in a low crouch and swept the gun from side to side, searching for a target.

The passage beside the Top-Notch was empty. That became obvious a moment later when Smithy emerged from the saloon carrying a lantern.

"What happened out here?" he asked. "Deputy, are you all right?"

"Yeah, no thanks to the polecat who took some shots at Mason and me," Jack said. He grunted with disgust as the light from the bartender's lantern washed over the sprawled form on the boardwalk.

Mason's eyes were wide open and staring sightlessly toward the street. A worm of blood crawled from the black-rimmed hole in his head, just below the right temple.

"Lord!" Smithy muttered. "He's dead."

"Yeah," Catamount Jack said, "and I never seen a dead man yet who could talk."

* * *

Dex Brighton leaned against the rear wall of a darkened building a couple of blocks away and caught his breath. He opened the cylinder of his gun and thumbed in fresh cartridges to replace the ones he had fired.

Black hate filled his mind. Mason had gotten what he deserved, but it would have been nice if he could have gotten rid of that meddling deputy, too.

And now Brighton had been forced to get his own hands dirty. He hated that. Killing didn't bother him all that much—he had done it in the past when necessary—but he greatly preferred to have other people do it for him. Things were just neater that way.

He had known he was taking a chance when he hired Mason to kill Claudius Turnbuckle. The bartender wasn't a professional gunman, by any means. Brighton had talked with him enough to know, though, that Mason was greedy and would do just about anything if the price was right. And having lived on the frontier, Mason had some experience with guns, enough so that he should have been able to hit Turnbuckle at that range.

But as soon as Brighton had seen Turnbuckle in the second-floor corridor of the hotel as the guests fled from the fire, he knew that Mason had failed. Turnbuckle was still alive, and by some absurd twist of fate, Mason had managed to start a fire in the hotel instead of killing the lawyer.

Brighton had seized the opportunity to slip up behind Turnbuckle in the crowd. The little dagger that Brighton carried in a sheath strapped to his forearm, under his sleeve, had come out, and all it should have taken was a quick thrust into Turnbuckle's spine from behind. No one would even know the lawyer had been stabbed until he collapsed.

Someone else in the mob had jostled Brighton's arm just as he struck, however, and even though he'd felt the blade go into Turnbuckle's body, he didn't know if it was a fatal wound, or even a serious one. Once again, luck had turned against Brighton at the last second.

A few minutes later, out on the street, he had seen Turnbuckle collapse. Tip Woodford and a man Brighton hadn't seen before had picked him up and carried him off, no doubt to the local doctor's office. Catamount Jack had started prowling around like he was looking for something, and it didn't take any great leap of logic to figure out what it was.

Brighton had known right then that he had better get to Mason as soon as possible.

The incompetent bastard wasn't at his shack on the edge of town, though, which was where Brighton had met with him before. That left the Top-Notch, and Brighton headed for it right away. He hadn't reached the saloon in time to stop the deputy from trailing Mason there. In fact, as he glanced through the front window, Brighton had seen Jack pushing an obviously wounded Mason toward the entrance.

Brighton didn't even have to think about what he did next. He knew that Mason wouldn't keep his mouth shut. He might have even talked already and implicated Brighton in the attempt on Turnbuckle's life.

But as Mason and Jack pushed through the

batwings onto the boardwalk, Brighton had heard the exchange between them from where he crouched in the shadows at the corner of the building. That had been enough to tell him that Mason hadn't spilled his guts yet.

And all it took to make sure that he never would was a quick, accurate bullet to the brain . . .

Brighton's lips pulled back from his teeth in a grimace. Twice tonight, Claudius Turnbuckle had come close to dying, but had escaped narrowly both times. At least Brighton's trail was covered. No one could prove he'd had anything to do with the attempts on Turnbuckle's life, just like they couldn't prove he had shot Mason.

Any scheme had its ups and downs, its failures and successes, its good luck and bad. His attempt to take over the Lucky Lizard Mine was no different. Even though things could have worked out better, the big payoff was still within reach. He had come too far to give up now, Brighton told himself. He was going to leave Buckskin a rich man.

No matter how many people had to die.

"Is he gonna live?" Catamount Jack asked as he came into Doc Garland's office and found Claudius Turnbuckle stretched out on the medico's examination table, apparently unconscious. Tip Woodford and Phil Noonan stood by watching anxiously.

Garland glanced up from the long gash in Turnbuckle's side that he was stitching together.

"Oh, undoubtedly," he replied. "Mr. Turnbuckle has a pretty messy cut in his side, but it's not going to kill him."

Jack frowned. "Wait a minute, Doc. You say he's got a cut?"

"That's right." Garland stepped aside so that Jack could get a better look at the wound, which appeared to be a fairly deep but nice, clean slash.

"That's not a bullet hole," Jack said, a little astounded.

"No, it was made with a knife or some other sort of sharp-edged instrument. From the looks of it, though, I really think it was a knife."

"I figured he was shot."

"Not this time," Garland said dryly.

"What's goin' on, Jack?" Woodford asked. "How come you were so sure Mr. Turnbuckle would have a bullet hole in his hide?"

"Because Mason, that no-account bartender from down at the Top Notch, bushwhacked him from the roof o' Patterson's Hardware Store across the street from the hotel."

The three men in the room who were still conscious stared at him. Jack spent the next few minutes explaining about what he had found behind the hardware store and how he had trailed Mason to the saloon and confronted him there.

"Somebody hired him to gun the counselor there," he said with a nod toward Turnbuckle, "and by somebody I mean that skunk Brighton. Mason would've admitted that, too, I reckon, if somebody hadn't put a bullet in his head."

"And by somebody, you mean Brighton again," Tip said.

"That's what I'm thinkin'." Jack shook his head. "Can't prove it, though. Brighton saw to that."

"What about the hotel?" Phil Noonan asked. "Do

they have the fire under control yet, or is it gonna burn down?"

"I stopped by there on my way here. The fire's out. Burned a couple o' rooms pretty bad, includin' Mr. Turnbuckle's, but they got it put out before the whole hotel could burn up. My guess is that while Mason was throwin' lead through the window from across the street, one of his shots hit the lamp and busted it. That'd be enough to start the fire."

Tip rubbed his jaw. "Makes sense to me. But that knife wound in Mr. Turnbuckle's side don't."

"I can think of one explanation," Doc Garland said as he continued his stitching.

"Well, don't keep it to yourself, Doc!" Jack burst out.

"I imagine there was quite a crowd in the hallway when everyone was trying to get out of the hotel. Someone could have come up behind Mr. Turnbuckle in all the confusion and stabbed him without anybody noticing."

Jack squinted at the doctor as he mulled over the idea. What Garland said made sense, and no other explanation really did.

There was something else in favor of the theory, too.

"Brighton's got a room in the hotel!" Tip Woodford exclaimed, reaching the same conclusion as Jack.

"Yeah," the deputy said. "Son of a bitch hired Mason to kill Turnbuckle. Then when he saw that the counselor was still alive, he made a try for him his own self. That didn't work either, so he went after Mason to cover his trail."

"You can't prove any of it, though. Brighton's still in the clear as far as the law's concerned."

Catamount Jack nodded. A bitter edge crept into his voice as he said, "Frank told me to keep Turnbuckle alive, and it's just pure luck that he is. But I reckon we ought to look on the bright side."

"There's a bright side to this mess?" Tip asked gloomily.

"Yeah. At least the whole damned town didn't burn to the ground. Think how bad it'd be if Frank came back from Carson City to find *that*!"

Chapter 23

Frank's plan worked. He kept an eye on his back trail all afternoon, and he was confident that no one had followed him from Buckskin. He followed roundabout routes, rode across rocky stretches and along streams just to make sure he threw off any pursuers.

As night fell, he made camp in a hollow underneath an overhanging bluff. The place wasn't quite a cave, but the overhang broke up what little smoke there was from the tiny fire he built to boil coffee and heat up some biscuits and bacon from his bag of supplies. Then he rolled up in his blankets and fell asleep, knowing full well that if anybody came poking around, Stormy and Dog would let him know about it.

The night passed peacefully, however, and Frank awoke the next morning refreshed and ready to go on to Carson City. He wondered briefly if there had been any trouble in Buckskin during the night. If so, Catamount Jack and Phil Noonan could handle it, Frank told himself. He was doing more good by fetching another judge, because the sooner the problem of Dex Brighton was dealt with, the sooner true peace would return to the settlement.

Frank saddled up and rode on, still checking warily behind him from time to time. He didn't see any sign of being trailed. By midday, he had reached Carson City. He didn't bother stopping at a hotel, but instead rode straight to the state capitol, an impressive, two-story building of light-colored brick, topped by a white bell tower with a flagpole on its summit. Trees dotted the green lawn in front of the capitol building.

Frank tied Stormy at one of the hitch racks and told Dog to stay with the stallion. The big cur sat down, and Frank knew he wouldn't move. Passersby on the street cast nervous looks at the shaggy, wolflife creature, but Dog ignored them and maintained his dignity.

A directory in the lobby of the capitol building sent Frank to the second floor in search of the governor's office. He knew the odds were against him being able to just waltz in and see the man right away, but he didn't see any harm in trying.

Sure enough, a pasty-faced gent with spectacles stopped him in the outer office.

"I'm sorry, sir," the man said in response to Frank's request to speak to the governor. "You'll have to schedule an appointment, and I'm afraid that Governor Sadler won't be able to see you for at least two weeks. He's a very busy man, you know."

Frank supposed that was true. Reinhold Sadler hadn't been governor for long; elected as lieutenant governor on the Silver Party ticket, he had assumed the top office following the death of Governor John

E. Jones, who was also a member of the Silver Party. Since the main thrust of the party's platform was to free silver mining and the silver trade from excessive federal regulation, close ties existed between Silver Party politicians and the mine owners in the state. Frank was aware of all that even though business and politics had never been consuming interests of his.

He played that card, telling the secretary, "Maybe you should ask the governor if he could make room in his schedule to talk to me for a few minutes. My name is Frank Morgan. I'm one of the owners of the Browning Mining Syndicate."

The secretary's eyes widened. Clearly, he had looked at Frank, with more than a day's worth of beard stubble and trail dust on his clothes and a marshal's tin star pinned to his shirt, and taken him for some small-town lawman. That was true, as far as it went, but there was a lot more to Frank Morgan than that.

For one thing, he was also a famous gunfighter. Maybe the last of the really famous gunfighters . . .

"Ah, Mr. Morgan," the secretary said as he got to his feet behind his paper-cluttered desk, "if you have some means of identification . . . ?"

Frank grunted. "My word's usually good enough." He allowed a tone of impatience to creep into his voice.

The secretary jerked his head in a nod. "I suppose I could let the governor know that you're here and would like to speak with him. Do you have a calling card?" Then, before Frank could answer, the man went on. "No, I suppose not."

For a second, Frank thought about taking a .45 cartridge from one of the loops on his shell belt and tossing it on the desk, so he could say, *There. There's my calling card.*

But he didn't. Such a dramatic gesture wasn't really in his nature.

Instead, he said, "You might mention to the governor that Conrad Browning is my son, too."

Conrad's name obviously meant something to the secretary. He nodded and said, "I'll be right back, Mr. Morgan." Then he disappeared through a door into Sadler's private office.

He wasn't gone for very long, maybe a minute. When he reappeared, he had a smile on his face.

"Governor Sadler said for me to send you right in, Mr. Morgan. I'm sorry for any, ah, misunderstanding."

"No need for you to be sorry, son," Frank told him. "You were just doing your job."

Frank went into the office, and found Governor Sadler standing at one of the windows that looked out over the lawn and the bustling streets of the capital, as well as the snowcapped Sierras that provided a picturesque backdrop to Carson City. Sadler turned away from the window and came toward Frank with his hand extended.

"Mr. Morgan," he said. "It's an honor to meet you, sir. I've heard a great deal about you."

"A little of it might even be true," Frank said with a smile as he shook hands with the politician.

Sadler laughed. The politician was a beefy man with thick dark hair and a graying Vandyke beard. He had a good grip, strong but not crushing. He waved Frank into a big leather chair in front of the desk.

"Cigar? Brandy?" Sadler asked before taking his own seat behind the desk.

Frank shook his head. "No thanks, Governor. I know you're a busy man, so I'll get right to the point. Despite what I told your secretary out there, I'm not really here as one of the owners of the Browning Mining Syndicate. I'm here as the marshal of Buckskin."

Sadler settled his bulk in the chair and frowned. "I'd heard that you had taken that job. Wasn't sure why Buckskin even needed a marshal. Then I found out it wasn't a ghost town anymore. There are, what, three mines producing regularly again?"

Frank nodded. "That's right. The Crown Royal— that's the one my son Conrad and I own, Tip Woodford's Lucky Lizard, and the Alhambra, owned now by a lady named Munro."

"Yes, I recall hearing about some trouble down there involving the lady's late husband. You were mixed up in that, too, I believe."

"Only as the local law," Frank said. "And that's my only interest in the trouble that's going on in Buckskin now. We've got a court case pending, a challenge to Tip Woodford's rights to the Lucky Lizard Mine, and Judge Grampis was supposed to be hearing it. Today, in fact."

Sadler leaned forward, suddenly even more interested.

"I heard what happened to Judge Grampis. A terrible, terrible tragedy. He was a fine, dedicated jurist for many years. It's a shame he had to run into those stagecoach robbers."

"That was no accident," Frank said.

The governor's bushy eyebrows rose. "What are you implying, Mr. Morgan?"

"I'm not implying anything, sir. I'm flat-out telling

you that Judge Grampis was murdered. Those owlhoots who stopped the stage were sent to get rid of him. The so-called robbery was just to make it look like the judge wasn't killed deliberately."

Sadler sat back to ponder what Frank had just told him. After a moment, he said, "That's a rather startling theory. Do you have any proof that it's true?"

Frank shook his head. "No, sir, not yet."

"Do you have any idea who would want the judge dead?"

"A man named Dex Brighton. He's the one who's challenging Woodford's ownership of the Lucky Lizard."

"I don't understand," Sadler said. "If the date for the trial was imminent, why would this man Brighton want anything to happen to Judge Grampis? That will just delay the legal disposition of the case."

"Exactly," Frank said. "Brighton has been pushing Woodford to accept a settlement offer. He's been doing that ever since he came to Buckskin, based on a document he claims that he has . . . a document that nobody except Brighton has ever actually seen."

"Ah!" Sadler said in sudden understanding. "You believe that Brighton has no real case, and if the trial actually takes place, that fact will be revealed. In other words, he's just a cheap crook trying to bully his way into someone else's hard work and good fortune."

"That's about the size of it," Frank said.

"But again, you have no proof."

"Not a bit, so far. All I have to go by is what my instincts tell me."

"I'm sure the instincts of a man such as yourself are quite reliable, Mr. Morgan, but . . ." Sadler spread his hands. "In the absence of any real evidence, I don't see how I can help you. This is not really a matter for the governor's office anyway."

"There's one thing you can do," Frank said. "I reckon the truth will come out at the trial. So if you appoint another judge right away to take Judge Grampis's place, and sent the fella back to Buckskin with me, we can bring the case to trial in a day or two, rather than the weeks or more that Brighton is probably counting on."

Sadler tugged at his beard and frowned again. "What you say makes sense, Mr. Morgan," he admitted. "If Brighton is truly a fraud, he wouldn't want the case to come to trial. But if he's telling the truth and can prove it, then rushing another judge to Buckskin will only hasten the legal defeat of Mr. Woodford . . . who, I take it, is a friend of yours."

Frank nodded. "Yes, Tip and I are friends. I wouldn't ever deny it. But he'll have to take his chances in court, and he knows it. I'll enforce whatever the judge decides, and Tip knows that, too. I just want him to get a fair shake and not be buffaloed into giving up something that's rightfully his."

Sadler took a cigar from a humidor on his desk, said, "You're sure you don't want one?" then lit it after Frank shook his head. The governor puffed a couple of times on the cigar, then said, "This is quite an interesting situation. *My* instincts say that you're probably right about Brighton, Marshal. I figure that given your history, you must be a pretty shrewd judge of character."

Frank didn't say anything to that, just waited for Sadler to go on.

"I'll have to appoint a replacement for Judge

Grampis, of course. I started thinking about that as soon as I heard what happened to him. I wasn't really planning on doing it right away, though."

"The longer you wait, the more it plays into Brighton's hands."

"Yes, I suspect you're right. I can't simply snap my fingers, though, and produce an acceptable candidate for the job. I have to sift through the possibilities and consider each one carefully—"

"Begging your pardon, Governor," Frank cut in, "but if you can find a fella who knows the law, can get around under his own power, and isn't drunk by ten o'clock in the morning every day, I reckon he'll do. One of my lawyers is representing Tip Woodford, and I reckon he'll knock down Brighton's case without much trouble."

"Confident, aren't you, sir?"

"I've never seen a reason to be any other way, sir," Frank said.

Sadler grunted. "As a matter of fact, I agree with you. Man's got to believe in himself before anybody else will." He shifted the cigar in his mouth, placed both hands flat on the desk, and concentrated for a moment. Then he plucked the cigar from his lips and said, "I have a man in mind. I'll see if I can locate him this afternoon. If he's agreeable to taking the job, you'll escort him to Buckskin personally?"

"We'll start first thing in the morning," Frank declared. "Make it there tomorrow evening, if we can, and hold the trial the next day."

"You don't believe in wasting any time, do you, Mr. Morgan?"

"Not when all hell keeps trying to break loose in my town," Frank said.

* * *

The governor saw to it that Frank had a room at the best hotel in town. After arranging for Stormy and Dog to be taken care of at a nearby livery stable, Frank took advantage of the opportunity to clean up and have a good meal.

His impatience grew stronger as the afternoon went on, and he was about to start back to the capitol building on his own when a messenger arrived from Reinhold Sadler, summoning him to the governor's office.

Another man was there with Sadler when Frank strode in. This second individual was shorter than the governor and had a fringe of graying red hair around a mostly bald head. He was clean-shaven and wore a rather belligerent expression on his face. His hands were clasped together behind his back, and he kept them there as he and Sadler turned to face Frank.

"There you are, Morgan," the governor said. "Meet Judge Cecil Caldwell."

The judge didn't offer to shake hands. He just gave Frank a curt nod instead and said, "Morgan. Gunfighter, eh? I've heard of you."

"I'm here as the marshal of Buckskin," Frank snapped. He didn't cotton much to this fella. Of course, he didn't *have* to like the judge who took Grampis's place. All that mattered was that the man be willing to go to Buckskin and render a fair, legal decision in the case between Tip Woodford and Dex Brighton.

And be willing to risk a bushwhack attempt or two along the way as well, Frank thought.

"We've got trouble brewing there," he went on, "and it's not going to settle down until a trial establishes who really owns the Lucky Lizard Mine. You see, this fella Brighton showed up and claimed—"

Caldwell jerked a hand from behind his back and held it up, palm toward Frank.

"Please don't say any more. I'll hear arguments from the attorneys in the case and testimony from any witnesses they may call, and whatever information comes out in those judicial proceedings will be the sole basis for any decision I render. As a lawman and an officer of the court, Morgan, you should know better than to try to prejudice a case before it comes to trial."

Frank glanced at Sadler, who chuckled.

"He wouldn't let me tell him anything about it either Marshal. Judge Caldwell has a very strict idea of judicial impartiality."

"There's nothing strict about it," Caldwell snapped. "A judge is either impartial or he isn't. The law doesn't deal in shades of gray."

Frank wasn't convinced that was completely true all the time, but he didn't argue the point with Caldwell. Instead, he said, "You're going to be taking Judge Grampis's place, Your Honor?"

"That's right. Governor Sadler told me you plan to return to Buckskin tomorrow."

"First thing," Frank said with a nod. "If we don't run into any trouble, we can make the ride in a day. Especially if you can travel by horseback, rather than in a buggy or something like that."

"I'm an excellent rider. I'll be ready to depart at first light."

That took Frank a little by surprise. Caldwell

might be an unfriendly cuss, but at least he was being cooperative.

"I know you don't want to hear anything about the case, Judge, but I have to tell you . . . there's a chance we'll run into some hombres who don't want you to make it to Buckskin alive. The same fellas would be just as happy to see me dead, too."

Caldwell nodded. "I appreciate the warning, Morgan. But I'm not going to let the possibility of danger stand in the way of dispensing justice."

"Well, then, we're in agreement, Your Honor, because I don't plan on doing that either."

Caldwell turned to Sadler and said, "Thank you for this opportunity, Governor. I'll do my best to live up to the honor."

"I'm sure you will, Judge," Sadler said. He didn't look surprised when Caldwell didn't offer to shake hands with *him* either, before stalking out of the office.

Frank watched him go, then waited until the door of the outer office had closed, too, before saying, "No offense, Governor, but that hombre's about as cold-blooded as a snake."

Sadler laughed. "You said you wanted somebody who knew the law and wasn't drunk by ten o'clock in the morning, Marshal. Cecil Caldwell qualifies on both of those counts. I don't think I've ever seen the man take a drink, and his record as a county judge is exemplary. He would have been appointed to the state circuit court before now except for one thing . . . He's one of the most thoroughly unpleasant individuals you'll ever meet."

"Yeah, I got that idea," Frank said with a shake of

his head. "But if he's honest and doesn't mind taking a chance, that's all I care about right now, I reckon."

A look of concern came over Sadler's beefy face. "You really think there's a chance Brighton's men will try to kill both of you to keep you from reaching Buckskin?"

"Governor," Frank said, "I reckon you can count on it."

Chapter 24

Luther wasn't quite sure where he was when he woke up. At first he thought he was in his hotel room, but then he recalled the shots shattering the window and the flames leaping and dancing around him. The attempt on his life came back to him with crystal clarity, shocking him so much that he tried to sit up without thinking about it.

The pain in his side and the bandages wrapped tightly around his midsection stopped him. His head fell back against the pillow. He lay there trying to piece together everything that had happened.

The bright sun shining around the curtains over the window told him that it was morning now, instead of night. Unless, of course, he had slept the clock around and it was late afternoon instead. Without knowing where he was, he couldn't orient himself as to east and west. All he knew for certain was that his arm ached, his side hurt, and he was lying in a reasonably comfortable bed on starched sheets.

"Ah, you're awake," a voice said.

Luther blinked his eyes and turned his head. He

saw a slender, brown-haired young man coming through an open doorway. After a second Luther recalled the man's identity—Dr. William Garland.

"How are you feeling this morning, Mr. Turnbuckle?" Garland asked.

For a moment, in his confusion, Luther had forgotten all about the masquerade he was carrying out. The doctor calling him Turnbuckle brought it all back to him . . . the train robber who shot the real Claudius Turnbuckle, Luther's arrival in Buckskin and the spur-of-the-moment deception he had carried out, Dex Brighton's claim on the Lucky Lizard Mine, Diana Woodford—especially Diana Woodford!—and the previous attempt on his life and the life of Frank Morgan . . . All of that and more crowded into Luther's brain and threatened to push his sanity out.

"What . . . what happened?" he managed to say. He figured it wouldn't hurt to see if Dr. Garland's version of the story jibed with his. At this moment, Luther doubted his own memories. "Where am I?"

"In one of the rooms in my house," Garland answered. "I thought it would be a good idea to keep you here overnight at least, because of the amount of blood you lost when you were stabbed." The doctor smiled. "Which brings us to your other question. You were attacked last night, Mr. Turnbuckle. Someone shot at you in your hotel room and wound up setting the place on fire when one of the bullets broke a lamp. Then—and this is only a theory, but I think it's a reasonable one—while you and all the other guests were trying to get out of the hotel, an assassin came up behind you and tried to stick a knife in your back. Luckily for you, he missed, at least to a certain extent, and succeeded only in inflicting a nasty cut on your side. It's now the next morning, and you're up to date."

Luther licked his lips and nodded. His own memories ended with the fire in the hotel and the mad dash to get out of the place. He vaguely recalled pain and blood, but he hadn't known that he'd been stabbed. Now the pain in his side and the bandages wrapped around his torso made sense.

Something else came back to him, and the memory brought with it an urgency that made him try to sit up again. He gasped with the effort and said, "I . . . I had some papers . . ."

Garland sprang to his side. "You need to take it easy, Mr. Turnbuckle. Lie back there . . . Are you talking about the papers that were stuffed in your sling when Mr. Woodford and Deputy Noonan brought you here?"

Luther nodded. "Do you have them?"

"They're right here." Garland stepped over to a chest of drawers and patted a stack of documents lying on top of it. "Some of them are a little burned around the edges, but they don't appear to be harmed otherwise."

"Did you . . . read them?"

"No. I could tell they were some sort of legal business and none of my affair. But even if I had, you could count on my discretion, Mr. Turnbuckle. Doctors are privy to all sorts of secrets, and it's part of our oath to keep them confidential."

Luther closed his eyes and let his breath out in a sigh of relief. He had risked his life to keep those papers from burning.

"Do you feel like eating something?" Garland asked.

Luther opened his eyes. "Now that you mention it, Doctor, I am rather hungry. Would it be all right for me to eat?"

"Of course. You need to keep your strength up. I'll bring you some food and some hot coffee. In the meantime, Catamount Jack wanted to know when you woke up, so I'll see if I can find a boy to run down to the marshal's office and tell him."

"Marshal Morgan's not back from Carson City yet?" Luther asked. Then, before Garland could answer, he muttered a reply to his own question. "No, of course he wouldn't be. There hasn't been enough time for that."

"No, I wouldn't think so," Garland agreed. "I'll be right back with some breakfast for you."

A few minutes later, the doctor returned with a tray containing a couple of biscuits, a bowl of soup, and a cup of coffee. He helped Luther sit up in bed with several pillows propped behind him and then placed the tray on his lap.

"Can you manage? My nurse isn't here today, and I have to get ready to see some other patients."

Luther nodded. "I'm sure I'll be fine."

He was able to use his wounded arm enough to balance the tray with it, and he could feed himself with his other hand without any trouble. Garland left the room, closing the door behind him.

The coffee was strong and bracing and made Luther feel better almost right away. The food helped, too, although he didn't rush it, fearing that his stomach might rebel if he tried to eat too fast. He was almost finished eating when the door opened again. Luther looked up, expecting to see either Dr. Garland or Catamount Jack, but instead he was surprised when Colonel Desmond O'Hara walked into the room.

The Chicago lawyer looked as urbane as ever and gave Luther a smile as he approached the bed. "Good morning, Counselor," he said. "I'm glad to see that you don't look too worse for your ordeal last night."

Luther didn't bother trying to sound gracious. "What are you doing here, O'Hara?"

"Tut, tut, Counselor, just because we're on opposite sides of a case doesn't mean that we have to be enemies. I heard about what happened and wanted to be sure you were all right. The doctor was busy with other patients and told me it would be all right for me to step back here and see you. Can't an attorney inquire as to the health of opposing counsel without worrying about such things as legal improprieties?"

"I didn't say anything about legal improprieties," Luther said. "And as for us being enemies, how can we be anything else when you're working for the man responsible for my injuries?"

O'Hara's smooth smile went away and was replaced by a frown. "If you made such a comment in public, it would be actionable," he said. "Mr. Brighton had nothing to do with what happened to you, and I would advise you *not* to repeat that statement if you don't want to find yourself facing a lawsuit for libel."

"Don't you mean slander?"

O'Hara waved that off. "Yes, yes, of course. The sheer audacity of it confused me for a moment. Slander, libel, whatever you want to call it, the idea that my client had anything to do with what happened to you is a damnable lie!"

"We'll see," Luther said. "We'll just see about that."

O'Hara's face hardened even more. "Speaking of damnable lies, Counselor," he said, "perhaps it's time we discussed the one that *you've* perpetrated."

"I don't know what you're talking about," Luther shot back with what he hoped was confidence, but at the same time, an icy sliver of fear struck deep within him.

"I think you do," O'Hara said, and the smug look on his face indicated real confidence. "I'm talking about the lie that you're a real lawyer."

With a supreme effort of will, Luther told himself that he had to brazen this out. No other course of action was open to him. "You're mad, Colonel!" he blustered. "Of course I'm a real lawyer. Haven't you ever heard of Turnbuckle and Stafford? We're one of the top legal firms in San Francisco!"

"I don't doubt that for a moment," O'Hara replied, smiling brazenly again now. "But you, sir, are *not* Claudius Turnbuckle."

"How . . . how did . . ."

The stunned words escaped from Luther's mouth before he could stop them, and they were followed by a triumphant look that appeared on O'Hara's face. Had it been a mere guess on the colonel's part? That was impossible. He had no reason to suspect such a thing. He had to have *known* somehow.

"I don't know who you are, but the real Claudius Turnbuckle is considerably older than you," O'Hara said. "Even allowing for the fact that you might not be as young as you appear to be, it's simply not possible for you to have been trying cases for as long as Turnbuckle has. I sent a wire from Carson City when I arrived there, prior to coming to Buckskin, asking an acquaintance of mine in San Francisco to find out as much as he could about the man who would be opposing me in court. The answer arrived on the stagecoach a couple of days ago, and I've been keeping it to myself for the time being, while I pondered what to do about it."

Luther recalled the old saying about desperate times calling for desperate measures. "I *am* Claudius Turnbuckle," he insisted. "Claudius Turnbuckle, Junior. I . . . I set out to prove to my father that I'm just as good a lawyer as he is."

That was a plausible story, Luther thought, and if it came out it wouldn't totally destroy him in the eyes of Frank Morgan, Tip Woodford, and most importantly, Diana Woodford.

But O'Hara was already shaking his head.

"That won't wash. Claudius Turnbuckle is an old bachelor. He's never been married."

"A . . . a man doesn't have to be married to . . . to have a son . . ."

"So now you're claiming to be Turnbuckle's woodscolt? That's absurd and you know it." O'Hara stepped closer to the bed and lowered his voice. "Who are you really? A confidence man? What do you hope to gain by impersonating Turnbuckle and fooling Woodford and Morgan?"

For a second, Luther felt like throwing the tray in O'Hara's face. Maybe that would knock the insufferable grin off the man's lips. But even if it did, that was all it would accomplish, and Luther knew it. He closed his eyes and groaned.

"Wait a minute," O'Hara said. "You're not trying to swindle them, are you? You actually want to win the case. And you seem to have some legal training . . . I've got it! You're either one of Turnbuckle's clerks, or a young associate for his firm. I don't know what you're doing here in his place or why you're trying to make everyone think that you're Claudius Turn-buckle, but that would explain why you know as much about what's going on as you do."

The colonel was shrewd; Luther had to give him credit for that much. With very little information to go on, he had cut right to the heart of the matter.

Luther wasn't going to admit anything, though. He said in a weak voice, "Get out of here. Leave right now or I'll call the doctor and tell him to send for the authorities."

O'Hara actually chortled. "I daresay that's the *last* thing you want to do, Counselor . . . and I use the term loosely. I have more reason to talk to the authorities than you do. You're perpetrating a fraud. You're the criminal, sir, not me . . . and that's exactly what I'm going to tell everyone in this town—unless you do as I say."

The boldness of it took Luther's breath away. Not only had O'Hara penetrated his masquerade, but now the man was trying to use it against him. Blackmail!

"What is it you want?" Luther asked in a voice that was barely above a whisper. "Do you want me to leave town? I can't. I can't abandon the case."

"I'm not asking you to do that. I'm merely asking you to see to it that my client emerges victorious in court."

"You mean throw the case?"

O'Hara shook his head. "At the trial, when Mr.

Brighton produces the document that proves his claim to the Lucky Lizard, you simply concede that it's authentic."

"But then the judge would have no choice but to hand over the mine to him!"

"Exactly. Justice would be served, without any more fuss and bother."

"Tip Woodford would be left with nothing."

"Less than nothing actually, since Mr. Brighton plans to ask for a share of the profits Mr. Woodford derived illegally from the mine. I warned you, Counselor." O'Hara laughed. "I suppose I'll just have to continue calling you that, since I don't know your real name."

Luther summoned up his courage, what there was of it, and asked, "What if I fight? What if I win the case?"

"Then the verdict will be thrown out immediately when I reveal your impersonation, along with the fact that you have no right to practice law. You'll be ruined in the eyes of all these good people, and I'd say there's a good chance you'll be arrested yourself." O'Hara reached down and patted Luther's foot through the sheet. "Think about it. I'm sure you'll see that there's only one thing you can do. Play along with me and at least you can leave town without winding up behind bars. You can go back to wherever you came from, and no one here will ever know the truth about you."

"I . . . I don't have any choice, do I?"

Luther hated himself as soon as the cowardly words left his mouth. He had no one to blame for this dilemma but himself, though. His own vanity had prompted him to assume Turnbuckle's identity, that and his infatuation with Diana Woodford. Now he was caught in his own snare, and like any animal, he would do whatever he had to do in order to free himself. A wild creature might chew off a limb to escape . . .

All Luther had to do was gnaw away some of his soul.

O'Hara smiled and patted his foot again. "No choice at all, young man, no choice at all. But you're doing the right thing." He turned and went to the door, paused to lift a finger to the brim of his hat. "Good day, Counselor. I'll see you in court."

Luther closed his eyes. His mouth was filled with a sour, bitter taste, and he realized after a moment that it was the taste of defeat.

He wasn't sure how long he lay there, wallowing in misery, before the sound of another footstep made him open his eyes. He saw the grizzled, rangy figure of Catamount Jack coming into the room, battered old hat clasped in one gnarled hand.

"Howdy, Mr. Turnbuckle," the deputy said. "How you feelin' this mornin'?"

"Oh, I'm . . . all right, I suppose."

"You look a mite stronger. You heard that I caught up with the hombre who took them pot-shots at you last night?"

Luther perked up a little as his natural curiosity asserted itself. "No. Who was it?"

"Fella name of Mason. He works as a bartender down at the Top-Notch Saloon." Jack paused. "That's the saloon where Brighton does most of his drinkin', if you get my drift."

Luther understood what the deputy was getting at, all right, and he didn't doubt for a second that

Brighton was the most likely person to be behind that ambush. Brighton had the most to fear from him, the most reason to want him dead.

"Did you arrest the man?" Luther asked. "Will he testify about who hired him?" Maybe there was some hope after all.

Catamount Jack grimaced. "He's dead. Some varmint gunned him from an alley 'fore he could say anything about who hired him. But I got me a hunch Brighton had somethin' to do with *that*, too."

So did Luther. Brighton had a knack for covering his trail. He was every bit as slick and slimy as that lawyer of his.

Luther's breath caught in his throat as a realization suddenly burst on him. If Brighton's case was as strong as O'Hara claimed it was, then why had the lawyer come here this morning to blackmail Luther into losing the case on purpose? O'Hara had asked him to stipulate as to the authenticity of the partnership agreement between Jeremiah Fulton and Chester Brighton. That document was the key to the entire case, and if it really was authentic, why would O'Hara need to blackmail opposing counsel into accepting it?

The partnership agreement was a fake. Frank Morgan had believed that all along, and now Luther knew beyond a shadow of a doubt that Morgan was right. O'Hara's heavy-handed blackmail proved it. Luther was filled with confidence that the trial strategy he had worked out would smash Brighton's claim once and for all.

And in the process, expose him as a liar and a fraud, lay him open to criminal charges, and worst of all, make Diana Woodford hate him forever.

"You want me to go on, Mr. Turnbuckle?" Jack asked. "You look like you ain't feelin' too good."

"When . . . when will Marshal Morgan be back with a new judge?" Luther forced the question out.

"Sometime tomorrow or the next day, I reckon, if they don't run into too much trouble. I'll bet you're anxious for the trial to get started, ain't you?"

Luther managed to nod. "I am feeling a little tired, Deputy. I should probably rest."

"You go right ahead and do that. Either me or Phil Noonan'll be somewheres close around here all the time, so don't you worry none about Brighton. That varmint ain't gonna get another chance to bushwhack you."

It was too late, Luther thought. Brighton didn't need to try anything else as crude as a bullet through a hotel room window or a knife in the back. The weapon that Brighton and O'Hara were using to destroy Luther now was the most unexpected one of all — the truth.

And Luther, for all his legal training, had no idea how to fight it.

Chapter 25

Judge Cecil Caldwell was at the livery stable bright and early the next morning, as he had promised. Frank waited until the judge got there and let Caldwell pick out his own saddle mount. Caldwell claimed to be a good rider, and if nothing else, he proved to be a good judge of horseflesh, selecting a sturdy chestnut gelding with plenty of bottom.

Caldwell wore a gray tweed suit and a dark gray derby. He carried a pair of saddlebags that he slung over the chestnut's back. They appeared to be heavy, and when Frank commented on that, Caldwell said, "Law books, just in case I need to refresh my memory about any of the finer points of the Nevada legal code. Not that I expect such a thing will be necessary. I know it backwards and forwards."

"That's good," Frank said. "Sounds like you're prepared."

"I've had my eye on a circuit judgeship for quite some time. I would have been appointed to it before now if not for influential enemies who conspired to retard my progress."

"Uh-huh," Frank said. He had a feeling that Caldwell was seeing varmints where there weren't any, because the man didn't want to admit it was his own sour nature that had kept him from getting what he wanted. It was human nature for a fella to blame other folks for his own shortcomings.

"It's a shame that Judge Grampis had to die to create an opening that needed to be filled right away," Caldwell went on.

"Yeah, I've heard that he was a good judge," Frank said as he cinched Stormy's saddle.

"One of the finest . . . Good Lord, what's that?"

Caldwell's startled exclamation made Frank glance up. He grinned as he saw Dog padding up the aisle that ran through the center of the livery stable.

"That's Dog," he said.

"It looks more like a wolf, not a dog. In fact, I think you should shoot it just to be sure."

"I didn't say it was *a* dog," Frank pointed out. "Dog's his name. He and I are old friends." He patted Stormy's flank. "The three of us have been trail partners for a long time."

Caldwell frowned in disbelief. "You're saying that's a domesticated canine?"

"Yep."

"Well, keep him away from me. I don't get along well with dogs."

Judging by the way Dog sat down, stared at Caldwell, and snarled a little, the feeling was mutual. Frank suppressed a chuckle and swung up into the saddle.

"Come on, you shaggy varmint."

Caldwell sniffed. "Are you talking to me?"

Frank pointed. "Talking to the dog." He couldn't

resist adding, "I don't reckon anybody's ever going to take you for shaggy, Your Honor."

Caldwell glared as he mounted up. Frank walked Stormy out of the barn. Dog loped out ahead of the two riders as Caldwell followed Frank. They would be on the trail most of the day, Frank reminded himself, and that was if everything went smoothly.

He wasn't looking forward to spending hours in the company of Judge Cecil Caldwell.

As it turned out, things didn't go too badly . . . at least, they didn't once Frank gave up on trying to carry on a conversation with the judge. Caldwell grunted curt, noncommittal answers to every question Frank asked, so after a while Frank stopped asking.

That was all right. The rugged countryside was pretty, with its forests and creeks and mountains, and anyway, Frank was busy watching for signs of trouble. Dog ranged out ahead most of the time, as reliable a scout as if he had been human. Probably more so, Frank thought, since no human possessed such keen senses.

They stopped on the bank of a creek at midday to boil coffee, fry up some bacon, and heat biscuits, while the horses grazed on the lush grass along the stream.

"Sorry if this isn't the sort of fare you're accustomed to, Judge," Frank said.

"It's fine," Caldwell said. "I've never cared all that much about what I eat. Meals are functional, that's all."

Frank felt a mite sorry for anybody who held that opinion, but he didn't say as much, knowing that

Caldwell wouldn't take it kindly. Instead, he asked, "Are you from Nevada, Your Honor?"

"Wisconsin actually. I came out here to practice law back in the seventies."

That was about the most responsive answer Frank had gotten from the man all day, so he pushed his luck a little.

"What brought you to Nevada, instead of staying in Wisconsin?"

Caldwell sipped his coffee, and for a moment Frank thought that the conversation had come to an abrupt end.

Then Caldwell said, "My father was a judge. He cast a rather large shadow. I thought my own career might flourish better elsewhere. As it turns out, I was correct."

Frank understood that. Some men had no desire to follow in their father's footsteps.

Caldwell surprised him by saying, "What about you, Morgan? What led you into a life as a wandering gunman?"

Frank took a sip of his coffee as he pondered the judge's question.

"Some folks would say fate," he finally answered. "When I came back to Texas after the war, I figured I wouldn't ever do anything except work as a cowboy. But then there was a fracas and a fella drew on me, and I wasn't going to stand there and let him shoot me. I slapped leather, too." Frank shrugged. "It didn't take long for word to get around that I was pretty fast with a gun. The more people knew about it, the more trouble dogged my heels. I figured it would be best to move on. I didn't want to bring anything bad down on my friends and family."

The fact that Mercy's father hated him had something to do with his decision, too. Mercy . . . his first love . . . married for years now to another man, a good man, and happily married to boot. To this day, he didn't know whether Mercy's beautiful daughter Victoria was actually his child, too, although he suspected that was the case.

There was no doubt, however, that Victoria's legs were useless because of the bullet that had shattered her spine. A bullet meant for Frank Morgan. Victoria would spend the rest of her life in a wheelchair because Frank had come home to Texas one time too many. Whether she was his daughter or not, that fact would always haunt him.

Luckily, she had her mother and her husband, Texas Ranger Tyler Beaumont, to look after her, and she was strong-willed enough not to let the fact that she was crippled destroy her life. That strong will was one more indication that Frank was really her father, but in truth, she could have gotten it from her mother, too.

Frank pushed those thoughts out of his mind. They came to him from time to time, like now, but he wasn't the sort to brood about the past. His eyes turned more toward the future.

"You couldn't just refuse to fight those men who challenged you?" Caldwell asked, bringing Frank's thoughts back to this noon camp on the trail between Carson City and Buckskin.

"I tried," Frank said, "but the Good Lord didn't put much back-up in me. When an hombre pushes me, I tend to push right back at him."

"You should have reported them to the law."

Frank felt a surge of irritation at the sanctimonious tone in the judge's voice.

"No offense, Your Honor, but you weren't there. And even if I'd backed down, in the long run it wouldn't have done any good. Sooner or later, one of the men who came after me would've shot me anyway, probably from ambush, and then lied about killing me in a showdown. Too many fellas wanted to be known as the man who killed Frank Morgan. Some of 'em didn't care how they did it either."

"Again, that's a matter for the law. If you're threatened, you let the proper authorities deal with it. Otherwise, we'd have nothing but anarchy out here. Why, every man would have to carry a gun just to protect himself and settle his own disputes! Can you imagine?"

Frank sipped his coffee and tried to figure out whether the judge was serious or not. What Caldwell had just described was exactly the way the frontier had been for many, many years. Those days were just now starting to pass away, probably for good.

Caldwell looked like he meant the question, though, so Frank nodded and said, "Yeah. I can imagine."

And if Brighton's hired killers were lying in wait for them, as Frank suspected they might be, then the judge might be able to imagine it, too, before they reached Buckskin.

If he lived that long.

After their meal, they mounted up and started along the trail again. Caldwell's claim that he was a good rider was true, as far as Frank could see. The judge sat the saddle well and didn't seem to be in any discomfort from the journey.

Around mid-afternoon, Frank reined Stormy to a halt and motioned for Caldwell to stop, too.

"What's wrong?" the judge asked. "The horses shouldn't need to be rested again this soon."

Frank pointed to a dim, narrow trail that led off in a zigzag path up a nearby slope, twisting through the thick growth of pines.

"That's the trail we're going to take."

Caldwell frowned. "That's hardly a trail. We've got a stage road right here that runs straight to Buckskin, I believe."

He gestured toward the ruts that had been cut by the wheels of countless Concords. At least the judge hadn't called it a perfectly good stage road, Frank thought wryly.

"Yeah, that's the main road to Buckskin, all right, but Dex Brighton and his men know that as well as we do. That's why they're liable to be waiting for us somewhere up ahead."

"There you go again, trying to prejudice Mr. Brighton's case before the trial even begins." Caldwell's mouth was a thin, hard line. "I'm going to disregard that statement, Marshal, and proceed along this trail."

"You do that and you'll be riding right into a bushwhacker's bullet, Judge. And it won't matter who paid for it . . . You'll be just as dead either way."

Frank wouldn't have thought it was possible, but Caldwell's back got even stiffer and straighter.

"Are you ordering me to come with you, Marshal?"

"As a matter of fact, Your Honor, I am. The only reason I came to Carson City to fetch a replacement judge was so that I could be sure you got there alive, instead of dead like Judge Grampis."

"You have no legal authority beyond the limits of Buckskin," Caldwell insisted. "You're only the town marshal."

"That's all I was until yesterday." Frank reached into his shirt pocket and pulled out a folded piece of paper. "That was before Governor Sadler appointed me a special deputy working for him, giving me jurisdiction in the entire state."

Caldwell stared at him for a moment before thrusting a hand out.

"Let me see that."

Frank handed over the special commission that Sadler had signed the day before. He hadn't said anything about it until now because he hadn't wanted to make use of it if he didn't have to. Wearing a town marshal's badge was still new enough to him; he wasn't sure he was comfortable with the idea of being a special agent for the governor. If this kept up, next thing he knew he'd be working for the president.

Caldwell unfolded the document and studied it for several minutes, even running a finger over the state seal that had been stamped into the paper. He finally looked up at Frank.

"This appears to be genuine."

"That's because it is."

Caldwell gave the commission back to him. Grudgingly, the judge said, "It seems that I have no choice but to follow your orders, Morgan. Lead on."

Frank put the paper away, then said, "Before we go . . ." He slid a hand into one of his saddlebags and pulled out a spare .45. "Do you know how to handle a gun by any chance, Your Honor?"

Caldwell's face flushed.

"Put that away," he snapped. "Special deputy for the governor or not, you can't make me carry a gun. I stand for law, not lawlessness, and that's what that gun represents."

Frank looked at Caldwell's determined expression and put the gun back in the saddlebag.

"All right," he said. "I reckon I can accept that decision. I just hope you don't regret it before we get to Buckskin, Your Honor."

"I'm already beginning to regret becoming involved in this entire matter. I think you would prefer it if you could just shoot everyone who's opposed to you and your friends."

Frank chuckled. "Well, it'd sure simplify matters if I could."

Caldwell looked appalled, but he didn't say anything else, just fell in behind as Frank pointed Stormy up the game trail that wandered over a mountain and into an adjoining valley. This was just the start of the roundabout route he had planned to take them into the settlement. He hoped that Brighton wouldn't have gunmen posted on every trail leading into Buckskin, but it wouldn't surprise Frank a bit if that turned out to be true.

He had to give the judge credit. Caldwell didn't complain even though the going got considerably rougher over the next hour or so. The trails they followed were so faint in places that Frank relied on Dog to sniff them out. Sometimes, they had to dismount and lead their horses when the slope was too steep up or down or the footing was treacherous. Sometimes, their route took them over ledges that crawled along the side of a cliff with sheer rock above and echoing emptiness below. In other places, they made their way through cuts so deep and narrow, the horses' flanks scraped against the sides and the sky was only a thin blue line hundreds of feet above them. Even though Frank was accustomed to country like this, it had to be a nerve-racking journey for Judge Caldwell.

By late afternoon, Frank judged they were about five miles west of Buckskin. They rode up out of an arroyo and into a relatively flat stretch of land that ran east and west, with the broken land through which they had come to the north and a line of vermilion cliffs jutting up to the south.

Frank pointed toward the cliffs and told Caldwell, "Those run for miles, and there's no way to get a horse up or down them. A man might be able to make it with ropes, but it would be a rough climb." He turned in the saddle and jerked a thumb toward the breaks. "Those badlands are volcanic in origin. Except for that arroyo we followed through them, the rocks are so sharp they'll cut a horse's hooves to ribbons in a few hundred yards. Same with a man's boots. But if we follow this open stretch for a few miles, we'll come out pretty close to Buckskin."

Caldwell was beginning to look a little worn and drawn, as if the long ride was finally starting to catch up to him. But he gave Frank a curt nod and said, "Lead the way, Morgan. I'll be right behind you."

Instead, Frank swung down from the saddle.

"Let's give the horses a breather," he suggested. "There's not much graze here, but they can rest a spell anyway, and so can we."

The men stood in the shade of a scrubby pine and watched as Stormy and the judge's chestnut plucked at the sparse clumps of grass growing from the rocky ground. Dog poked around some bushes about fifty yards away, probably looking for a small animal to chase.

"You think you'll be able to hold the trial tomorrow morning, Your Honor?" Frank asked.

"I don't see why not," Caldwell replied. "From what you've told me, both litigants are represented by capable counsel, and they've had adequate time to prepare their cases. I'll call the court to order at nine o'clock tomorrow morning, and if either party requests a delay, they'll have to show cause why such a delay should be granted. Otherwise, we'll proceed with the trial immediately."

"Sounds good to me," Frank said, "and I'm sure it will to Tip Woodford, too. He's had this hanging over his head for too long already."

"It shouldn't take long to hear the evidence. I expect the trial won't last more than a day or two."

"I hope you're right, Judge." A frown creased Frank's forehead as he watched Dog, who had abandoned his exploration of the brush and now stood stiff-legged, gazing off to the west. "What's got into that critter . . . ?"

Even at this distance, Frank heard the deep-throated growl that suddenly came from the big cur.

"Hit the saddle, Judge!" he snapped as he reached for Stormy's reins. "We've got to get out of here!"

"Blast it, Morgan, what are you—"

Caldwell didn't get to finish his indignant question, because just then a bullet slapped through the air next to him, followed instantly by the crack of a rifle.

Chapter 26

The judge stood there openmouthed for a heartbeat, as if he couldn't believe that he'd just been shot at. Frank hadn't swung up into the saddle yet. He lunged toward Caldwell, grabbed the man's arm, and practically threw him at the chestnut.

"Mount up, Judge!" Frank ordered. "*Now!*"

A bullet struck a nearby rock and screamed off in a ricochet. That sound seemed to penetrate Caldwell's brain and convince him that he was in deadly danger, because he took hold of the reins and began scrambling up onto his horse's back. He missed his first try at the stirrup and almost fell, and Frank bit back a curse as he wondered if he was going to have to help the judge mount.

Caldwell made it on his second try, though, grabbing hold of the saddle horn and awkwardly swinging his leg over the chestnut's back. Two more shots rang out while he was doing that.

Frank pulled his Winchester from the saddle boot while he was mounting up. He hauled Stormy around and looked off toward the west, where four riders were galloping toward him and the judge. The horsemen were about three hundred yards away.

"They should've gotten closer and then opened up on us," Frank called to the judge. He pointed east, toward Buckskin. "Get moving, Your Honor, as fast as you can that way!"

The shots had spooked the chestnut a little. Caldwell fought against the reins and asked, "What are you going to do, Morgan?"

"Try to slow those varmints down a little." Frank jerked his Stetson from his head, leaned over, and slapped the hat against the chestnut's rump. "Go!"

Caldwell went. He didn't have any choice, because the horse underneath him took off in a lunging gallop. The chestnut was heading in the right direction, though, so all Caldwell had to do was hang on and let the horse do the work.

Meanwhile, Frank swung Stormy around and lifted the Winchester to his shoulder, working the lever to jack a cartridge into the chamber as he did so. Stormy was well accustomed to gunfire; the rangy gray stallion didn't budge as Frank cranked off three rounds as fast as he could work the rifle's lever.

The attackers—some more of Brighton's hired gunnies, Frank was sure—were still firing as they gave chase, but the hurricane deck of a racing horse was no place for accuracy. Their bullets either went over Frank's head or well off to the side.

By contrast, Frank's aim was deadly. One of the men was knocked backward out of the saddle as a round fired by The Drifter plowed into his chest. His left foot hung in the stirrup as he tumbled off his mount, and his limp body bounced high off the ground, again and again, as the horse continued its gallop.

Another of Frank's shots had found the mark. A man sagged forward, clutching at a bullet-shattered shoulder, but managed to stay mounted and gradually slowed his horse as it veered off to the side.

That left two of the ambushers, and since they were still more than a couple of hundred yards away, Frank whirled Stormy around and trusted to the stallion's speed and strength to outdistance them. He heeled Stormy into a run, following Judge Caldwell toward Buckskin. Frank saw the judge about fifty yards ahead of him. The chestnut was still running full tilt. Caldwell grasped the reins with one hand and held his derby on with the other.

It didn't take long for Stormy to cut down the gap between Frank and the judge. When Frank glanced over his shoulder, he saw that he had pulled away even more from the pursuers.

He would have to slow down when he caught up with Caldwell, though. It would be touch and go whether or not the judge's horse would be able to outrun those bushwhackers.

Caldwell must have heard the pounding beat of Stormy's hooves on the hard ground, because he looked back to see who was closing in on him. His face was white with fear. Frank waved him on. They couldn't afford to slow down.

Stormy drew even with the judge's horse. Frank gave Caldwell an encouraging nod and pulled back a little on the reins, slowing Stormy so that they wouldn't sweep right on past. He didn't know if the pursuit would continue all the way to Buckskin, and another worry on top of that had occurred to Frank.

The sound of gunshots traveled a long way. If Brighton had other gunmen in the area, they might hear the shooting and start to close in. It was possible that Frank and Caldwell might still be cut off from Buckskin.

A few moments later, Frank saw that he had been right to worry about that. Three riders appeared on the right, angling toward them from the direction of those vermilion cliffs. The men were riding hard on a course to intercept them, and Frank didn't have any doubts about their identity. They were more of Brighton's killers.

"Follow me, Judge!" he shouted over the thundering hoofbeats. He veered Stormy to the left, toward the breaks. They couldn't escape by going through those badlands; it would be suicide to try. The horses would be hobbled and unable to go on before they went a hundred yards.

But maybe they could skirt the edge of that wasteland, Frank told himself. If he and Caldwell could get around the horsebackers coming from the right, it would still be a horse race to the settlement.

Within minutes, Frank knew that the men had too much of an angle on them. He and the judge couldn't avoid the pursuit.

That meant they would have to fight their way through. *He* would have to fight their way through, because Caldwell wasn't carrying a gun.

But this was why he had gone to Carson City to fetch the judge in the first place, he reminded himself. He had fully expected this trouble. Now he had to deal with it.

Frank hauled back on the reins, slowing Stormy. Caldwell and the chestnut shot ahead. Caldwell noticed that Frank was gone and started looking around wildly for him, but by then Frank had Stormy moving up on the other side of the chestnut.

"Over here, Judge!" Frank called. "Keep moving! Head straight along the edge of the breaks when you get to it! I'll give you some cover!"

Caldwell nodded to show that he understood.

From time to time, Frank saw a spurt of dirt and gravel from the ground nearby, an indication that the two men behind them were still shooting. The three closing in from the right had opened up, too; Frank saw spurts of orange muzzle flame from their six-guns. Again, they would have been better off stopping their horses, dismounting, and using their rifles. Frank was grateful for any luck he and Caldwell could get. In this case, the killing frenzy that no doubt gripped the gunmen made them want to charge in and blast their quarry with their revolvers. That was a break for Frank and the judge.

Frank still had his Winchester in his right hand as he used his left to hold the reins. He wasn't trying for accuracy as he thrust the rifle's barrel toward the three bushwhackers on the right and pulled the trigger. He just wanted to come close enough to maybe slow them down a mite.

Then he twirled the Winchester like it was a handgun, using the weapon's own weight and motion to cock the loading lever again. It was a fancy move, the sort of thing that Bill Cody or some other showman might do to impress an audience of Easterners at a Wild West performance, but from time to time it came in handy in real life . . . like now. A man needed a mighty strong wrist to be able to pull off the maneuver. Frank Morgan had what it took.

Since he was grandstanding anyway, he took the reins in his teeth, shifted the Winchester to his left hand, and used his right to draw the Colt on his hip. He guided Stormy with his knees as he fired both weapons, twirling the Winchester with his left hand while the Colt in his right bucked and roared.

It must be spectacular as hell to watch, he thought fleetingly.

More importantly, the hail of lead he was throwing toward the attackers actually had an effect. One of the men threw up his arms in death and slid from the saddle, crashing to the ground. Another lost his gun when one of Frank's slugs smashed his elbow. That left only one man coming from this direction, and suddenly it seemed like he wasn't sure if he wanted to catch Frank and Caldwell or not. He peeled away, still shooting but no longer closing in.

Frank threw a glance over his shoulder. He and the judge were still well ahead of their original pursuers. Hope began to rise in him.

As always, that was a jinx. Puffs of smoke came from a clump of boulders at the edge of the badlands as Judge Caldwell galloped past them. The chestnut stumbled. Frank grated a curse as he saw the horse slow down. The next second, the judge's derby leaped off his head, no doubt plucked from it by a bullet. The chestnut came to a stop, leaving Caldwell an easy target on its back.

Frank holstered his Colt and took the Winchester in both hands again. A few rounds remained in it. He brought the rifle to his shoulder and emptied it into the rocks where more of Brighton's gunmen were hidden. He wanted to make things hot for those gunnies by boucing a lot of hot lead around inside the clump of boulders. They'd be too busy ducking for cover to ventilate the judge.

It must have worked, because no more shots came from the rocks as Frank galloped up to Caldwell. He saw that the chestnut was wounded, but ought to still be able to run. Frank jammed the Winchester back in the saddle boot and leaned over to grab the other horse's reins.

"Come on! We've still got a chance!"

With Frank holding the reins in an iron grip, the chestnut broke into a run again, trailing just behind Stormy. Frank leaned forward over the stallion's neck to make himself a smaller target as gunfire resumed from the rocks. He hoped that Caldwell had enough sense to do the same thing. A glance back told him that the judge was following his example. Bullets sang through the air around them, but they were moving fast again now and none of the slugs found their mark.

The men coming up from behind had cut into the lead while Frank was slowed down, but they were still well back. The chestnut was moving slower now, however, and Frank was no longer confident that he and Caldwell could outdistance the pursuit to Buckskin. The settlement was only a few miles away now, but that distance might as well be a hundred miles, he thought.

His rifle was empty, too, as was the Colt, and he couldn't pause to reload either. Nor could he manage that task on the run, because if he let go of the chestnut's reins, the injured horse would probably stop again. Frank didn't know how long the animal could go on before it collapsed. He hated to ask for such sacrifice from the horse, but he had no choice.

He realized he hadn't seen Dog for a while, and looked around, trying to spot the big cur. At that moment, he heard a faint shriek somewhere behind him, and looked back to see that one of the two men who had been giving chase was now on the ground, trying to defend himself from a shaggy grayish-brown shape with flashing teeth.

Good old Dog! Frank had to grin as he realized that the cur had hung back and let the bushwhackers go past him, then unhorsed one of them with a well-timed leap. The other man stopped and swung his six-gun toward Dog in an attempt to save his partner from having his throat ripped out.

He was too late on both counts. Dog sprang aside as the gun roared, leaving a bloody corpse on the ground behind him. Then he took off after Frank and Caldwell, a gray streak moving too fast for the remaining gunman to draw a bead on him.

Even at a distance, Frank's keen eyes saw enough of that for him to know what was going on. He grinned, and kept Stormy and the chestnut moving as Dog raced after them.

His hope now was that he and Caldwell had successfully run the gauntlet of Brighton's hired killers. More of the gunmen might be in the area, but Buckskin wasn't far away now and the one man who was left on horseback behind them wasn't giving chase anymore. He had abandoned the pursuit, perhaps realizing that he didn't particularly want to catch up anymore, since that would mean facing The Drifter alone.

The chestnut slowed down, and Frank slowed Stormy's pace to match that of the injured horse.

They were moving at a fast trot now, slow enough for Frank to talk to the judge.

"You can see now why I wanted to give you a gun, Your Honor."

"I wouldn't have been able to help, even I had taken the weapon," Caldwell said with a shake of his head. "I've never fired a gun in my life."

"Even some wild shots might have been enough to distract those hombres."

"Yes, and I might have shot *you* by accident, Morgan, or myself."

Frank couldn't argue with that. He just said, "I hope we're past the worst of it now."

Caldwell looked behind them.

"They're not chasing us anymore."

"Nope. We made them pay too high a price for trying to catch us."

Caldwell's mouth quirked in a bitter twist. "You say those men work for Dexter Brighton?"

Frank was a little surprised by the question, after Caldwell's earlier insistence that he not listen to anything against Brighton.

"That's my best guess. I don't have any proof of it, of course. But I don't know of anybody else who would want to stop us from getting to Buckskin."

"I see." Caldwell pulled a handkerchief from his pocket and wiped sweat-streaked dust from his face. "I plan to ask Mr. Brighton about that."

"He'll just deny it," Frank said.

"That's his right."

"Seems to me you're worrying a mite too much about the rights of a man who wants to kill you."

"Somebody has to worry about those rights,"

Caldwell snapped. "Otherwise, sooner or later, no one will have them. That's the rule of law."

Frank shrugged. Caldwell was like a lot of other people; he believed that a fella's rights came from a court, or a piece of paper, instead of his own heart—and his own strong right hand. You couldn't argue with folks like that, but sometimes you could show them the error of their ways.

Caldwell would see for himself when they got to Buckskin.

Chapter 27

Vern Robeson was the first to spot them as they rode into the settlement, just as dusk began to ease down out of the mountains. The hostler came out of Amos Hillman's livery barn carrying a pitchfork. He saw Frank and Judge Caldwell, dropped the pitchfork, and turned to run back inside and tell his boss that the marshal was back.

Hillman came out of the barn as Frank and Caldwell stopped in front of the big structure. A grin creased the liveryman's weathered face.

"Howdy, Frank. Glad to see you made it back from Carson City."

"No gladder than I am to be here, Amos," Frank said. He swung down from the saddle and handed Stormy's reins to Hillman. "The judge's horse got nicked by a bullet along the way. Reckon you can tend to it?"

Hillman ran a hand along the chestnut's blood-streaked flank and grunted.

"I see that. Looks like you fellas ran into some gun trouble."

"More than our share," Frank agreed.

"Well, don't worry about this horse. I'll take good care of it." Hillman looked up at Caldwell. "Need a hand gettin' down, Judge?"

"No, I . . . I'm fine." Caldwell's hands were wrapped around the saddle horn. "It's just that I've been holding on so tightly, for so long, that I'm having a bit of a problem . . . letting go."

He pried his fingers off the saddle horn at last and then climbed down from the chestnut's back. He paused beside the horse and patted its shoulder, taking Frank a little by surprise.

"A gallant mount," Caldwell muttered. He looked at Hillman. "Do your best for her, sir."

"I sure will, Your Honor. I reckon you *are* the judge Frank went to Carson City to fetch back with him?"

"He's the judge, all right," Frank said. "Judge Cecil Caldwell. Your Honor, this is Amos Hillman, owner of this livery stable and one of our town councilmen."

Caldwell gave the liveryman a curt nod, then turned to Frank and said, "If you'd show me the hotel, I'd really like to get a room and rest a bit."

"Sure thing."

Frank shucked the Winchester from the saddle boot. He had reloaded it as they approached the town, along with his Colt, and it felt good to know that he had fifteen rounds in the rifle along with the five in the revolver. As a matter of habit on Frank's part, the Colt's hammer rested on the empty sixth chamber in the cylinder as it rode in its holster. Too many rash hombres who liked to carry a full wheel in their guns had shot their own toes off.

With the rifle held slanted across his chest, Frank accompanied the judge down the street toward the hotel. It seemed unlikely that Brighton would try to kill Caldwell right here in the middle of town, but after all he and the judge had gone through to reach Buckskin, Frank didn't want to lose Caldwell now.

Besides, some of Brighton's men might have already brought word to him that the ambush attempt had failed, and Brighton might be desperate enough to try just about anything to keep that court case from going ahead. Frank was more convinced than ever that the man's claim on the Lucky Lizard was fraudulent and that Brighton had never intended for the case to go to trial. That was just another weapon in his effort to steal the mine from Tip Woodford.

Even though night was falling and the streets of Buckskin weren't as crowded as they were sometimes, enough people were around so that word of Frank's return with the judge spread quickly. Catamount Jack and Phil Noonan came out of the marshal's office and hurried to meet them.

"I'm mighty glad to see you, Frank," Jack greeted him. He looked Caldwell up and down. "This must be the judge."

Frank performed the introductions, then asked, "Everything quiet around here while I was gone?"

Catamount Jack's disgusted snort gave him the answer.

"Not hardly," the deputy said. "You know Mason, works down at the Top-Notch?"

"Yeah."

"Well, he tried to kill Mr. Turnbuckle. Opened up on him with a Winchester from the roof o' Patterson's Hardware Store while Mr. Turnbuckle was in his hotel room."

Frank's eyes widened in surprise at the news.

"Is Turnbuckle all right?"

"Mason wasn't too good a shot. He missed Mr. Turnbuckle, but hit the lamp instead. Set the room on fire and pert near burned the hotel down."

"Good Lord," Frank muttered. "Have you got Mason locked up?"

"Nope." Jack jerked a thumb over his shoulder. "We planted him in Boot Hill this afternoon. I tracked him from the back o' Patterson's store to the Top-Notch and had a showdown with him there. At first he denied tryin' to bushwhack Mr. Turnbuckle, but then he tried to plug me. I figured that was a good enough confession."

"You figured incorrectly, Deputy," Judge Caldwell snapped. "Involvement in an altercation doesn't constitute a legal admission of guilt."

Jack frowned and went on. "Anyway, I let daylight through the skunk, but I didn't kill him. Whoever did that was lurkin' outside the Top-Notch, and he put a bullet in Mason's brain 'fore Mason could say who hired him to kill that lawyer fella. We all know who it was, though."

Caldwell opened his mouth to say something else, then thought better of it, shook his head, and rolled his eyes. Obviously, he thought that he had landed in a place gripped by total anarchy.

"That ain't all, though," Catamount Jack went on.

Frank nodded. "I was afraid you were going to say that. What else happened?"

"While Mr. Turnbuckle and the other folks stayin' in the hotel were tryin' to get away from the fire, somebody come up behind him and stuck a knife in him."

"My God!" Caldwell exclaimed. "Is there a murder attempt every five minutes in this town?"

"No, it just seems that way sometimes," Frank told him. "Go on, Jack. How's Turnbuckle?"

"Healin' up down at Doc Garland's. Turns out he wasn't hurt too bad, just sliced up a mite. He says he'll be ready for the trial, soon as His Honor here gets around to it."

"Trial will convene at nine o'clock sharp tomorrow morning," Caldwell said stiffly. "I can't think of any place that obviously needs some law and order more than this godforsaken town!"

Frank might have taken offense at that, but he was too tired. He said, "Come on, Judge. We'll get you settled at the hotel, if there are any rooms left. Jack, I want you and Phil to take turns standing guard outside the judge's room tonight."

Caldwell started to protest. "I don't think that's really necessary—"

"After everything that's happened, Your Honor, I'd appreciate it if you'd just humor me. I don't want anything to stop that trial from going on tomorrow."

Grudgingly, Caldwell nodded and said, "All right. Is there somewhere I can get something to eat . . . ?"

"Jack, see if Lauren can fix up a tray for the judge and bring it over to the hotel later."

The deputy said, "Sure, Frank. What are you gonna do?"

Frank's hands tightened on the rifle. "I'd like to go have it out with Brighton . . ." He glanced at the judge. "But I reckon I'll let the law handle that. I'll go have a talk with Mr. Turnbuckle instead, let him know that the judge is here and everything's set for tomorrow morning. Judge, if you do what Jack and Phil tell you, you'll be all right, and this whole thing will be over before you know it."

"It can't be too soon to suit me," Caldwell said.

Frank felt the same way. The showdown was coming, one way or another, and it was damned well about time.

Luther Galloway had had an early supper and was propped up in bed, trying to study the notes he had salvaged from his burning hotel room a couple of nights earlier, along with the ones he had made since then. He had written out his opening statement and clutched a pencil in his hand as he revised it, crossing out a word here and there, sometimes substituting another word, sometimes not.

It was an exercise in futility, though, and Luther knew it. No matter how convincing his oratory was, Tip Woodford's case would collapse once Luther buckled under and accepted the authenticity of Brighton's phony claim. With the sword of truth that Colonel O'Hara was holding over his head, there was nothing else he could do.

Weariness was stealing over him along with the despair that was his constant companion now, and he was having a hard time keeping his eyes open. He was suddenly wide awake again, though, as the door of the room opened and Marshal Frank Morgan stepped inside.

Luther sat up straight and said, "Marshal Morgan! You're back. Do you have the judge with you?"

Morgan nodded. "I sure do . . . no thanks to seven

or eight of Brighton's gunhawks who tried to stop us."

"Are you hurt?"

"Nope. Neither is the judge, although I reckon he was shaken up a mite by being shot at." Morgan took his hat off as he came closer to the bed and grinned. "He's not used to having bullets flying around his head like you and me, Counselor."

"I wouldn't say I'm that used to it, and I hope I never am!" Luther replied fervently.

"I hear you were wounded again, by a knife this time . . . after somebody took some potshots at you."

"You must have talked to your deputy. Jack caught the man who tried to kill me. One of the men, I should say. We don't know who cut me as I was leaving the hotel."

"I'll bet you can hazard a guess, though," Morgan said.

"Brighton's going to get his comeuppance in court," Luther said, the angry words coming out of his mouth before he remembered that the case he was going to present was doomed before it ever began. All the evidence he had gathered would go unused and unknown to anyone except him.

And Dex Brighton would win. That was the bitterest pill of all, even more bitter than the disappointment that Woodford and Diana would feel and the humiliation that would follow Luther all the way back to San Francisco. Luther hated Brighton, and the idea of him triumphing was almost intolerable.

Then fight back. Don't let him get away with it.

The voice was an insistent whisper in the back of Luther's brain. It had been nagging him more and more as time passed and the trial approached.

He had what he needed to win. He could destroy Brighton's claim once and for all. But to do so, he would have to expose his own deception.

To get his mind off that depressing subject, he asked, "Who did the governor appoint to replace Judge Grampis?"

"A fella called Cecil Caldwell. Have you ever heard of him?"

"No, but it's unlikely that I would have heard of a Nevada judge, since I've always practiced law in California."

How easily the lies came now. Ever since arriving in Buckskin, Luther had told one falsehood after another . . . and these people had believed him. They had put their faith in him to make sure that justice was served and Tip Woodford's claim to the Lucky Lizard was protected.

They had done more than believe him. They had believed *in* him.

And he was going to let them down, in the most devastating fashion possible. That knowledge wrenched at Luther's heart.

The pain he felt inside must have been evident on his face, too, because Frank Morgan suddenly frowned and asked, "Are you all right, Luther? For a second there you looked like somebody stepped on your grave."

"No, I . . . I'm fine," Luther said. "Just weak from losing so much blood, the doctor says, and the shock of being wounded again. From time to time I have a . . . dizzy spell."

"I'd say you've earned it. You'll be ready for the trial tomorrow, though, won't you? Judge Caldwell intends to call the court to order at nine o'clock sharp."

"I'll be ready," Luther promised. Another lie. He would never be prepared for what was going to happen tomorrow. "Where did you say that court is usually held?"

"In the Silver Baron. That's the only place in town with a room big enough. Maybe one of these days Buckskin will have a real courthouse."

Luther frowned. "Colonel O'Hara is likely to object to the trial being held in a building owned by the defendant. He might ask for a change of venue."

"I don't think he'll get it. Judge Caldwell is eager to get this over with."

"So am I," Luther said, and for once it was the truth. Like getting a bad tooth pulled, maybe it would be better if he suffered through this without delay. What was that old saying about a brave man dying but one death, while a coward dies a thousand times?

Luther knew all too well which category he fit into.

"I've got Jack and Phil Noonan guarding the judge tonight," Morgan went on. "I think I'll stay here, as long as it's all right with Dr. Garland, and make sure that Brighton doesn't try one more time to get rid of you."

"Do you really think that's necessary?"

"I don't know, but I'm not going to take the chance. After everything that's happened, I don't want anything to interfere with that trial. It's time to end this."

It was going to be the end, all right, Luther thought. The end of the case, the end of Tip Woodford's hopes and dreams, the end of Luther's masquerade, the end of any respect and affection that Diana might have for him . . .

"You go ahead with your work," Morgan told him. "I'll be right outside if you need me."

"Thank you, Frank. You've been a stalwart throughout this entire affair. But tomorrow . . . when the judge calls the court to order . . . then it's my turn."

Morgan rested a hand on Luther's shoulder.

"We all know you won't let us down, Claudius," he said.

Chapter 28

"This court is now in session!"

Those words had different effects on everyone in the Silver Baron Saloon as Judge Caldwell's gavel came down with a sharp bang to punctuate them. Frank Morgan assumed that was true anyway. He knew that in his case, he was just glad that the trial was finally under way. He hoped it would work out in Tip's favor, but either way, it was time to settle things.

The poker tables and most of the other tables had been moved into the back of the room, except for a couple that would be used by the lawyers and their clients, and the chairs where the cardplayers and drinkers usually sat were now lined up in neat, orderly rows facing the longer table where Caldwell sat. A sheet had been draped over the big painting of a rather plump nude that hung behind the bar. There was only so much decorum you could achieve in a saloon that was doubling as a courtroom, but having a naked gal and a bunch of cavorting nymphs watching the proceedings would just make it more difficult.

A few minutes earlier, Frank had served as bailiff,

calling out, "All rise!" as Judge Caldwell came in through the door at the end of the bar that led into the office. Now, from his post at the side of the room, Frank looked around at the people who were lowering themselves into chairs in response to the judge's order to be seated.

Tip Woodford looked tense and worried. He had a lot riding on this. So did Dex Brighton, and he looked just about as nervous as Tip did, Frank decided. So did Colonel O'Hara. Frank had been watching O'Hara and Brighton talking in low tones at one of the tables before Judge Caldwell came in, and he knew neither man was happy that things had come to this point. Frank was more convinced than ever that Brighton didn't want a trial, had never really wanted a trial.

But he was about to get one anyway.

The makeshift courtroom was packed with spectators. All the chairs were full, and men stood behind the chairs and crowded around the batwings. Catamount Jack had posted himself at the entrance, his arms crossed over his chest and a scowl on his face, to keep anybody else from trying to crowd in. The boardwalk was full of men peering through the windows, too.

Only two women were in the room. One was Frank's daughter-in-law, Rebel, who sat with her husband, Conrad Browning, both of them taking an intense interest in what was going on. The other was Diana Woodford, who occupied a chair behind the table where her father and Claudius Turnbuckle were seated. She looked worried, too, but she mustered up an encouraging smile when Turnbuckle turned and glanced back at her.

The most nervous-looking man in the room, Frank decided, was Claudius Turnbuckle himself. Large beads of sweat dotted his pale, drawn face. Maybe that was from the strain of the wounds he had suffered, but Frank didn't think so. It was more than that. Turnbuckle looked like a man who was scared to death.

Like a lawyer who was about to try his first case.

Frank frowned as he wondered where that thought had come from. Claudius Turnbuckle had plenty of experience; he was one of the top lawyers in San Francisco. Frank had trusted a lot of his business affairs to Turnbuckle and Stafford for several years now, and he was satisfied with the job they'd done. Turnbuckle wasn't accustomed to practicing in such rough surroundings, though. That had to be it.

Judge Caldwell cleared his throat and picked up some papers he had brought with him to the table.

"I've read the briefs submitted to the court by both parties," he said. "Colonel O'Hara, do you have an opening statement?"

O'Hara came to his feet.

"I do, Your Honor, if it please the court."

Caldwell nodded and said, "Proceed."

O'Hara hooked his thumbs in his vest in what had to be a practiced move, and began striding back and forth in front of the table where Caldwell sat as he proclaimed in a loud, clear voice, "Your Honor, this is a simple matter, little more than a mere misunderstanding. There is no good or evil here, only a cloud of misperceptions and hard feelings that must be dispersed in order to shine the light of truth and justice on the proceedings. My client, Mr. Dexter Brighton, is the true and legal owner of the mine known as the Lucky Lizard, but he bears no ill will toward Mr. Thomas Woodford, who holds the sincere but incorrect belief that *he* owns the Lucky Lizard and the silver it produces. Because of Mr. Woodford's sincerity and the mitigating circumstances under which he mistakenly believes that he acquired the rights to the Lucky Lizard, Mr. Brighton has attempted on numerous occasions to reach an accord with Mr. Woodford, an agreement that would divide the disputed property equitably. Mr. Woodford has refused these generous attempts at graciousness on the part of my client . . . and so we find ourselves in court, come here to settle the matter in the fashion of all true Americans who believe in the rule of law!"

The fella sure could talk, Frank thought . . . and not say much except a pack of lies.

"But make no mistake about it, Your Honor," O'Hara continued, "the facts of the case are on our side, as we shall demonstrate. Although Mr. Woodford had no way of knowing otherwise at the time, the deal he made to buy the Lucky Lizard was illegal, because the individual from which he purchased it had no right to dispose of the property in that manner. Therefore the sale is null and void, and as the only surviving descendant of the original partnership between Jeremiah Fulton and Chester Brighton, my client, Dexter Brighton, is, as I said, the true and legal owner of the Lucky Lizard Mine." O'Hara stopped and bowed slightly from the waist. "That's all, Your Honor."

Caldwell nodded and said, "Thank you, Colonel." He turned his head toward the table where Tip Woodford and Claudius Turnbuckle sat. "Mr. Turnbuckle? Do you have an opening statement?"

Looking like he had the weight of the world on his shoulders, the young attorney rose to his feet. He had to clear his throat a couple of times before he was able to say, "Yes . . . yes, Your Honor, I do."

The judge nodded gravely. "Proceed."

Instead of stalking back and forth like a caged mountain lion, Turnbuckle stayed where he was behind the table, as if his feet were rooted to the floor. The fingertips of his right hand rested on the table in front of him; his left arm was still in the black silk sling. The bandages wound around his midsection where the knife had wounded him made him stand stiff and straight.

"Your Honor, opposing counsel speaks of a misunderstanding. He speaks of misperceptions. There is no misunderstanding in this case. There are no misperceptions. But I agree with the colonel when he says that this is a simple case. It is very simple. That man—"

Turnbuckle swung toward the other table and flung out his right hand, the index finger pointing directly at Dex Brighton.

"That man is trying to steal the Lucky Lizard Mine!"

Luther had easily adapted his opening remarks to counter those made by Colonel O'Hara. That was something he had learned from the real Claudius Turnbuckle, to take advantage of whatever openings opposing counsel gave you. Now, as a buzz of startled conversation swept through the makeshift courtroom in response to his deliberately dramatic gesture, he felt a surge of confidence.

He could do this. Despite his lack of experience, he could win this case if he wanted to.

If he dared.

Judge Caldwell cracked the gavel on the table and said, "Order! Quiet down, you people!" As the hubbub died away, he pointed the gavel at Luther. "Proceed, Counselor, but remember . . . despite the surroundings, this isn't an opera house. There's no need for melodrama."

"Yes, Your Honor. I apologize to the court."

Caldwell sniffed and motioned for him to go on.

Luther didn't pause to think about the threats O'Hara had made. He plunged ahead, ignoring the icy, hate-filled stare that Dex Brighton gave him.

"Ever since Mr. Brighton has arrived in Buckskin, he has been making unsubstantiated claims and trying to pressure my client, Mr. Thomas Woodford, into signing away that which is rightfully his."

O'Hara shot to his feet.

"Whether or not Mr. Brighton's claims are unsubstantiated is what these proceedings will decide, Your Honor," he said. "I move that Mr. Turnbuckle's prejudicial characterization be stricken."

"He's making an opening statement, Counselor," Caldwell said. "This is when he gets to be prejudicial . . . within reason. Sit down."

O'Hara inclined his head in acceptance of the judge's ruling and sat down.

"As I was saying, Your Honor," Luther continued, "we will prove that my client is the rightful owner of the Lucky Lizard Mine and that Mr. Brighton's claims are false. It is indeed as simple as that. Thank you."

"Very well." Caldwell looked at O'Hara, who

was rising to his feet again. "Call your first witness, Counselor."

"I have only one, Your Honor," O'Hara proclaimed. "I call my client, Dexter Brighton."

Brighton stood up, cast a quick, hostile glance toward the table where Luther and Tip Woodford sat, and then walked over to the chair at the end of the judge's table. Frank Morgan stepped forward with a Bible, and Brighton was sworn in, promising to tell the truth, the whole truth, and nothing but the truth.

His testimony would really be far from that, Luther knew.

O'Hara asked only a few questions, allowing Brighton's testimony to fill in the background: the partnership between Jeremiah Fulton and Chester Brighton, Dex Brighton's father, and the agreement they had made to sell out only to each other.

"And where was your father, sir, when Mr. Fulton carried out his fraudulent sale of the mining claim now known as the Lucky Lizard to Mr. Thomas Woodford?"

Luther stood up and said, "Objection, Your Honor. As opposing counsel pointed out earlier, we're here to determine what's fraudulent and what's not . . . and he's questioning a witness now, not making an opening statement."

"Quite right, Counselor," Caldwell said. "The objection is sustained."

O'Hara smiled slightly, as if having the ruling go against him didn't bother him at all.

"Very well, Your Honor, I'll rephrase the question." O'Hara turned to Brighton again. "Where was your father when Jeremiah Fulton sold the mining claim to Thomas Woodford?"

"They had parted company temporarily," Brighton said. "My father was in poor health and had returned to the East to recuperate while Fulton continued prospecting. But the partnership was never dissolved. I have the original agreement, written and signed by Jeremiah Fulton himself, to prove that. My father gave it to me before he died and asked me to reclaim what was rightfully his. Rightfully mine now, of course, since my father has passed on."

"What, exactly, does this agreement stipulate?"

"That each of the partners could only sell his interest to the other, and that if either of them died, his interest would go to the other partner."

"And when did Jeremiah Fulton pass on?"

"January 22nd, 1882," Brighton said.

"Do you have proof of that?"

Brighton nodded. "A copy of the death certificate from Ford County, Kansas, where he died."

"What about your father?"

Brighton said, "My father died on July 17th, 1894, in Pennsylvania. I have a copy of that death certificate, too."

"Therefore, when Jeremiah Fulton died in 1882, his interest in the mining claim was inherited by your father, and then in turn that interest became yours upon your father's passing?"

"That's correct."

O'Hara turned to look over at Luther, and he couldn't keep from smirking for a second. Luther saw the look and knew why it was there. O'Hara believed that the case was almost wrapped up now. Only one thing remained.

"Do you have the documents in question with you today, Mr. Brighton?"

"I do." Brighton reached inside his coat and took out a small bundle of papers. He held them out toward O'Hara, who took them and placed them on the table in front of Judge Caldwell.

"I'd like to enter these documents in evidence, Your Honor," O'Hara said. "If you'll examine them, you'll see that they are exactly as my client has described, two death certificates giving the dates of death for his father and Jeremiah Fulton, and the original partnership agreement between the two men."

Luther stood up and moved around the end of the table.

"I'd like to examine those documents, too, Your Honor."

Caldwell nodded and waved him forward.

"Of course, Counselor. You should have had an opportunity to look at them before now."

"I would have liked to, Your Honor, but Mr. Brighton refused."

Caldwell frowned at Brighton and O'Hara and said, "If I had been here earlier, I would have ordered him to comply with your request, Counselor."

"I didn't trust him," Brighton snapped. "You don't know what's been going on around here, Your Honor. The whole town's against me. Woodford's got the local law in his pocket—"

Caldwell snatched up the gavel and slammed it down on the table.

"That's enough, sir! Please confine yourself to answering questions from counsel."

"Sorry, Your Honor," Brighton said with a surly grimace.

Caldwell separated the documents and spread

them out on the table, faceup. Luther looked them over. The two death certificates appeared to be legitimate, and he didn't really doubt that they were. He was much more interested in the so-called partnership agreement. It was scrawled on a piece of brown paper with ragged edges, evidently torn off of a larger piece. He kept his face carefully expressionless as he studied the document.

Everything he wanted to see was there. The case was won. Luther knew he could end the trial, right here and now, with only a few questions.

O'Hara thought it was over, too. With a hint of that smirk still lingering on his face, he said, "Now that counsel has had a chance to study the documents, I would ask that he stipulate as to their authenticity."

All Luther had to do was say that he agreed to that stipulation. As soon as the words were out of his mouth, O'Hara would move for an immediate ruling. Judge Caldwell would probably refuse, but it wouldn't matter. There would be no way to repair the damage to Tip Woodford's case, no defense Luther could mount. If the partnership agreement was authentic, then Caldwell would have to rule in favor of Dex Brighton. The judge wouldn't have any choice.

Caldwell knew that, too. Luther could tell as much from the suddenly concerned look in the judge's eyes. Everything was riding on what Luther said next.

"I'm not prepared to so stipulate at this moment, Your Honor."

Caldwell looked relieved, but O'Hara was visibly shocked. Luther was double-crossing him, and they both knew it. That knowledge was in the look that passed between them as they locked eyes. Luther saw the anger and the threat that lurked there. He couldn't help it. He couldn't just cave in to O'Hara's blackmail, not with so much at stake for Woodford and Diana.

The truth had to come out. *All* the truth. And if he was ruined in the process, then so be it.

"The documents are entered into evidence," Caldwell said. "Do you have any more questions for this witness, Colonel O'Hara?"

With a shake of his head, O'Hara said, "No, Your Honor."

Caldwell looked at Luther and asked, "What about you, counselor?"

"Yes, Your Honor, I have a few questions."

"Proceed then."

Luther turned toward the witness chair. Brighton knew that Luther had double-crossed them, too, and in that instant, as he saw the cold hatred in the man's eyes, Luther was certain that Brighton was the one who'd tried to stick that knife in his back. He figured Brighton had killed Mason, too, although he might not ever be able to prove either of those things.

But he *could* prove that Brighton was lying about the partnership agreement and his claim to the Lucky Lizard.

Luther tapped a finger on the document, below the signatures.

"Mr. Brighton, you said this agreement was written by Jeremiah Fulton."

"That's right."

"And it's signed by both men, Fulton and your father, Chester Brighton."

"You can see that for yourself," Brighton answered with a sneer.

Luther pushed the piece of brown paper toward Brighton.

"Would you mind reading what it says?"

"Out loud, you mean?" Brighton asked, frowning.

"That's right."

Judge Caldwell leaned forward and said, "The document is already entered into evidence, Counselor. It doesn't have to be read aloud for that to be true."

"I'm aware of that, Your Honor," Luther said. "I'd still like for the witness to read it."

"Very well." Caldwell looked at Brighton. "Proceed, Mr. Brighton."

Looking impatient and irritated, Brighton picked up the paper and started to read.

"This agreement is made between Jeremiah Fulton and Chester Brighton on February 21st, 1872, that we will be partners from now on in the mining claim we have been prospecting in the Wassuck Mountains of Nevada. This claim runs from Juniper Creek in the south to Skunk Ridge to—"

"That's enough," Luther said. "I believe the rest of the document spells out the location of the claim and then specifies that the two men could sell out only to each other, as well as the agreement that in the event of death, the surviving partner would inherit the entire claim."

"That's what it says. You saw it for yourself, Turnbuckle. Satisfied?"

Before the judge could admonish Brighton, O'Hara was on his feet, saying, "My client apologizes for his tone, Your Honor. You have to realize how much of a strain this whole affair has been for him. To have his rightful inheritance stolen from him—" O'Hara stopped short, then said, "And now

I apologize, Your Honor. It's just that this case seems so cut and dried . . ."

"Yes, it does," Luther agreed. "Just a few more questions for this witness."

Caldwell nodded for him to go ahead.

"Now, you didn't read exactly what that document says, did you, Mr. Brighton?" Luther asked.

"I certainly did." Brighton waved the paper in the air. "Now that it's been entered into evidence, I'll let anybody look at it who wants to."

"When is it dated?"

"February 21st, 1872."

"How is the name of the month spelled in the document?"

Brighton frowned again. "What?"

"How is February spelled?"

Brighton looked down at the document and said, "F-e-b-r-a-r-e-y."

"And the date? The twenty-first?"

Brighton's jaw tightened. He didn't say anything.

"Mr. Brighton?" Judge Caldwell prodded.

"I don't see what this has to do with anything!"

"Neither do I, but counsel has asked the question and you have to answer." Caldwell paused. "Besides, as you said, it's written down, right there on the paper."

Like the letters were being pried out of him, Brighton said, "T-w-e-n-n-y-f-u-r-s-t."

Luther said, "So the agreement is actually dated *Febrarey Twenny-furst*, is that correct?" He drew the words out to emphasize them.

"Yes," Brighton said between clenched teeth.

"And how is *agreement* spelled?"

"A-g-r-e-m-i-n-t." Brighton slapped the paper back

down on the desk. "What the hell difference does it make?"

O'Hara jumped up to apologize, Judge Caldwell reached for his gavel, and Frank Morgan started forward to head off any trouble. Luther overrode them all by raising his voice and saying, "I'll tell you what difference it makes, Mr. Brighton! I'll tell you why it's so important that nearly every other word in that document is either misspelled or used incorrectly. Jeremiah Fulton never wrote it! It's a fake!"

Luther stood there, the pulse hammering in his head almost as loudly as the tumult that broke out inside the Silver Baron. Brighton and O'Hara were both yelling, Judge Caldwell was pounding his gavel, and the spectators joined in the general commotion. It didn't quiet down in the courtroom until Frank Morgan lifted his voice and shouted, "Everybody hush!"

In the sudden silence that fell, Morgan grinned at Luther and went on. "I want to hear what else Mr. Turnbuckle's got to say."

O'Hara leveled a finger at Luther and started to say, "He's not—"

Morgan cut him off.

"I said pipe down, Counselor, and I meant it!" Morgan nodded to Luther. "Go ahead, Mr. Turnbuckle."

Luther took a deep breath and glanced at Tip Woodford and Diana. For the first time in a long time, he saw hope in their faces, and it made him feel good. It made him feel that what he was doing was worth whatever it cost him.

"Mr. Turnbuckle," Judge Caldwell said, "do you have any proof of your accusation?"

"I do, Your Honor." Luther stepped back to the defense table and picked up the bundle of telegrams Phil Noonan had brought from Carson City. "I have here evidence that Jeremiah Fulton was far from the semiliterate bumpkin this so-called partnership agreement makes him out to be. In actuality, he attended Harvard, studying geology, engineering, and natural history. He not only graduated with honors, he went on to obtain his master's degree and his doctorate, studied in Europe, and overall was a highly educated man whose work was published in numerous scientific and academic journals before he decided to come West and put his education to use in searching for gold and silver. You have the witness's own testimony that Jeremiah Fulton wrote that error-riddled document, and I submit to you, Your Honor, that such a thing is patently impossible!"

Luther didn't say anything about how Fulton had been broke and in a Virginia City whorehouse when he sold the claim to Tip Woodford. Just because a man was highly educated didn't mean he always showed the best judgment.

"Let me see those telegrams," Caldwell said. He ignored the objections that O'Hara called out. Meanwhile, Brighton sat in the witness chair, visibly seething with rage. His plot had collapsed. He had never wanted things to get this far because he had known that the document was a phony. A smart lawyer might be able to knock it down. That was exactly what Luther had done.

Judge Caldwell put the telegrams aside and smacked the gavel on the table until things quieted down again. Then he cleared his throat and said to

Luther, "Do you have any further questions for the witness, Counselor?"

"No, sir."

"Step down," Caldwell told Brighton. "I believe you said you had only one witness, Colonel O'Hara?"

"Yes, Your Honor," O'Hara grated.

Caldwell looked at Luther. "Do you have any witnesses, counsel?"

Luther shook his head and said, "No, Your Honor. I believe you have enough evidence to make a ruling."

"Then I'll hear closing arguments. Colonel?"

O'Hara paced forward and said, "I have a closing argument, all right, Your Honor. That man is a fraud!" He pointed a shaking finger at Luther. "He's not Claudius Turnbuckle!"

Chapter 29

O'Hara's accusation didn't exactly take Frank by total surprise. He had felt all along that there was something not quite right about the man who called himself Claudius Turnbuckle. He was just too young, and there had been that time when he was wounded and only semicoherent when he had started talking about Turnbuckle as if he were somebody else.

Now the man stood there, pale and haggard but victorious in his effort to prove that Brighton was lying, and he said simply, "Colonel O'Hara is correct, Your Honor. I'm not Claudius Turnbuckle. But that doesn't change the facts of the case."

"Then who are you?" Caldwell demanded, a dumbfounded expression on his face.

"My name is—"

"Luther!" Frank burst out as the realization hit him. "That's what you were trying to say that day. Your name is Luther."

The fake Turnbuckle gave him a wan smile. "That's right. I'm Luther Galloway. I was Mr. Turnbuckle's law clerk."

"Was?" Caldwell asked.

"He was killed during a train robbery on the way here."

Frank's gaze turned toward Brighton. "Are you sure it was a real train robbery, Galloway? Brighton's gunnies held up a stagecoach just to get rid of Judge Grampis and delay this trial."

"That's slander!" O'Hara howled. "I mean libel! I mean—"

Luther Galloway said, "I don't believe the colonel is actually an attorney either, since he doesn't know the difference between slander and libel. I think he's an actor hired by Mr. Brighton as part of the swindle he was trying to pull here."

Everybody was yelling now, and nobody paid any attention to the pounding of Judge Caldwell's gavel. Frank knew he couldn't shout them down again, so he slipped his Colt from its holster, pointed the barrel toward the ceiling, and pulled the trigger.

The thunderous slam of the gunshot made silence fall on the room like an avalanche. Frank looked at Tip Woodford and said, "Sorry about the bullet hole in the ceiling, Tip. I'll pay for it."

Tip waved off the offer and said, "Don't worry about that, Frank. We got more important things to take care of." He lumbered to his feet and addressed Judge Caldwell directly. "Your Honor, you still got to rule on this case, don't you?"

"Indeed I do, Mr. Woodford."

"But . . . but," O'Hara sputtered, "opposing counsel isn't really a lawyer!"

"I'm not convinced you are either, *Colonel*," Caldwell said, scorn dripping from his words. "But as Mr. Turnbuckle . . . I mean, Mr. Galloway, was it? . . . has pointed out, whether or not either of you are actually lawyers, the facts of the case remain the same. And based on the evidence in these telegrams, weighed against the testimony given by Mr. Brighton, I can only conclude that Mr. Brighton is a bald-faced liar and his so-called partnership agreement is a fake." The judge picked up the gavel. "Therefore, I dismiss his claim and affirm that the Lucky Lizard Mine belongs to Mr. Thomas Woodford."

The gavel cracked down on the table, making it official.

Frank moved over to the judge and nodded toward Brighton. "What about arresting him for trying to pull a swindle?"

Brighton surged to his feet. "My father gave me that paper!" he insisted. "I had no way of knowing it wasn't real!"

"He tried to kill me and Mr. Turnbuckle . . . I mean, Luther . . . a couple of times," Frank said. "Not to mention what happened to Judge Grampis."

Brighton shook his head. "Lies, all lies!"

Caldwell looked up at Frank and asked, "Can you prove that Brighton was involved in any of that, Marshal?"

Frank took a deep breath and shook his head. "No, I reckon not. But I know it's true."

"That's not enough," Caldwell snapped. He looked at Brighton. "Mr. Brighton, you're free to go." He lifted the gavel to emphasize his next point. "But I suggest that you leave Buckskin and never return. The same holds true for you, Colonel O'Hara. The law can only protect a couple of tinhorn chiselers so far."

That unexpected bluntness on the part of the

judge brought a chuckle from Frank. Maybe Caldwell wasn't so bad after all.

Brighton and O'Hara grabbed their hats and pushed through the crowd in the saloon. Catamount Jack stood aside from the door to let them go.

"Good riddance!" he snorted after them.

Tip Woodford grabbed Luther's hand and pumped it.

"Thanks to you, I've still got my mine!" he said.

Diana came up and hugged the young lawyer—or whatever he was—and said, "Thank you, Mr. Galloway. I don't know what we would have done if you hadn't come here and saved the Lucky Lizard for us!"

Luther looked stunned. "You . . . you're not all furious with me?"

Frank came up beside him and rested a hand on his shoulder, saying, "Maybe pretending to be Turnbuckle wasn't the smartest thing in the world, but I don't reckon you meant any harm, young fella. I'm sorry to hear that the real Turnbuckle's dead, though. I never met him, but he was supposed to be a mighty fine lawyer."

"Don't see how he could be any better'n Luther here," Tip said. "He won the case, didn't he?"

Frank nodded. "And in mighty slick fashion, too. You knew all along that the key was that partnership agreement, didn't you?"

"It had to be," Luther said. "And there had to be a reason Brighton wouldn't let anyone see it. I just tried to find out as much about Jeremiah Fulton as I could, hoping there would be something to prove that he couldn't have written it. I knew Brighton couldn't be too confident in it, or else he wouldn't have kept trying to delay the trial. He just wanted to use the threat of a legal defeat to pressure Mr. Woodford into signing over the mine."

"Say," Tip said, "I was supposed to be charged with assaultin' Brighton for that punch I threw at him."

Judge Caldwell had been listening to the conversation. Now he said, "Since Mr. Brighton has left the court, I see no reason not to dismiss any charges he might have pending against you, Mr. Woodford. In fact . . . court is dismissed!"

Again, the smack of the gavel punctuated the declaration.

"So it's all over?" Diana asked. "We don't have to worry about anything anymore?"

"It appears that we don't," Luther Galloway said. "Brighton is gone."

Frank glanced toward the street where Brighton and O'Hara had disappeared. He wished he could be as sure as Luther appeared to be that the two crooks were going to accept defeat so easily.

"A fine lawyer you are!" Brighton snorted as he and O'Hara left Buckskin in the phony attorney's buggy. "You let a flunky from the real Turnbuckle's office beat you!"

O'Hara struggled with the reins as he said, "I never dreamed he would admit to his deception like that. I thought we had an agreement—"

"You saw how much agreements are worth. If I ever catch up with the bastard who faked that one for me, I'll kill him. He should have found out more about Jeremiah Fulton, instead of assuming that just because he was a prospector, he couldn't be an educated man."

Deep down, Brighton knew that the fault really

lay with himself. He should have done a better job of researching Fulton's background. His father really had known Fulton, back in the days when both of them had been looking for gold and silver, although they had never been partners. Chester Brighton had told his son about how Fulton had sold his claim for a pittance, only to have it turn out to be fabulously valuable. At that moment, the idea of getting his hands on the Lucky Lizard had been born in Dex Brighton's mind. It had taken several years to set up the scheme—he'd had to wait for his father to die—but once things were in motion, he had been confident that they would lead to the big payoff that had always somehow eluded him.

Now the plan was ruined, but he wasn't going to leave here empty-handed, he vowed. He was going to come out of this with something for all his trouble . . . and he thought he knew how to do it.

"Where are we going?" O'Hara whined as he struggled to keep the horses on the trail.

Brighton reached over and snatched the reins away from him. "Give me those," he snapped. "I'm going to do what I should have done to start with. I'm going to take what I want."

O'Hara frowned worriedly, but didn't say anything else except to mutter, "I never claimed to be a real lawyer."

Brighton ignored him.

A short time later, they approached the abandoned mine where Cy Stample and the rest of the hired gunmen were waiting. Stample strode out to meet the buggy, an eager expression on his craggy face.

"Is the trial over?" he asked, getting right to the point. "Did you win?"

The bleak expression on Brighton's face gave Stample the answer to his question. The gunman cursed and smacked his right fist into his left palm.

"You didn't get the mine!"

"No," Brighton said. "The judge ruled against me."

"Damn it," Stample grated, "the boys ain't gonna like it when they find out they came all this way and did the things they did for nothin'."

"It won't be for nothing," Brighton insisted. "We won't come out with as much as we hoped, but there's a considerable amount of silver on hand out at the Lucky Lizard. We're taking it."

"Raidin' the mine, you mean?"

Brighton jerked his head in a nod. "That's right. I've been paying attention, and I happen to know that it's been a while since any silver shipments left the mine. There has to be quite a bit of bullion stored at the stamp mill, enough for you to pay your men and leave good shares for the two of us."

O'Hara protested, "You're talking about being outlaws! You can't do that!"

Brighton gave him a cool look. "Why not?"

"You'd be fugitives from now on. And I'm sure men would be killed when you raided the mine. You'd have murder charges hanging over your heads."

"Mister," Stample drawled, "there ain't a one of us who ain't already killed somebody who got in our way."

"Well, *I* haven't!" O'Hara snapped. "I may have been a criminal, but I've never been a murderer and I'm not going to start now. You can count me out of this madness."

"I already have," Brighton said as he turned toward O'Hara and pressed the barrel of the pistol he had slipped from his pocket against the phony lawyer's side. O'Hara's body muffled the faint crack of the weapon as Brighton fired. His eyes bulged in shock and pain, and he groaned as he slumped to the side. Brighton gave him a shove that finished the job. O'Hara fell from the buggy and landed on the ground with a heavy thud. Blood trickled from his open mouth.

"Figured that's what you had in mind when you said there'd be good shares left over for the two of us," Stample said. "I'll go tell the boys to get ready to ride. You comin' with us, Boss?"

"Damn right I am," Brighton said. "I haven't come this far not to be in at the finish."

Luther still had a hard time believing that everyone in Buckskin didn't hate him. Once the Silver Baron had been transformed from a courtroom back into a saloon, though, Frank Morgan insisted that he sit there at one of the tables, along with Tip Woodford and Diana, and Conrad and Rebel Browning, and explain everything about his masquerade.

He did so, and when he was finished, Morgan said, "Maybe you shouldn't have done it, but everything worked out all right, Luther."

"Mr. Stafford's going to fire me when he finds out what I did," Luther said.

"Maybe not. I'd be willing to write a letter to Stafford saying what a fine job you did of handling Tip's case. Might make him think twice about getting rid of you. I reckon in the long run you'd be an asset to the firm."

"But I can't pass the bar exam!"

Diana rested a hand on Luther's arm and said, "I think you're just too nervous about it, Luther. You're smart, you know the law, and you've got common sense." She smiled. "Well, some common sense anyway. I'll bet you do fine when you take that test again."

"Well . . . perhaps. I suppose I should try."

Morgan said, "Nobody accomplishes anything without trying. You just remember that, Luther."

"I will. And I appreciate the offer of that letter, Mr. Morgan—"

"Call me Frank, remember?"

"That was when I was Claudius Turnbuckle."

Frank picked up the cup of coffee that Johnny Collyer had brought to him and sipped from it.

"I sent for Stafford or Turnbuckle because I wanted Tip to have the best legal representation he could. As far as I can see, that's just what he got."

A warm feeling filled Luther's chest as he looked around the table at the smiling faces. He was beginning to understand these people a little better. Here on the frontier, what a man did was the most important thing. Luther had lied, but he had come through when he needed to, and he had learned his lesson about deception. It wasn't necessary. A man who stood up and did what was right would always be respected here in the West, no matter who he was or what failures lurked in his past.

Tip Woodford got to his feet. "I'm gonna go out to the mine and let the fellas know they're still workin' for me," he said.

"I'm sure they'll be glad to hear it," Frank said.

Diana stood, too. "I'll go with you, Pa. I need to check on some things in the office." She smiled at

Luther. "We'll see you later, Mr. Galloway? For supper at our house tonight, maybe?"

"I . . . I'd like that," Luther said. "I'd like that very much."

When Tip and Diana were gone, Conrad Browning said, "I'd be willing to write a letter to John Stafford, too, Galloway. I like a man who's not afraid to take a chance and seize an opportunity. If Stafford doesn't want to continue employing you, I might be interested in finding a spot for you in one of my companies." He looked over at Frank. "Our companies, I should say."

Frank waved a hand and said, "I leave the running of them to you, Conrad, you know that. That includes who you want to hire. Can't say as I think it would be a bad idea, though. Luther here is pretty sharp, and he's tough, too. He's been shot and stabbed and blackmailed, and he kept right on fighting."

"I did, didn't I?" Luther said.

"Just remember to tell the truth in the future," Frank said, "and you'll be all right."

Luther smiled, but that smile suddenly froze on his face as he glanced toward the saloon's entrance and saw who was just now pushing his way through the batwings. Shock sent his heart racing. The man strode into the Silver Baron, moving a little slower than usual and leaning more on his heavy walking stick, but his voice was as strong as ever as he spotted Luther at the table and bellowed, "Galloway!"

"Who in blazes is that?" Frank asked with a frown as he turned his head toward the newcomer.

"Claudius Turnbuckle," Luther said in a voice as hollow as death. "The *real* Claudius Turnbuckle."

Chapter 30

Well, *this* was an unexpected development, Frank thought. Luther had seemed pretty sure that Turnbuckle was dead.

But the lawyer had been alive when Luther left him, Frank recalled from the story Luther had told. The doctor who had been tending to Turnbuckle's wounds had assured Luther that his boss couldn't survive. Obviously, that diagnosis had been incorrect . . .

Because here was Turnbuckle in Buckskin, big as life and twice as angry.

"Mr. Turnbuckle!" Luther gasped as he shot to his feet. "I . . . I thought—"

"I know what you thought!" Turnbuckle snapped. "You thought you could leave me for dead and take my place! I heard all about it from some fellow called Catamount Jack, when I stopped at the marshal's office." His gaze swung toward Frank. "You'd be Frank Morgan?"

"I would," Frank said as he got to his feet and extended his hand. "It's nice to meet you at last, Mr. Turnbuckle. I figured I'd never have the pleasure."

Turnbuckle snorted, but he shook Frank's hand.

"After the pack of lies this young whippersnapper fed you about me being dead, you mean," he said. "*After* he lied and claimed to be me."

"The doctor told me you wouldn't live," Luther said with a hard, nervous swallow. "He said you couldn't possibly survive the wounds you received in that train robbery."

Turnbuckle snorted again. "Clearly, he was wrong about that, wasn't he? He underestimated how strong I was, and how determined to live."

"Are . . . are you all right?"

"A bit weak, still, but I'll be fine." Turnbuckle shook the head of his cane at Luther. "Marshal, why isn't this man behind bars?"

"Charged with what crime, sir?" Frank asked.

"Impersonating one of his betters!"

"It's true he lied to us about who he is," Frank admitted, "but you can't arrest a man for lying unless he's doing it to carry out some crooked scheme. Luther here was just trying to help. After you got shot, he could have turned around and gone back to San Francisco, you know."

"No, he couldn't have," Turnbuckle insisted. "I ordered him to come to Buckskin and tell you what happened to me."

"Well, he carried out half of that order," Frank pointed out.

Luther cleared his throat. "Mr. Turnbuckle, you told me that the client had to come first. I thought I should try to help Mr. Woodford, just as Mr. Morgan wanted. But I didn't think anyone would pay any attention to a lowly law clerk, so I . . . I pretended to be you. I admit that. But I meant no harm. I just wanted to help."

"And he did," Conrad said. "He won the case, and quite handily, too."

Turnbuckle glared at him and demanded, "Who are you?"

"Conrad Browning."

Turnbuckle's attitude changed, but only subtly, Frank noted. He wasn't the sort of man to kowtow to anyone, even a business magnate like Conrad who provided a lot of income to the firm of Turnbuckle and Stafford.

"Good to meet you, Browning," he said as he shook hands with Conrad. "No offense, but you're younger than I expected you to be."

Frank chuckled. "That's what we all told Luther when we thought he was you."

Turnbuckle was still angry, but he seemed to be slightly mollified. He told Luther, "You should be grateful that I haven't sacked you on the spot, young man."

"I am, sir."

Turnbuckle gestured toward the sling in which Luther's left arm rested.

"What happened to you?"

"I, uh, got shot."

"And stabbed," Frank added. "In fact, the varmints who caused all the trouble around here tried to kill him several times. That would have been *you* on the receiving end of those bushwhack attempts if you'd been here, Mr. Turnbuckle."

The lawyer's bushy eyebrows rose.

"Is this true, Galloway?"

Luther nodded. "Yes, sir."

"And yet you carried on and won the trial anyway?"

Luther looked like he didn't want to answer, so Frank said, "He sure did. Brighton and his phony lawyer never had a chance."

Turnbuckle frowned. "Well, that's . . . surprising."

Frank clapped a hand on Luther's shoulder and said, "You've got the makings of a mighty good lawyer here, Mr. Turnbuckle. If I was you, I wouldn't let him get away."

Turnbuckle rubbed his jaw for a moment before saying, "I'm going to have to think about this . . ."

"Go right ahead," Conrad said, "but you should know that if you decide to terminate Mr. Galloway's employment, I intend to hire him myself."

"I never said I was going to fire him, just that I ought to."

Frank expected Turnbuckle to say that Luther could have his old job back, with a chance to become a practicing attorney and join the firm, but that decision was postponed by a sudden commotion. Phil Noonan ran into the saloon and said, "Marshal, come quick!"

Frank picked up his hat from the table and put it on as he headed for the entrance. He heard footsteps behind him and glanced over his shoulder to see the others following him.

"What is it, Phil?"

"A fella just brought in that other lawyer, that Colonel O'Hara. He's in bad shape, Marshal. He's been shot."

"Shot!" Frank exclaimed. "Who'd shoot him?" He looked at Luther. "Although I reckon you might've felt like it."

Luther held up his good hand and swore, "I've been right here in town the whole time, Frank."

"I know that. Come on. Let's see what it's about."

As the group hurried toward Dr. Garland's house, where O'Hara had been taken, Phil explained that a rider had come into town with the phony lawyer's body slung over his saddle.

"Jack took him on down to the doc's place and sent me to fetch you, Frank."

"Do you know who found him?"

"Monte Calhoun. He was on his way into town when the fella came staggerin' out of some trees alongside the trail. Monte said he looked like he'd been wanderin' around for a while and Monte thought at first that he was just lost, but then he saw that somebody'd shot him."

Frank knew Calhoun; the man was a drifting cowpoke who had worked for all the spreads south of Buckskin at one time or another. He was honest and not a troublemaker, other than the occasional saloon ruckus that cowboys were prone to on payday.

Catamount Jack was waiting on Dr. Garland's front porch when Frank and the others arrived. The deputy shook his head and said, "The doc says it don't look good for O'Hara, Frank. I figured you'd want to talk to him if you could, before he cashes in his chips."

"Did he say who shot him?"

"Yeah," Jack replied with a grim nod. "Dex Brighton."

Somehow that didn't surprise Frank. A falling-out among thieves, complete with gunplay, never did.

They went inside and found an equally grim-faced Dr. William Garland standing beside the bed where Desmond O'Hara lay. O'Hara's eyes were closed and his face was as pale as the sheets on which he lay. His chest still rose and fell, but the movements were feeble and ragged.

"Is he unconscious?" Frank asked.

"I'm not sure if he can hear you or not, Marshal," the doctor replied.

Frank took off his hat and moved closer to the bed. "O'Hara? It's Frank Morgan. Listen to me, O'Hara. Did Brighton do this to you?"

O'Hara's eyelids fluttered. He forced them open with an obvious effort and looked up at Frank with bleary, pain-wracked eyes.

"B-Brighton . . . shot me," he rasped. "Dirty . . . double-crosser . . ."

"Where is he now? I'll track him down and see that he pays for what he's done."

"Gone to . . . mine . . ."

Frank frowned and bent closer as O'Hara's voice weakened.

"What mine?"

"L-Lucky . . . Lizard . . ."

Frank sent a sharp, worried glance toward the others who had crowded into the little room, then said to O'Hara, "Brighton's gone to the Lucky Lizard? Why?"

"He and his . . . gunmen . . . raid the mine . . . steal silver . . ."

Frank stiffened. If O'Hara was telling the truth—and the dying man had no reason to lie under these circumstances—Brighton was trying to salvage what he could from his failed plot by openly turning outlaw and stealing the bullion that was on hand at Tip

Woodford's mine. Frank had no trouble believing that Brighton would resort to such a thing.

"How many men does he have?"

"D-don't know . . . for sure . . . He said . . . thirty or . . . forty . . ."

The grotesque rattle that came from O'Hara's throat following the last word was vivid evidence that he would never speak again. Death had claimed him.

"Good Lord!" Catamount Jack exclaimed. "Thirty or forty owlhoots fixin' to raid the Lucky Lizard? We got to get out there, Frank!"

"Round up as many men for a posse as you can, Jack," Frank said. "Let them know it'll be dangerous, though." He clapped his hat on his head. "You and Phil follow me as soon as you can, with as many men as you can find."

"You're headed out there now?"

"Might still be time to warn Tip and his men. He rode out there a while ago."

Luther Galloway clutched Frank's arm as Frank started past him.

"Diana was going to the mine with her father," he said.

Frank nodded. "I know."

"I'm coming with you."

A grimace tugged at Frank's mouth as he said, "You're not a fighting man, Luther. You're better with words than guns."

"But I'm tough," Luther insisted. "You said so yourself."

"Suit yourself. I don't have time to argue with you."

Luther hurried after him as Frank left the doctor's house. Claudius Turnbuckle called after them, "Galloway, wait! Have you lost your mind?"

Luther ignored him.

By the time they reached the livery stable, Conrad and Rebel had caught up to them.

"We're going, too," Conrad said.

"Thought you said Tip Woodford's problems weren't any of your concern," Frank said.

"They're not, but you are. If you get yourself killed, it'll mean a lot of paperwork for me straightening out your half of our holdings."

Rebel added, "And Diana and I have gotten to be friends. I want to help her if I can."

"I don't think you should go," Conrad complained. "It's too dangerous."

Frank couldn't suppress a chuckle. "I figured you would have learned by now that you can't win that argument, son. Anyway, Rebel's a better shot than you are."

"Damn straight," she agreed with a grin.

With the help of Amos Hillman and Vern Robeson, they had horses saddled within minutes. Frank handed one of the two spare pistol from his saddlebags to Luther, and Conrad took the other one. Rebel already had a gun in her handbag, a silver-plated .38. The four of them rode out, pounding along the trail to the Lucky Lizard.

The mine wasn't far out of town, and within minutes of leaving the settlement they heard gunfire coming from that direction.

"It's too late," Luther said. "Brighton and his men have already attacked."

"Too late to warn Tip and Diana maybe," Frank said, "but not too late to lend a hand. The fight's still going on."

And from the sound of the shots, it was quite a

battle. Frank knew it wouldn't last too long, though, if Brighton really did have forty gun-wolves with him. The miners would have been taken by surprise, and they wouldn't be a match for such a crew of hardened killers.

Frank signaled a halt before they reached the mine. They couldn't just gallop in blindly. That would be a good way of getting themselves shot to pieces. Instead, he swung down from the saddle and motioned for the others to dismount. Then he shucked his Winchester from the saddle boot and trotted forward through a screen of pines to get a look at the situation. The other three followed him carefully.

Frank saw that Brighton's gunmen were spread out in a long line, using trees, rocks, and anything else they could find for cover as they poured hot lead at the office building, the stamp mill, the miners' barracks, and the entrance to the mine tunnel. Puffs of gun smoke from the buildings and the tunnel mouth showed that the men who worked there were putting up a fight.

However, as Frank watched, some of the outlaws began to circle around, coming at the office, barracks, and stamp mill while the others covered them, and he knew that in a matter of moments the defenders in those buildings would be caught in a cross fire and overwhelmed. In fact, a group of four men had just reached the rear of the office building. Dex Brighton was among them, and although Frank snapped a shot at him with the Winchester, the bullet missed and Brighton kicked the rear door open. He disappeared inside the building, followed by the three killers with him.

Frank bit back a curse as shots roared inside the office. That was the place where Tip and Diana were most likely to be. He was about to tell the others to cover him and make a dash for the building when Luther Galloway suddenly burst out of cover, streaking toward the office. He had pulled his left arm out of the sling, and the black silk flapped behind him as he ran, the borrowed pistol clutched in his other hand.

"Blast it!" Frank looked toward Buckskin and saw the cloud of dust rising in that direction. Catamount Jack and Phil Noonan were on their way with that posse, but it would be another few minutes before help arrived. "Stay here!" he told Conrad and Rebel. "See if you can pick off a few of the varmints!"

Then he ran after Luther.

Neither of them reached the office before the front door opened and Dex Brighton stepped out onto the porch, holding a pale and obviously frightened Diana Woodford in front of him. She didn't look like she had been hurt yet, but the barrel of Brighton's gun was jammed cruelly into her side.

Behind them came another man, craggy-faced and ugly, with Tip Woodford as his prisoner. Blood dripped down Tip's face from a gash on his forehead, and crimson stained the left sleeve of his shirt, too.

"Morgan!" Brighton shouted. "Stop right there!"

Frank threw on the brakes, and Luther had no choice but to do the same.

"It's over, Morgan," Brighton called. "Unless you want Woodford and the girl to die, you'll back away from here, and if that dust I see is from a posse, you'd better call them off. I'll kill everybody here if I have to."

"Take it easy, Brighton," Frank said, hoping to keep the man from getting trigger-happy. "Nobody's got to die."

"You're wrong there," Brighton snarled. His eyes were those of a rabid animal. Hate and greed had turned him mad. "The man who ruined everything has to die."

With that, he jerked the pistol he held away from Diana's side and pointed it at Luther Galloway, his finger whitening on the trigger.

Chapter 31

Luther didn't hesitate. He charged forward toward Brighton and Diana even as flame jetted from the barrel of Brighton's gun.

But Diana had lurched backward against Brighton just as he pulled the trigger, and the bullet whistled past Luther's left ear. Before Brighton could fire again, Luther bounded onto the porch and crashed into both of them. That knocked Diana free of Brighton's grip. All three of them tumbled to the planks.

At the same time, Tip Woodford began struggling with his captor, wrestling desperately with him over the man's gun. The craggy-faced outlaw slammed a fist into Tip's face and knocked him over, but that proved to be a mistake because he had knocked Tip out of the line of fire. The man must have realized that a split second later, because he tried to turn back toward Frank Morgan and bring his gun up . . .

Frank let the outlaw's revolver come level before he fired. The bullet punched into the man's chest and knocked him back a step. The gun in his hand sagged, but he struggled to lift it again. Frank's Colt roared twice more, the slugs crashing into the outlaw's body and driving him into the log wall of the office building. He dropped his gun and slid slowly down the wall, his face already going slack in death.

At the other end of the porch, Dex Brighton hammered a couple of savage blows into Luther's face, stunning him. Brighton rolled away, snatched up the gun he had dropped when Luther barreled into him and Diana, and leaped to his feet. Splinters flew from the corner of the building next to him as a shot from Frank's gun narrowly missed him. Brighton fled around the corner.

Frank went after him, ducking as Brighton twisted and fired. The bullet came close enough for Frank to feel the wind-rip of its passage next to his ear. But then the hammer of Brighton's gun clicked on an empty chamber. His face contorted as he flung the gun away.

Frank holstered his Colt and pounded after Brighton. Like most men who had spent a great deal of their lives in the saddle, Frank wasn't a great runner, and his boots weren't made for it either. He had the advantage of wanting Brighton to answer all the crimes the man had committed, though, and it gave him the extra burst of speed he needed to bring Brighton down with a flying tackle.

Both men crashed to the ground with stunning impact. Brighton recovered first, by half a second, but that was long enough for him to lash out and slam his boot against Frank's chest in a brutal kick. Frank went down again and Brighton leaped after him, snatching up a rock and lifting it over his head so that he could bring it down in a bone-crushing blow on

Frank's skull. Frank jerked his head aside at the last second. The rock scraped his ear as it went by.

Frank sledged a blow against the side of Brighton's head and sent the man rolling away. Now it was Frank's turn to pounce. He landed on Brighton with a knee in the belly and chopped a couple of punches into his face. Brighton heaved up and threw Frank to the side.

They came up slugging.

Left, right, fists hammering home, eyes swelling, blood dripping . . . Frank Morgan and Dex Brighton were approximately the same size and weight, and they were evenly matched in fighting ability. Brighton was younger, but Frank had justice on his side. He bored in as Brighton stumbled back. A left hook to the midsection doubled Brighton over, putting him in perfect position for the looping right that Frank brought around.

Brighton flew backward, his feet leaving the ground, and crashed down in a limp sprawl. He groaned once and then was out cold.

The popping of gunshots made Frank swing around. He saw that the posse had arrived from Buckskin, and now Brighton's gunnies were the ones caught in a cross fire. They tried to shoot their way out of the jaws of this unexpected trap. Several of them were cut down by the deadly accurate fire of the miners and the possemen before the others flung their guns down and shoved their hands in the air. The battle of the Lucky Lizard had been fierce for a while, but now it was over.

Frank would have dragged the unconscious Brighton back to the office building, but Catamount Jack and Phil Noonan showed up to do it for him. When he got back there, he found Luther sitting on the steps next to Tip Woodford while Diana fussed over both of them.

"You get winged, Tip?" Frank asked his friend, pointing to the bloody sleeve.

Woodford grinned. "Just a scratch. I'll be fine. How about you, Frank? You look a mite like you tangled with a wildcat."

"Just Brighton. And I'm all right, too."

Luther asked, "Where's Brighton? Did you get him?"

"Jack and Phil are bringing him back. He's busted up worse than I am, but he'll live to stretch a rope for killing O'Hara, I reckon. He deserves it for plenty more than that, but they can only hang him once."

Tip Woodford grunted. "Once'll do it. He's got it comin', sure enough."

Dog had accompanied the posse from town, and now the big cur was nosing around the body of the craggy-faced outlaw Frank had shot. A deep, angry growl came from Dog's throat, and the fur on his neck rose.

Frank looked down at the man and nodded. "This must be the fella who took those potshots at us, Luther. Dog caught his scent a couple of times, and he never forgets the smell of no-good skunk." He looked closer at the young man. "Are you all right?"

"Yes," Luther replied with a sigh. "I just wish I'd been able to capture Brighton myself. I guess I'm not cut out to be a hero."

"Are you crazy?" Diana asked. "You charged right into the barrel of his gun when he tried to shoot you, just to save me! How much more of a hero could you be, Luther?"

"Hero . . . or fool."

She sat beside him, took his chin in her hand, and turned his head to face her.

"Sometimes it's the same thing," she said, and then she kissed him.

Tip Woodford stood up and came over to join Frank. "Boy ain't too big of a fool," he said with a chuckle. "He's lettin' her kiss him."

"Looks to me like he's kissing her right back," Frank said with a grin. "Yeah, Luther's pretty smart. Reckon he'll be a real lawyer before you know it."

The craggy-faced owlhoot was Brighton's lieutenant, Cy Stample. Frank found that out from questioning some of the hired gunmen who had surrendered rather than be killed in the fight. Frank had reward dodgers on him that said he was wanted from Oregon to Texas, for rustling, bank robbery, murder, and just about everything else under the sun. Nobody was going to miss him or the other hired killers who had crossed the divide during the ruckus.

Judge Caldwell and Claudius Turnbuckle promised to see to it that Dex Brighton answered for his crimes. He would be taken to Carson City to be tried, but given O'Hara's deathbed indictment of him, a conviction and a hanging seemed like foregone conclusions.

Frank wouldn't be around to see it. He had reached a decision.

He came into the Silver Baron the next day and found Tip and Diana there, along with Conrad and Rebel. Luther was there, too, sitting next to Diana, who didn't look too happy.

As he pulled back a chair and sat down, Frank asked, "What's wrong?"

"Luther's going back to San Francisco," Diana said.

"I have to," the young man explained. "I still work for Mr. Turnbuckle, you know. He decided not to fire me after all."

Conrad said, "My job offer is always open, Luther."

"Thank you, Mr. Browning. I appreciate that. And I may take you up on it one of these days, depending on how my other plans work out."

"What plans are those?" Frank asked.

"To become a lawyer for real . . . and come back here to Buckskin to practice."

Diana's face lit up at that. "Really?"

Luther nodded and said, "Really."

Tip reached over and patted him on the shoulder.

"Buckskin can always use another good citizen, son. We'll be happy to have you hang out your shingle here."

Frank wondered briefly how things were going to work out with Diana and Luther and Garrett Claiborne. He had a feeling the mining engineer wasn't going to give up his budding romance with Diana without a fight. But again, they would have to just work that out among themselves, because Frank wasn't going to be here to get involved . . . not that he would have, even if he hadn't reached the decision he had.

"I've got something for you, Tip," he said.

"What's that?"

Frank unpinned the badge from his shirt and slid it across the table toward the mayor.

Tip's eyes widened and he started shaking his head.

"Now, dadgum it, Frank, you can't do that—"

"It's already done," Frank said. "I'm resigning as marshal of Buckskin, Tip. Give the badge to Catamount Jack. He deserves it, and he'll do a fine job for you. He's spent more time being the marshal lately than I have."

"He can't handle the same sort of trouble that you do, though. He's not a—"

Woodford stopped short and looked embarrassed.

"He's not a gunfighter," Frank finished for him. "That's what you were going to say, Tip. It's all right. And it proves my point. Buckskin doesn't *need* a gunfighting marshal anymore. Things are settling down a little more every day. You'll still have some trouble, but Jack and Phil Noonan will be able to take care of it. They're mighty good men."

"You can say that after everything that happened with Brighton?"

"Varmints like Brighton are few and far between." Frank tapped the badge. "My mind's made up, Tip. It's time for me to be riding on."

Rebel spoke up, saying, "You've already stayed here longer than I thought you would, Frank. If you're not careful, you'll put down roots."

Frank grinned at his daughter-in-law. They understood each other and always had.

"Wouldn't want that, would we?"

"Not when there's a good reason people call you The Drifter."

"You'll come back this way sometime, though, won't you?" Conrad asked.

"Probably." The question took Frank by surprise. "What would it matter to you?"

"Well," Conrad said, "if you're in this area, you

can stop by Carson City and see us. We're moving there from Boston."

A grin broke out across Frank's face. "I knew you were thinking about moving West, but I figured you'd wind up in Denver or some place like that."

"We considered that," Conrad said, "but Rebel liked Carson City when we passed through there, and with the way the Browning holdings are expanding all through the West, it's centrally located. Handy for any troubleshooting I need to do."

"You have any trouble you need me to shoot, just let me know," Frank said, still grinning.

"I always do."

Tip Woodford leaned forward and put his hand over the badge that still lay on the table.

"You sure I can't talk you out of this, Frank?"

"Positive."

Tip sighed. "All right. When are you leavin'?"

"Later today. I've never seen any point in waiting, once my mind's made up."

"Well, then, you'd damned well better have a drink with me before you go."

"With all of us," Luther said.

Frank looked around at them and nodded, feeling the warmth of their friendship filling him, easing the ache of the long, lonely years he had spent on the trail.

"I reckon I can manage that," he said.

Frank led Stormy and Goldy out of Amos Hillman's livery stable. Dog padded alongside them. Goldy was saddled, and Stormy would carry the supplies Frank was taking with him, for now anyway. He planned to switch back and forth between the mounts.

He had already shaken hands with Amos and said his good-byes. He was going to miss the irascible old liveryman. In fact, he was going to miss a lot of people in Buckskin . . . Claude Langley at the undertaking parlor, Leo and Trudy Benjamin at the general store, Johnny Collyer and Professor Burton and Doc Garland and Vern Robeson . . . Lauren and Ginnie and Becky at the café had all hugged and kissed him and shed tears when he told them good-bye, and Lauren's kiss had been especially bittersweet. If Frank had stayed in Buckskin, there might have been something between the two of them, and they both knew it. But the time had come for him to move on, and even though he felt plenty of regrets, he knew it was the right thing to do.

"Frank!"

He looked around and saw Catamount Jack walking toward him. The marshal's badge shone on the old-timer's vest, but Jack didn't look happy about it.

"Doggone, Frank, this ain't right," Jack insisted. "I'll talk your ear off if I got to, but I got to make you see you need to stay right here in Buckskin."

"I've got two ears, Jack," Frank said with a smile. "Don't worry, you'll do just fine."

"Aw, hell, I know that! I been carryin' you ever since you took the marshal's job."

"And don't think I don't appreciate it."

"But it just ain't gonna be the same around here without you. This is your home now."

To tell the truth, Frank thought, that was why he was leaving. He was starting to feel too much that way himself.

Before Jack could continue his attempts at persuasion, another voice spoke up, calling, "Mr. Morgan! A word with you, please."

Frank and Catamount Jack swung around to see Claudius Turnbuckle coming toward them. The San Francisco lawyer wore an even more worried look than usual.

"What can I do for you, Mr. Turnbuckle?" Frank asked.

"There's a rumor going around town that you're leaving," Turnbuckle said.

"It's no rumor, sir. I've resigned as the marshal of Buckskin."

"What are your plans now? Where are you going?"

Frank shrugged. "Don't have any plans, and I reckon I'll go wherever the trail takes me."

"Then perhaps I could ask a favor of you. Before I came down here to Buckskin to find out what that young pup Luther was up to, I received a telegram from my partner, Stafford, that's causing me a considerable amount of concern. He's down in southern California, tending to some affairs for another client of ours in Los Angeles, and he's run into some trouble. I had to read between the lines of his wire, you understand, but I'm afraid it's the, ah, sort of trouble in which you frequently become involved."

Frank's smile disappeared. "Gun trouble, you mean?"

"That's what I'm worried about. Since you're leaving Buckskin anyway, is there any chance you could see your way clear to riding down that way and checking to see if Stafford needs help?"

Frank pondered the request for a moment. Claudius Turnbuckle has been willing to leave San

Francisco and come to Buckskin on a moment's notice to help him. Just because things hadn't worked out quite that way wasn't Turnbuckle's fault. And it had been Turnbuckle's law clerk Luther Galloway, Frank reminded himself, who had saved the Lucky Lizard for Tip Woodford, at considerable risk to his own life.

Finally, Frank nodded. "I reckon I could do that."

"Excellent!" Turnbuckle reached inside his coat and took out a folded telegram. "Here's Stafford's wire, telling you where he can be contacted. I appreciate this more than you know, Morgan. Stafford can be a cantankerous old badger, but he *is* my partner."

Frank shook hands with Turnbuckle and said, "I'll do what I can for him."

Then he turned to Catamount Jack, pumped the old-timer's hand, and slapped him on the back in a rough hug.

"Take care o' yourself, you ol' gunfighter," Jack rasped.

"You, too, you old pelican."

With that, Frank swung up into Goldy's saddle and heeled the horse into a trot that carried them out of Buckskin. Stormy paced them to the right, and Dog bounded along on the left. Frank didn't look back.

The Drifter was on the drift again.